# TARNISHED EMPIRE

# AVA HARRISON

Tarnished Empire
Cover Design: Hang Le
Editors: Editing4Indies, Polished Pen
Proofreader: Marla Selkow Esposito, Amy Halter
Formatting: Champagne Book Design

Dedicated to my mom.
Thank you for always listening to me ramble about
my crazy plot ideas.


P.S. Please skip all scenes where the characters are . . .
kissing.

*Knowing your own darkness is the best method for dealing with the darknesses of other people.*
*~ Carl Jung*

# PROLOGUE

## Alaric

L IFE IS PRETTY FUCKING GOOD.
My business is thriving. Money is plentiful, and a willing girl is always available to entertain me.

Tonight, I have a business meeting that could change the whole trajectory of my life. Word around town is Michael Lawrence is thinking of retiring. When I heard this, I jumped on the opportunity to speak with him. Apparently, he'll sell for the right price, which is cause for a celebration, considering he's the leading distributor of guns in the Southern Hemisphere.

The honey-colored liquor beckons to me from across my desk. Leaning forward in my chair, I reach for the decanter. My staff always knows to keep it full.

This information almost seems too good to be true, but it's exactly what I need to get to the next level. To make this business my own instead of the floundering one my father left me when he passed away a few years back.

A person will always show their true colors, you just need to be watching them to see. I wasn't watching my father.

A valuable lesson learned.

One I will not forget.

But all the anger in the world won't change the past, so instead, I need to look toward the future.

I'm lost in thought until a sound coming from across the room has me looking up from my desk. My office door swings open, and my brother, Damian, walks in.

I haven't seen my brother in what seems like forever. He looks different standing there. Older. His dark eyes are the same—a complete contrast to my light ones—but his hair is longer and disheveled. Like me, he always looks like he has bedhead, but this is more. He looks like he just doesn't care.

He strides across the room toward my desk as if he owns the place, and he should.

Hands in his pockets, head cocked, he asks, "What time is the meeting?"

Despite his absence, I apprise him of my dealings.

"In an hour."

His mouth thins with displeasure. "You sure you want to do this?"

"Yes."

"Don't you think—"

My hand lifts to silence him. "Damian. When you run your own business, you can do what's best for you. This is my business, and this is what we need." Low blow, even for me, talking about the big fucking elephant in the room.

Years ago, when my father was still around, and Damian's actions mattered, he was reckless. He spent the early years of his life doing things he shouldn't, and it cost him everything.

What should have been his life is now mine.

He hates me for it—resents me—and I don't blame him. I'd hate me too. I took his birthright.

But his loss is my gain, or at least that's what my father told me when he handed me the keys to the almost crumbled castle.

My father was always quick to tell me this wasn't my fault, but rather Damian's. He deserved everything he got because he let a woman come before family.

When he should have been working, he was nursing a broken heart.

A lost love that was never his to have.

In the world I live in, there is no time for love. No place for it.

Always my father's punching bag, I listened and learned not to show weakness at an early age.

The most important thing is the "Business."

Family second.

And a wife …

That wasn't on his radar.

My mother was easily forgotten once she left. After he knocked her up, not once but twice, she was more than happy to leave with fat pockets of cash.

Damian is an idiot who let his feelings get in the way.

When my father died, drugs and booze were Damian's only friends.

Even if he's never around, he still works for me.

"Lawrence could be up to something."

I shrug. "The old man wants out."

"Ever think it could be a ruse?" His question takes me off guard. Rarely did anyone question my judgment, let alone him.

"No," I answer firmly. Damian is silent, but then his hands reach out and rest on my desk, his fingers tapping out a beat. I wonder if he realizes he's doing it. He's always had that nervous tic. I cock my head and wait for him to say what he so badly wants to.

"You should consider it. Never can tell who to trust." His words cut through me. They reach their intended mark. The thing is, even if I do care, even if I feel guilty for my part in his dismissal from the family business, I don't respond to his dig.

I narrow my gaze at him.

"You want to go for me?" I ask.

"What?"

My eyes search his face as I take him in. "Do you want to go in my place?"

"Because ..." His jaw is tight as he inhales in deeply before continuing. "Why would I do that? You already took everything from me. Do I really need to be your errand boy now, too?"

Sitting forward in my chair, I hit my fists on the desk. My scotch glass shakes, and the amber liquid inside swooshes toward the edge. It doesn't spill, though it made its point. "It's not my fault you fucked up your life."

A heavy silence falls upon us. My brother's face is unreadable as he coughs and then speaks. "This should have been mine." His voice is lower and more somber than normal.

"*Should* have," I stress, "but you fucked that up when you were banging hookers and snorting coke." No need to mince words. My brother was a real fuckup.

"I was in mourning."

Even fifteen years later, he still hasn't learned. I shake my head at his ridiculous comment. "You act like she was your wife."

"She could have been ..." His eyes bore into mine. I can feel the pain in his words. She was never his.

But in his mind, she could have been. Should have been.

He's loved her since we were children.

She was the daughter of my father's colleague. We all assumed that one day they would marry and combine the families. And maybe that would have been the case, but fate had other plans.

He continues to stare at me, his unwavering gaze making me uncomfortable. The old scar that runs from his left brow down his cheek looks darker than normal. A stark reminder of all the ways I hurt my brother in the past. Pain and regret seep into my blood, making me want to take away his pain. It's not an easy task, but emotions like this have their way of making me want to drink.

When I look at him, I still see the man who crumpled upon

the news, who vanished into a shell from the loss he suffered. The loss he blames on me. He thinks her death is my fault, and maybe it is. I can still feel the heavy burden of guilt that sits on my shoulders. And if he's right, and it is my fault, it's made even worse because I'm also the asshole who stole his life.

"It wasn't meant to be," he repeats.

"It's my business," I remind him. Regardless of whether my actions brought us here, his inaction sealed the deal.

"Would it kill you just to stop?"

On a large exhale, I stare at the man who I once looked up to. The man who helped me become who I am today. The clarity and resolution in his eyes haven't been present for years. He looks like the brother I lost, and I realize what a fool I've been.

My anger from the years I lost with him has blinded me to the fact that he's here now, and maybe he's right. Maybe we could run this business together. It's what my father was training us for before Grace.

"Sit." I gesture to the chair across from me, and he doesn't think twice before he takes a seat. Maybe this can be the beginning of something new. It always should have been two brothers working together. I reach for the glass to hand him one.

"What are you doing?" His deep brown eyes watch my every move.

"Isn't it obvious? I'm inviting you to have a drink with me."

Dark eyebrows slant into a frown before he nods. Still uncomfortable, still waiting on my answer.

"You're going," I finally say, and he stares blankly at me. Knowing my brother, he probably doesn't want to get his hopes up. "You will go in my place. You want in? This is what you have to do. No objections," I say smoothly.

His expression freezes. "Are you serious?"

"It's not the final meeting. It's only a talk to go over details. But if you want to be active in this, you have to start somewhere."

His face continues to be unreadable, but I expect little from him. I won't tell him my plans until I'm sure he can handle it. But when the time comes, I'll give Damian the keys back to his portion of the castle.

"To the end of an era." I lift my glass to make a toast.

"Only the dead have seen the end of war." He smirks as he says his signature catchphrase that he stole from Plato, making me chuckle in response. I hadn't realized I missed it until now.

"This is the beginning."

"We shall see." He rubs the back of his neck as he stands from his chair.

"Take my car. And pass along my apologies. Tell him something unavoidable came up."

"Will do, brother."

The word brother causes a stabbing pain to radiate inside me. It's been too long since we've interacted like this.

As he walks out the door, he puts his phone to his ear. I'm not sure who he's calling, but I lean back in my chair.

For the first time in a long time, things don't seem so heavy.

# CHAPTER ONE

## Phoenix
*Four years later ...*

M Y FATHER PACES THE OFFICE.
Back and forth. Back and forth.

What's wrong with him? This isn't normal behavior.

Right after college graduation, he demanded my presence back home. Then he tells me to come to his office to talk about "work." A part of me wonders if he's planning to pass down the company to me, but that wouldn't make any sense. He refuses to ever talk about it, but something is obviously driving him to act like a madman because no sane person acts this way at two p.m.

Sure, the pacing isn't necessarily a sign of an issue, but it's his office that has set off red flags.

Disarray.

Complete and utter disarray.

Those words clearly depict what is going on inside the four walls of this office.

I pull my gaze away from my father and allow myself to take in what should be a clean sanctuary for him to do business. Instead, it looks like a construction site that just had demo work done.

The first thing I see is the desk. It's turned over. My forehead scrunches as I look at it.

Wow.

That takes real strength to knock it down like that.

I can't believe the man who raised me could do that.

I'm impressed.

Not only is the desk on the floor, but so are the papers that should be resting on his desk. The phone is smashed.

I have to assume whoever called him pissed him off.

"What happened?" I take a step closer, and he steps back. From the way his brows knit together and his fist clenches, it's apparent that he's hanging on by a thread and trying not to snap at me.

"Leave, Phoenix," he grits out through clenched teeth.

I advance toward him, shaking my head on my approach. When I'm standing close enough that I can touch him, I place my hand on his shoulder.

"You asked me to come, so I'm here. Talk to me," I say. He turns his head and looks at me. Then he closes his eyes. They don't stay closed for a long time—just a beat—but long enough for his chest to rise and fall with his breaths.

With his gaze on mine, the look in his eyes begins to soften. "I don't want—"

"No." I place my hand on my hip, indicating I mean business. "You no longer get to push me away. You summoned me here for a reason. I'm your daughter, and this is my legacy too …"

"Don't you want more?"

"No. Dad." I say the word and let it hang in the air. He might not be my biological father, but he raised me, and this is my choice. "I want to help."

His shoulders drop, and he walks toward the couch in the corner of his office. I follow suit and sit across from him.

"If we are going to talk business, we might as well drink."

"Agree."

Sitting down, he pours himself a glass of scotch and me

another one. I'm not one for scotch, but if I'm trying to prove myself, I'll accept.

"What's going on with the business?"

My father rubs at his chin. "Nix, there is something I need to tell you ..." he says, and I laugh. He used my nickname, one he rarely uses. It's reserved for times when he thinks he'll disappoint me.

"Dad, I know what you do." My voice is nonchalant. He can pretend all he wants that he's simply in the import-export business, but I'm no fool.

I watch as he opens his eyes wider, surprised by my revelation. "How?" he asks.

"You might have sent me to boarding school and then away to Switzerland for college, but I have always known."

From where I sit, I can see the muscles in his jaw tighten. He's not happy, and I know it. It doesn't matter, though. This day was going to happen sooner or later.

"You have?"

"Of course."

His eyes go wide at that, and his mouth hangs open. He rights himself rather fast and cocks his head, still staring at me in complete shock. "And you don't hate me?"

"You saved me. How could I ever hate you?" My voice drips with emotion. I don't like to think about my life before, but it doesn't stop it from being true. He saved me. After my parents died, he took me in and raised me as his own. I owe my life to him. So even if he's a criminal, I'll always love him.

He mulls over my words, but eventually, he nods his head in acceptance then lifts his glass to take a swig.

I lift my own, placing it to my lips. When the first drop touches my tongue, I bite back the urge to cough. I need my father to take me seriously, and coughing would probably show my lack of maturity.

He treats me like his little girl. Capable and smart, but still a little girl. Now that I'm out of college, I want him to see me as the adult I am—if I have any hope that he'll let me help him.

After everything he's done for me, I owe him. I have to repay him for taking me in and caring for me.

Most girls my age would be okay living in the lap of luxury, but I'm not most girls.

Being taken care of isn't for me. I want to earn my keep and show my worth.

I let the scotch pour down my throat, allowing it to scorch a path as it pools in my stomach and makes me warm.

This makes my dad smile. "It's an acquired taste." He takes another swig, and the sound of the glass against the wood echoes through the quiet of the room as he places the glass on the coffee table.

It reminds me of the noises that come from a grandfather clock ticking in the dead of night, dark and ominous. But there's no need to baby me, and he'll find out soon enough. "How much do you know?" he asks. Leaning forward, he balances his elbows on his thighs.

"Everything," I admit.

He's silent, taking in this information. A girl can learn a lot about her family while attending a private school. Some good, most bad. Bratty rich girls love nothing more than to tear a fantasy down. It's fine. I'm happy I'm no longer blind to the truth. I'm about to open my mouth when he lifts his hand to speak.

"The guns ..." He lifts his right brow, checking to see just how far my knowledge goes.

"I know *everything*," I clarify. I know that my adoptive dad is one of the largest arms dealers in the world. "I know what you do. I know you sell guns."

"My clients—"

"Dad." I hold up my hand. "I know your clients aren't

honorable people. Probably none of them are law-abiding citizens, either."

Deep lines full of worry form along his brow. "You *really* don't hate me?"

"Of course not. Who you are isn't defined by what you do. You are my father, and I'd love you no matter what you did. Now tell me what happened and let me help you."

As if my words are waging war inside him, he takes a deep drawn-out breath.

"I didn't want you to be a part of this. I wanted more for you." His soft and powerful words are full of love, but it's my life, and I'll make him understand.

"I'm an adult now, and this is what I want." I level him with my eyes. "Now talk." There is no room for objection. He knows me well enough to know this.

"Very well." He lets out a throaty laugh before grabbing his drink, leaning back, and getting comfy on the couch. I know this conversation will be long. "My guns were seized."

I didn't expect that, and I'm instantly on edge, praying he's not going to jail.

"By …?"

"The competition. A piece of shit who is trying to destroy me. I never wanted this to touch you."

"Tell me."

The hand holding his glass tightens, his knuckles turning white. This can't be good.

"His name is Alaric Prince, and he's the worst of men. He has been systematically trying to ruin me for years. Not to mention the hit he put on my life that by some chance I've avoided."

Hit?

It feels like I've been sucker punched. There's a hit on my father. The one word is like a puzzle piece that has been lost for years but is now placed in its slot. Everything that's happened over the years begins to make more sense. The reason my father hides in his compound. There's a hit on his life. I need to know more.

"I don't understand. Who is he?"

"A little shit." The force in his voice takes me off guard. There is a story here, and he has to fill me in so I can help him.

"You will have to give me more than that." I lift my right brow at him in challenge. "We've come this far. If we are doing this, you might as well tell me everything."

"It's a long, complicated story."

I lean my body forward, placing my elbows on my knees. Cocking my head, I smile. "Well, then it's a good thing I'm home for good. Because time is something I have in spades. I have all the time in the world, Dad. Tell me. How long have you been at war?"

"Four years."

Suddenly, more things come together. The reason he shipped me off to a private college in the middle of nowhere. Why he never let me take his name when I asked. Why he doesn't publicly acknowledge me. I thought it was because I hadn't proved myself, but he was at war. He was protecting me. A warm feeling spreads inside me, followed by one as cold as ice. This Alaric person has hurt the one person who has tried to protect me. I need to do something; I need to know more. But first, I need to make sure I'm hearing him right. That all this time, I was enough.

"This is why ..." Tears well in my eyes.

Lifting his hand, he reaches across the coffee table and takes mine. "I was never embarrassed by you. You are my daughter. Maybe not by blood. But because I loved you, he couldn't know about you."

The love and devotion I have for this man makes me stand and start pacing. I am now where he was only a few short minutes ago. Nervous energy courses through my body as I think of what all this means.

I walk back and forth a few times, but no words form in my mouth. They feel dry as though I am chewing on sand. But I need to say something. Ask something. "And now? Does he know?"

"I have no reason to believe he does." Behind his words is doubt.

"Why does he hate you?"

He shrugs, but I level him with a stare. He needs to tell me. Whatever it is, I need to know.

"Because he thinks I murdered his brother."

It doesn't surprise me to hear my father has killed someone. Michael Lawrence is a ruthless man, but from the way he looks at me, I don't believe he did it.

But I still ask, "Did you?"

He looks at me, eyes widening. "No."

That makes me stop pacing. I nod to myself, knowing there is only one solution. "Then we must stop this war."

"Trust me, I've tried. There is nothing I can do. We are well beyond him listening or believing."

We both sit in silence, and a million thoughts run through my brain. My knee starts to shake from nerves, but I squash it down. Inaction is not feasible, and even if I'm not sure about my idea, I have to voice it. "Then I guess there is only one thing we can do."

"And that is?"

"Make him." My lips part into a large smile. My father doesn't return the sentiment, instead choosing to give me a look that says, *Okay, captain obvious, but how.*

"How do you suppose we do that?"

"Leverage. Take everything from him, and once we burn him to the ground, he will."

"By then, it will be too late."

"Why?" I ask.

"There is no way to get close enough to him."

More ideas start flying through my mind, but they are darker and dirtier, and I'm so sure my father will hate every single one.

"I can. He doesn't know me. No one does. I can get the information you need."

"Phoenix."

"No, Dad. Don't *Phoenix* me. This is my choice. I'm not the little girl you sent away. Let me help you."

His lips form a thin line as he stands and starts pacing again. He doesn't like the idea, but at least he's considering it.

"I don't want you to get hurt," he implores.

"I won't."

"You don't know that …" His hand reaches up to pull at his hair. "Alaric Prince is out for revenge. He is the worst of men. I should know."

I move around the fallen desk to where he stands so I can get closer to him. When I'm directly beside him, I look up at him. "Don't doubt me."

"I don't. I just can't—"

I can see the love, fear and desperation deep in my father's eyes.

"Trust me. Believe in me. Let me help you."

*Let me save you the way you did me.*

"Okay." And with that, we seal my fate and the fate of Alaric Prince.

I will find the leverage needed to bring the enemy down. No matter what.

# CHAPTER TWO

## Alaric

WITH BUSINESS SETTLED IN THE STATES, IT'S TIME FOR A change of venue. My guns are secure—or better yet, the AK-47s I stole from Michael Lawrence are secure in Cyrus Reed's estate. Normally, I wouldn't store my guns outside my warehouses, but since I lifted these off the competition, I can't have them in circulation yet. The voyage from Cyrus's to the Caribbean only takes a week, but it's the perfect opportunity for me to relax before work picks up again.

I'm headed to the Bahamas first, then making stops and detours along the way. At some point, I need to go to Venezuela and then while in South America I'll schedule the rest of my meetings.

But it's not just business for me on this trip. I plan on indulging in a few pleasures.

Which is why I'll kick off my trip in the Bahamas.

Mathis has opened a new club at the large hotel on the island, and he's throwing a gigantic party next week.

It's an excellent place to hold a few meetings.

One might not think of a club as a suitable location to sell guns, but I have found since taking over the business that clubs are the perfect place. Women, booze, drugs, and guns are, in fact, the perfect mix.

Men are more apt to spend when a pretty young thing is grinding on their dick.

---

By the time the yacht docks, I'm ready to let loose. I used my time at sea as an opportunity to schedule meetings for this weekend, the first one being with Xavier. He wants fifteen thousand guns for a government coup.

I don't give two shits what he's using them for; all I care about is the money. This deal alone will gross me twenty million.

In my office on the main deck, I pick up the phone and dial Cristian's extension. He answers on the first ring. "Be ready to leave at eleven," I order before he can speak.

"Yes, Boss," he replies, and I hang up. There isn't much else to say. My men know the drill. They accompany me everywhere—a night out clubbing on a tropical island included.

Cristian is my right-hand man and my head of security. I don't mix business and pleasure with my staff, so these men are not my friends. I run a tight ship and have no attachments to anyone. It makes life a hell of a lot easier.

The only person I ever truly cared about is dead. It was my fault, and I won't make that mistake again. If I don't care, then everyone is dispensable.

Standing from my desk, I head to my master stateroom in the front of my boat. Once inside, I strip out of my clothes and step into the shower.

My yacht is my home. Although I own a few residences scattered around the world, I rarely stay in any of them.

I stay in the Caribbean during winter and spring, and I usually spend the summer in Europe. But this year, because of business, I never made the transatlantic crossing, which is fine. I like how empty the islands are right now.

Every once in a while, I stay put. In my business, it's better not to be in one place too long.

Where most people have storage in the bottom of the boat, I keep my smaller shipment of guns that still need to be transported. My boat is large enough. At over one hundred and seventy feet, it's large enough for all my needs but still small enough to float under the radar. Pun intended.

I finish showering and head to the main salon. My men are standing in all-black suits, wearing their earpieces, ready to go. It doesn't take us long to arrive at the club.

And once I get there, Mathis has a beautiful woman waiting for us. My friend isn't in town. Apparently, he's in the South of France somewhere, St. Tropez probably, but he knows how to make a guy feel special. When the beauty in the red dress shows me to my table set up high above the club in the roped-off section of the VIP lounge, half-naked women are already dancing nearby.

There's no need even to order, as the table has already been prepared to my liking. Vodka, tequila, scotch, and champagne—something for anyone who comes by with guests.

The first person to arrive is Xavier.

"What can I get you?" I ask.

"Vodka," he answers, and I nod to the waitress who goes about pouring us both drinks.

"How many?" I know the number we agreed upon during our earlier phone calls, but things change, so it's always smart to double-check.

"Fifteen thousand," he confirms. Maybe not enough for a war, but I wouldn't put it past him to be getting guns from my competition too.

Not for long, though. If all goes as planned, Lawrence will be as good as dead by month's end. Now just to find the right bait to lure him into my trap.

Lifting my glass, I take a swig, shutting down all thoughts of revenge so I can deal with the matters at hand, the reason I'm here at this club to begin with. "When?"

"End of the month."

"Location?"

"Same as before."

Good. I know the area. Lawrence also keeps some of his gun shipments there, which means Xavier is double-dipping. He knows Michael will probably not come through, not after the last smaller shipment I lifted from him, but it appears my buddy over here is giving him one more chance to right his wrongs.

I can feel the smile growing on my face. I'll steal that shipment too, and in turn, after I ruin him, I'll make Michael Lawrence beg.

"It will be the same price as before."

"Thank you, my friend."

I wish he wouldn't call me that. He's no friend of mine. He's a client, plain and simple, but worse, he's not a very loyal one. But that's okay. He doesn't even realize he's just a pawn in my game.

"Anything else?" I ask. He shakes his head at my question. "Then let's drink."

"And get laid." He laughs. They are all the same—every damn one of them. As much as I would love to do that, looking around the room, I have yet to see anyone who catches my attention. They all scream desperate the way they seductively shake their bodies for me to appreciate. I lift my drink and allow my gaze to skate across the vastness in front of me. In typical Mathis form, he designed this club for decadence and sin. Most of the space is modern. Cold and sterile, with a metal ceiling and metal bars. But it's the VIP room where I am that really stands out.

Each private banquette has the ability to be closed off to the public, with white chiffon drapes that you can pull shut to hide all manner of business. At the moment, mine are open, allowing me the perfect vantage point to watch.

Mathis did an excellent job.

As we both bring our drinks to our mouths, I notice that Cristian isn't looking at me, so I follow his gaze. It doesn't take me long to see what or rather who he is staring at. There, at the end of the row of banquettes, is the most exquisite woman I have ever seen.

Long brown hair that flows down past the swell of her breasts. It's her eyes, though, that keep me from looking away. From where I'm sitting, I can't see the color, but when she sees me, they are mesmerizing. She only glances my way for a second before turning around and giving me the cold shoulder.

Few women have done that. Not at a place like this.

Most women throw themselves at me. She, however, stands with her back to me. Her behind is not the worst view I've seen. Her short dress that looking from the front seemed modest is anything but.

No. Here, from this angle, nothing is left to the imagination. Two thin straps lower to an open back that dips to the dimples of her ass.

Possessed, I stand from my seat, needing to know who this girl is—and why she so casually dismissed me.

I'm a man on a mission as I stalk over to her. My team is quick to follow, so I'm intimidating as hell as I make my approach.

I should tell them to stand down, but I want to see her squirm. There's no way that a little thing like her won't.

When I finally make my appearance, I'm towering behind her. She hasn't seen me, but she must feel my presence because I watch her back muscles tighten.

Slowly, and with purpose, she turns around to face me.

She has to crane her neck up, but when her gaze reaches mine, her pupils dilate.

I hadn't come here tonight hoping to fuck, but after watching the way her mouth parts and a slight puff of oxygen escapes her pouty yet full lips, I want to fuck her. I want to feel those lips wrapped around my cock.

"I'm not interested," she spits out before I can even speak. Her response has me throwing back my head, laughing—something I rarely do these days.

"You don't even know what I was going to ask."

"You were going to ask me if I wanted a drink. And seeing as I already have one …" She lifts the glass that I hadn't previously seen in the air. It's new, the bubbles still bouncing on the glass from the pour. "I don't need another."

"And what if you're wrong?"

"So, you weren't coming to ask me if I wanted to … what?" Her eyebrow lifts. "*Talk* with you?"

"Again, wrong." Not entirely wrong, but wrong enough.

"Well, color me intrigued. You came all the way here—"

"You noticed me." I smirk, and she must realize her mistake, and my smile broadens. "Here's what I think. I think you wanted me to come over here. I think you like the game of cat and mouse."

"I think you know nothing."

"Pity," I say, before turning and walking away.

"That's it?" she asks from behind me.

"Yep." I turn my head over my shoulder. "But …" I pause for emphasis. "If you have a different answer for me, I'll be back tomorrow. Same time. Same place." And with that, I walk away, right out of the VIP area and then right out of the club.

Once we step outside, I stop. Turning to the right, I look at Cristian.

"Yes, Boss?"

"Her name. Her social security number. Find me everything there is to know about that woman by tomorrow."

He doesn't ask me why I need the info. I plan to fuck that girl, but I don't touch anyone without doing my due diligence.

# CHAPTER THREE

## Phoenix

I DID IT.

I can't believe I pulled it off.

The moment he turns and walks away, I refrain from the need to slump to the floor and let out the breath I have been holding through the entire exchange. I'm not sure if he'll turn around again, so I have to stay composed for a few more moments.

Come on. Come on. Leave already.

I watch intently as his body disappears in front of me. His men flank his side, a layer of protection that is intimidating. My heart is hammering in my chest, as the fear I was keeping at bay rattles inside me like a snake ready to attack.

They're almost completely out of sight, and then I can breathe. Then the panic will subside.

Maybe a few more moments.

The time passes slowly as I wait, like tiny grains of sand that get stuck in an hourglass. I want to shake it to make it go faster, but I know it's no use. Instead, I inhale deeply and will my hands not to tremble.

*One, two, three, four* … By the time I hit ten, they have faded into the crowd, and there is nothing left other than a throng of women who desperately want that handsome man to return. Not me. No, it doesn't matter how completely devastatingly handsome that he is; I'm happy he's gone. Because now I can finally let out the breath I was holding.

My gut reaction is to run out of here and go straight to my hotel to call my father. But I don't allow myself to do that.

I need to act cool and collected, just in case.

With my shoulders pulled back, I walk to the bar. I'm still in the VIP area, so there's no wait. Most of the guests in this section have bottle service at their tables. As easy as it is to just sit with some desperate man to get a drink, I don't. Not after my time with Alaric Prince.

On the outside, I might have looked cool and collected, but inside I shook the whole time we spoke. I wasn't prepared. Photos didn't do him justice. I knew he was attractive, but what I met at the bar tonight was so much more than attractive.

The word god springs to mind.

Like a real-life Poseidon. King of the ocean.

I knew from pictures that he had brown hair, but what I couldn't see in a picture was that nestled amongst the brown locks were streaks of blond from his time on the yacht. Sun-kissed features and crisp blue eyes.

He's gorgeous. Although, that might not be even strong enough of a word.

Needing to calm myself from the interaction, I smile at the handsome man behind the bar.

"Tequila." My hands still shake beside me.

"Any brand in particular?"

"Your best." Whatever will take the edge off. I don't normally drink this much, haven't since I graduated from college, but this calls for one or two. I wish my best friend Hannah were here. She would know how to talk me down from my crazy.

My nerves knot up tight. My breaths lodge in my throat from fear that I would misstep.

This is my time to show my father that I can help him. I know I don't have to, but after everything he's done for me, I want to.

It's not long before I'm settling my tab and heading to my hotel. I'm not drunk per se, but I'm not sober either. I have a large tolerance to alcohol despite my size. I'm short and petite, a combo that shouldn't bode well for heavy drinking, but I can hold my own. I thank my days at boarding school for that. No matter how much I have, I never really get drunk. Now with a healthy buzz going on, I just want to relax and climb into my hotel bed and fall asleep.

I'm not sure how long I've slept, but when I open my eyes, streams of light peek in through the curtains.

Turning to my side, I swipe my phone and look at the time. It's eleven a.m. I must have had more to drink than I thought.

Even though it's late, I have plenty of time to get ready. Tonight is the night that I approach him again, but first I have to call my father.

The phone only rings once before he answers. I pace the floor as he says hello.

"Hi," I respond, more timidly than I want. I'm not afraid of what he will ask of me. I'm afraid I'll disappoint him.

"I was worried about you." He has every right to be. I'm sure I'll wear a hole in the carpet with all this pacing back and forth. He can't see it, but I'm just as nervous as he is.

I stop in front of the mirror across from the bed and stand stiffly, holding my body.

Not a good look for me. Nope. This face has seen better days. I look tired. My eyes are normally harder, but now I just look exhausted.

"I'm good."

"Did you make contact?" he asks. He wasn't on board with my plan, but it was the only one we had.

"I did," I respond, and it makes me smile. I hadn't thought about it yet today, but I did it. I did what I was supposed to do. I contacted Alaric Prince. "I set the bait." My voice already sounds stronger with purpose.

"And what exactly is the bait? Please tell me you—"

"I have it under control. I did nothing but stand there. He did the rest."

"The rest being …?"

I can hear the concern in his voice. My adoptive dad might have sent me away for half my life, but he's always shown how much he cares for me. His voice is inaudible and reminds me of when I first came to be in his custody.

The muscles around my heart tighten, but I shake my head. I will not go there right now.

I push down all my past and think about the future. The future, meaning tonight.

"Phoenix, tell me what you have planned." He practically begs me.

His nerves make mine flare. "He's invited me to the club tonight. I plan to drink and find out more."

"You truly think he will tell you where my guns are?" I can hear the doubt in my father's voice, and it makes me want to work that much harder to succeed.

"Well, no, obviously not. But maybe I can find a way to get to his phone—"

"This is too dangerous. I'll send—"

I know what he's about to say—*he'll send his men in*—but that would be war. When I saw Alaric yesterday, he had a minimum of twenty men with him, and that was only the ones I could see. The man has an entourage larger than any celebrity.

"You can't send anyone in. I saw it last night. There is no getting close enough to him. Unless you want a war."

"I don't want that. There have already been too many

casualties. I want to shut him down, but I don't want to kill innocent people …" His voice is soft and sad. He doesn't sound like the businessman I have grown to know over the years. Yes, he has always loved and cared for me, but this is different. I just don't know why. I shake off these thoughts and let out a breath.

"I promise I'll be safe. I'm just going to find out where he's staying. Try to figure out a way to get his phone. It shouldn't be that hard."

Lies. It will be impossible, but I'll figure something out. I'm resourceful.

Like my namesake, they burned me to the ground, but I rose. That's why I go by the name Phoenix.

From the ash, I was reborn, and I have no intention of failing in this.

I owe Michael Lawrence, my father in every way that matters, for my life, and if ending this war is how I can repay him, then that's exactly what I will do.

# CHAPTER FOUR

## Alaric

I T DOESN'T TAKE LONG FOR CRISTIAN TO ARRIVE. I EMPLOY AS many men as I do because they all have a unique skill set that I need. When he opens the door to my office, I recline in my chair and continue to drink a glass of scotch.

We're docked, so the boat only sways slightly but enough for the amber liquid to resemble a wave.

"What do you have for me?" I ask between sips.

"Actually, a lot," he answers, and that's when I notice his hands aren't empty. That fact alone has me placing the glass down and leaning forward. I place my elbows on the desk in front of me, tilting my head to signal for him to sit.

The sound of the chair pulling back echoes through the space as he takes a seat. "Remember that adoptive son you've been searching for?"

I know exactly who he's talking about. Word around town is my enemy has one weakness. A man with no family has a secret son. I've been searching for him ever since my brother died.

An eye for an eye—or in this case, a brother for a son.

"Phoenix, right?"

But that's all I had. No last name. Nothing. Word has gotten back that Phoenix means something to Michael, but no one knows more than that. Since Michael ignited the flames of war four years ago, no one has seen him. He has been a complete recluse, which makes seeking vengeance nearly impossible.

"Well, it seems we had a few of the details wrong."

"Speak." My voice comes out rough and abrasive, but I have waited years to find ammunition to use on him.

Sure, I have bled him dry by stealing his merchandise as often as I could, but affecting his profit margins doesn't pack a punch. It stings, but it doesn't burn.

I want to burn this motherfucker to the ground.

Take and torture whatever he holds dear.

We only just got word six months ago that there might be a son.

A lot of chatter, but no location. I'm not sure that this has anything to do with the task at hand, but I'm intrigued.

"He doesn't have a son."

That can't be right. We had good intel on this "Phoenix." My jaw tightens, and I can feel myself becoming impatient. Why is he telling me this, especially if it will only lead to a dead-end?

"Then how does this help me?"

His lips spread, and an enormous smile appears on his face.

"What aren't you telling me?"

"It appears he has a daughter. An adoptive daughter named Phoenix Michaels. She doesn't even have his last name."

He throws the file down, and staring back at me are the big blue eyes of the goddess from last night. Her image is attached to the front of the file with a paper clip. I open it and see the school transcripts. It appears she went to a private school in Switzerland.

I keep turning, but there isn't much there.

"She wasn't formally adopted."

That piece of information has me placing the file down on my desk and looking up toward Cristian. "Then how do you know she's important to him?"

"He paid for her school. We tracked her credit card, and from there, we got a name. It wasn't too hard to piece two and two together once we knew where to look. Plus, it can't be a coincidence that she uses his first name as her last name."

My fingers begin to tap a rhythm as I take in this information. A habit that makes me think of my brother—and apparently, I've picked up as my own after losing him. "Seems too easy."

"Not if we didn't know Michael had a son. That was a stroke of luck. The man gave no indication that anyone meant anything to him."

I nod my head. It's true. All these years, I could never find a thing, and now, she found me.

"It can't be a coincidence." Cristian bobs his head in agreement.

"No. It can't." We both fall silent as I continue to stare at the exotic beauty. Last night she was gorgeous, but in this picture, she's even more so.

Full lips, small freckles dot her nose, long wavy dark brown hair falls to her breast, and bright blue eyes.

She was a knockout last night. Someone I could imagine myself drowning in, but seeing her without a stitch of that shit on her face is better. She looks innocent, and it makes me want to corrupt her even more.

"What are you going to do about it, Boss?"

I lean back in my chair. Thoughts and ideas run through my brain a million miles a minute.

What to do with Phoenix? The name isn't really fitting for her. She's too small and weak. What to do with the little dove?

I look up and reach for my glass, lifting it to my mouth and taking a long swing.

What to do?

What to do?

I'm halfway through my glass, and I meet Cristian's stare.

"You have that look, Boss." He laughs.

"Grab a glass." I'll need a few minutes to concoct a plan, and while I do that, we'll have a drink. Cristian stands from his chair and moves over to the side table, followed by the sound of the tumbler being lifted and then scotch pouring into the glass. When he finally takes his seat in front of me again, I lift my own to make a toast.

I don't offer words, just a wicked and devious smirk. She came to me, and she will get what she deserves, but first, I'll play with my new pet.

"So, what will it be?" he asks. His brow furrows as he waits. He leans forward, and I smile brightly, placing the glass down. Standing, I walk to the door to return to my stateroom so I can get ready for the night. My hand reaches for the knob, and I pull open the heavy door, but just as I'm about to step through, I turn, looking over my shoulder at Cristian.

"Isn't it obvious?" My lips pull up into a sardonic smile.

"Not to me," he responds.

"Well …" I like the idea more and more the longer I think about it. "Obviously, we are going to catch a bird."

"And once we do?"

His question makes me laugh.

"We put her in a cage."

---

Someone rarely pulls one over on me. It's even rarer that I find myself surprised. But here I am.

She doesn't know that I know her.

I do.

I know everything.

Including her face.

If she thinks she can pull a fast one on me, she is wrong. Deadly wrong.

The thing is, she has no clue, and I plan to use that weakness against her. So here I am at the club in the VIP lounge yet again—trap set.

She's not here yet, but if I know anything about her, I don't expect her to be. No. No, she will make me wait.

Lure me in.

Maybe another guy would be fooled, but another guy isn't me.

I almost find it insulting that Michael thought this plan would work. That he thought he was clever enough to use his daughter against me.

Shows just how desperate he must be.

I take a seat on the soft velvet bench of the banquette that Mathis reserved for me. Women dance to the left and right of me, but I don't have eyes for any of them. I'm waiting for one bird, a little dove.

That's what she is. She might think she's a phoenix, but to me, she's a small, helpless little bird that Michael tried to pull out of his hat for a trick.

As if she can hear my inner ramblings, she enters. Now that I know who she is, I shouldn't find her as gorgeous as I do. But even if she had a knife to my heart, she'd still be the most beautiful woman in the room.

Tonight, unlike in the pictures, she's wearing makeup. Soft streams of light bounce around the room, hitting her with each step she takes.

With shoulders pulled back, she stands tall and proud. She's sexy as all fuck with her regal persona. Now that I know who she is, it fits.

She's the dethroned king's princess. *But that's not necessarily true*, I tell myself. She was hidden away. Like a fairy tale. Far away in a tower. But I'm not a prince, and she's not my princess.

No, instead, she's the means to an end.

I'll bait her to fall into my trap and use her to kill my opponent. It's time this war ends once and for all.

She gets closer with each step. She hasn't noticed me yet, which allows me to admire her from afar without her knowing. My disdain is probably palpable at this moment. As gorgeous as she is, I hate her with every fiber of my being.

No, hate is too strong a word. I don't give a shit about her. I hate her father.

The world stops when our eyes finally lock. She's an exotic beauty. Blue eyes stare at me as if I have all the answers in the world, which is impressive. She must be a talented actress.

I stand and place my glass down, heading over to where she is. She stops in her tracks as I approach, making me come to her.

Well played.

If I were a normal fool, I would eat that shit up and be desperate to have her in my arms. But like her, I know the game I'm playing.

Unlucky for her, she's ignorant.

If she thinks she can get the upper hand on me, she is dead wrong.

Once in front of her, I stare down at her, not smiling and not welcoming. But I don't smile often, and anyone who knows me knows this.

If my intel is correct, she knows I'm lethal, and anything more than a smirk would give me away.

"I wasn't sure you would come …" This time, the smirk reaches my eyes. *Lies.* I knew she would come.

"You didn't leave me time to answer. You were in a rush to leave."

"I had business," I respond before turning toward the table. "Sit," I instruct, and she gives a small nod. "I'm Alaric."

"Raven." Another lie. They slip off her tongue with little resistance. *Impressive.*

She takes a step forward until our bodies are side by side, and I reach out my arm and splay my hand on the small of her back. My fingers touch the soft slope of her spine until it rests on her warm skin.

I can't see her full dress, but from what I can tell from my touch, it's open in the back. Without further delay, I lead us back to the table and have her sit beside me.

"What do you want to drink?"

She looks around the table, scanning all the bottles in front of her.

"Tequila," she responds.

You can learn a lot about a girl from the drink they pick. Yesterday, she drank champagne, today tequila. She needs liquid courage for whatever the next part of her plan is.

I lift my hand and signal the waitress. "Two shots of Don Julio. Extra chilled."

There might be a bottle already at my table, but it's not good enough for me. To get the drink to the right temperature, it needs a shaker, something that is not at my disposal right now. However, the waitress in front of me knows that even though I'm a scotch drinker, when I do indulge in tequila, I like it prepared a certain way, so she has one in her hand already as she smiles down at me.

It doesn't take long before the shots are poured, and with glasses now in hand, I raise mine for a toast.

"What shall we celebrate?" I ask.

"Letting loose. Having fun. Getting drunk?"

"New friends?" I respond, my voice dropping an octave. All the wicked things I want to do to her are evident in my tone.

Her pupils widen a fraction, but not enough for someone to notice unless they were watching.

*Good.*

Keep her on her toes.

# CHAPTER FIVE

## Phoenix

I'M READY TO LEAVE. HAVING A CONVERSATION AND flirting are hard to do at a location like this.

Sure, I could throw myself at him, but from what I saw the day before when I was watching him, that would not hold his interest for long.

The night before, plenty of women approached him. They rubbed their barely dressed bodies against him, but not one of them held his attention. I was the only one, and that's because I paid him no mind.

I know plenty of assholes like him.

Not only from my early upbringing, but also from my experience at the private schools I went to in Switzerland. I learned there that men want what they think they can't have.

So, I played coy. Now, it's time for me to go, and I'm not sure the gamble paid off.

Maybe I misread the situation. Maybe he's not falling for it.

I stand from the table, and he looks up at me.

*Please take the bait*, I silently pray. Please. This is my last chance to help. To prove I can help.

"And where do you think you're going?" His deep voice cuts through my nerves, and when he smirks, I think I might fall over from the anxious feeling coursing through me. If what

I'm doing isn't bad enough, him being this handsome makes it even harder.

I do my best to plaster on a sweet yet sexy smile.

"I'm going home," I respond.

"Already? You just got here." He shifts in his seat and then moves to stand. When he's directly in front of me, I can barely breathe. He's too close. Way too close. Then if his proximity wasn't enough, he pushes his sleeves up, showing me his tanned and heavily tattooed arms.

Shit.

This is not okay.

This man needs to come with warning labels.

It should be illegal to be this sexy.

He's stealing the oxygen from my lungs. Everything about him—his eyes, the way he holds my gaze—demands respect. He commands attention, and I hate the way I feel when he looks at me because I hate him for hurting the only person I love.

Why does he have to be so damn handsome? And why does he have to know it? We stare at each other, and my breath stills in my chest, wanting to come out in ragged bursts from the pounding of my heart. I will it not to and demand my heart to hold a steady beat of indifference. Being so close to the objective, I can't falter now.

I'm too damn close to mess this up. I've come too far.

Inhale.

Exhale.

Breathe, goddammit. Breathe and act like you aren't affected by him and his larger-than-life presence.

"I have to go. Plus ..." I start to say, trying desperately to set the trap. "It's too loud in here." I gesture around to the club and all that it entails—music, dancing, and debauchery.

He cocks his head to the left. "Come to my place." His words are powerful. He's not asking. He's telling.

I shake my head. "I can't." I really freaking can't because the way I'm all jumbled up, I'd forget why I'm here and end up kissing this man. My gaze dips on instinct, and I look at his full and majorly kissable lips.

Shit.

*Look up, Phoenix.*

His forehead. That's a safe place to look.

I watch as his brow furrows, and I wonder if he will say more to convince me, but he shakes his head. "You misunderstand me. I wasn't inviting you tonight."

"Oh." I sound like an idiot, but I'm confused. Isn't that what he said?

"What I was going to say, had you let me, was that tomorrow I'm having a small gathering on my yacht. Come. It will be much quieter than this." He gestures to the crowd, dancing and milling around us.

The answer is yes. This invitation is exactly my goal. I have to say yes, but I keep quiet for a minute.

Again, my heart pounds. This is my in.

But I don't want to seem too desperate, so instead, I lower my gaze to the floor, and then I count slowly in my head.

*One.*

*Two.*

*Three.*

When I get to ten, I look up from the speck of imaginary dirt I was staring at. It's too dark for me to have seen anything, but in my head, I know it was there.

"There will be people there?" I ask.

"Yeah."

I finally meet his eyes when I ask, "What time and where?"

"Party starts at eight p.m. My yacht is docked at the pier. It's the last one docked, and it's called the *Empire*."

I want to barf in my mouth. Of course, it is. An empire he stole.

"Interesting name."

"You would think that," he smarts, his smirk dangerously close to detonating my underwear. This hits too close to home. I bite the inside of my cheek until I'm sure it will bleed.

"I guess I'll see you tomorrow," I finally say, and without waiting for him to say anything, I give one last smile and turn my back on him.

Then I'm walking out of the VIP area and the club. When I leave the building, and the warm air hits my face, it makes me feel like my skin is on fire.

I need to calm down.

I need to come up with a plan.

I walk to the street and make a quick left. As soon as I'm out of distance from the club, I fish my phone out of the pocket of my dress. Who doesn't love a dress with pockets?

The phone rings as I walk closer and closer to my hotel.

Finally, I hear my father's voice.

"Nix?" he answers in a low and troubled voice. He's not happy with my plan, and from his tone, I can tell he's nervous.

"Job done. I have my in."

"Not the phone, Nix," he responds, and I feel silly for not thinking of that. "George will meet you at the bar in your hotel. Ten minutes," my father says before hanging up.

I knew he had men here, but I didn't realize they were that close.

Knowing what I'm about to do, it makes me feel safer. Knowing George is here will help calm my nerves tomorrow.

After a few more blocks, I'm back at the hotel and head straight to the bar. The woman standing behind it smiles. "What can I get for you?" she asks, her French accent curling around each word. She appears to be around my age, and I wonder what brought her to work at this hotel? Is she a fresh graduate like me, trying to find her place in the world? Or maybe she came here on vacation and fell in love? A million scenarios run through my brain as I realize I haven't answered her yet. Instead, I've been gawking.

"Vodka martini straight up," I respond before pulling my attention away from her as I wait. I'm halfway through my drink before George sits down. George has been a loyal employee of my father for as long as I can remember. I don't know him well, but I trust him with my life.

We don't look at each other as we drink our drinks.

"He invited me to his boat tomorrow," I tell him, never looking at him.

"When and where?" he asks. His voice is low as though he's trying extra hard not to alert anyone to the fact we are talking to each other.

I fill him in on the details, and then I turn to meet his stare even though I shouldn't. "I'm going."

"Your father won't like that."

"It's on his yacht. He could keep information ..."

"Be that as it may, he won't let you do that."

"Then we won't tell him."

"Nix, you know I can't do that." He tilts his head to the side and pleads with his eyes.

"Then find a way to be on that boat."

"I'll be there," he responds, but his voice is tight, and I know this will be no small feat.

"How?"

"Let me worry about that." He chuckles, and I nod in agreement. "Okay."

"I'll only be there long enough to look around. He must have a place where he puts his stuff. In and out. It will be easy."

"I'm still telling your father."

"Fine."

Then I lift my drink and take a swig. With that out of the way, my nerves grow even more. The plan is set, so now I just need to follow through on it.

# CHAPTER SIX

## Alaric

I'M STILL IN THE CLUB DRINKING MY SCOTCH WHEN CRISTIAN approaches my table. Placing my drink down, I tilt my head to look up at him.

"You take care of it?" I ask, and he nods. I stand from my seat and move until I'm right before him. "And …?"

"Tom is following them as you requested. They're at a hotel."

My brow lifts. "Is that so?"

"They're at the bar. How would you like me to tell them to proceed?"

"Tell Tom as soon as the girl is gone that I want whoever she was speaking to in the warehouse by the pier. I'll be there shortly to see what the little dove is up to."

With that settled, I don't bother to tell my men I'm leaving. I pay them to watch and follow. When I stride out the door, my men, as expected, flank me. As soon as the warm air hits my face, my caravan of SUVs comes to a stop at the sidewalk; they're here for me and my men.

I walk toward the second one. Pulling the door open, I step inside and sit. Some of my men go to the first SUV and some to the third. Cristian is the only one to join me, sitting in the front with Peter.

There is no need for me to speak. My team runs like a well-oiled machine. Everyone knows where we are going, what we are doing, and most importantly, who we will torture.

If Michael Lawrence thinks he can make a play against me, he is grossly mistaken.

Sending his daughter in to do his work will be a grave mistake.

Not just for him but also her.

I don't relish in the thought of killing a woman. In fact, I've never killed one. But seeing as he sent her in, I might have to reconsider my stance on that. I govern myself by one strict rule: Never murder anyone who doesn't deserve it.

Guess time will tell with this one.

The ride to the warehouse at the dock doesn't take long, and eventually, we pull up to what appears to be an abandoned building from the outside.

I pay good money to keep up the appearance that nothing is here. I also pay very good money to the owner of the building to leave me undisturbed.

Luckily for me, the owner is a friend, not a foe, and although he takes the money, he would turn a blind eye regardless if I paid him. But I loathe being in anyone's debt.

The only time I have ever asked for a favor was from Cyrus Reed, but I have long since returned that one.

When the SUV pulls to a stop, I throw my door open and step into the warm salty air. My men are out of their vehicles before my foot even hits the pavement so they can walk by my side. Once we reach the entrance, they throw open the rusted metal door for me. This warehouse stores guns—my guns—but more than that, it currently holds Michael's man, sitting front and center tied naked to a chair.

As much as I don't want to see him naked, it's a necessity.

Having him in his birthday suit is the only way I can, with

one hundred percent certainty, know that he isn't wearing a listening device or any form of tracking device.

He hasn't noticed me yet. I'm still lurking in the shadows, but the moment my feet echo in the large cavernous space, he lifts his head and meets my stare.

The moment recognition sets in, I can see his pupils dilate in fear.

His body begins to shake the closer I get.

Yep, bastard. You're caught.

He knows it. I know it, and the tiny beads of sweat that roll down the side of his face tell me he knows what this means for him.

He's dead.

The only question now is if his death will be painless or if I will have to torture him for the information I need.

As soon as I'm standing directly in front of him, Cristian hands me a folder similar to the one from last night.

It contains all the pertinent information on the man in my custody.

"What do we have here?" I step closer, and with each move, I allow my lips to tip up into a smile. "It seems we have caught vermin," I state to Cristian.

"That we have," he responds.

"And what do we do when we find vermin?" I ask, mocking the tied-up man.

"We kill it."

My men laugh.

"But not before we play." A table loaded with instruments to make his demise very painful sits beside the man.

I look over what they have set in front of me. A knife, pliers, scissors …

"What to use first?"

"Pliers," I hear from my right and look over at Cristian. My mouth opens on a chuckle.

"Always so violent. Maybe we should let"—I pick up the dossier and look for his name—"George here decide if we need to make this painful before I start to rip his fingernails out one by one."

"So, what's it going to be, Georgie boy? Painful or …" I pull the gun out of the back of my pants. "Not so painful."

"Please, I don't know anything." He sounds like a blubbering baby as he begs for his life. I take a step over to the table, grabbing the knife.

"It seems you don't want to take the painless way out. Maybe there's more to you than I thought." With the knife in my hand, he watches me. "Listen, we don't have to make this hard. All you have to do is tell me what I want to know. If you do that, I won't go looking for your family. I won't pay your brother a visit."

His eyes widen at that, but apparently, I misjudged his love for his brother because he still doesn't speak.

I drag the knife up his leg. The blade cuts into his skin, leaving a trail of blood in its wake.

It's obvious where my knife is leading.

"Okay, let's try another approach. Tell me what Phoenix is planning."

His head lifts, and he meets my stare again with wide eyes full of surprise. Interesting.

He thought he was here for something else and didn't realize we'd put two and two together.

"Yes, that's right, George, we know all about Phoenix … Nix. Michael's daughter."

"She has nothing to do with this." His voice cracks.

"No. That's where you're wrong. She has everything to do with this."

I remove the knife from where it rests on his thigh and angle it up.

"I wouldn't shake too much if I were you. Here's how it's

going to go. I'm going to kill you regardless. But if you don't tell me what Phoenix has planned, then I will feed you your balls, and then I will keep torturing you before I find your brother and bring him here." Smile. Yep. I'm a sick motherfucker, but no one fucks with me.

"She wants on your yacht."

"This I know. More."

He shakes his head, but I lift the knife upward. "She plans to seduce you enough to get into your office."

"Was she sent in to kill me?"

"No. Please don't hurt her. She's had a rough enough life." Interesting. "She just wants to find out where you keep her father's guns. She wasn't planning on hurting you. We can't afford to miss this delivery, so she's stepped in to get the intel."

"And no one is backing her up?"

"I was."

"What is her father's role in this plan?"

His lips form a thin line, not answering me.

"Does he approve?"

"He agreed reluctantly. He didn't want her to do this, but he knows his daughter, and he knows once Nix wants something, she gets it."

I flick the knife in my hand, twirling it around to decide if this is enough information. I'm not surprised by what he is telling me. I knew there was a plan, but a part of me had hoped I wouldn't have to kill her.

I still don't.

Except he killed my brother, so it would only be fair for me to kill the one person who means something to him.

The idea holds weight but still tastes bitter in my mouth.

"What are you going to do to me now?" he asks, wondering if I'm going to torture him for more information

I could.

I could use this moment to find out more, but I am a man of my word. I told him if he told me her plan, then I wouldn't hurt him more than I have to. Death not included.

As much as this is an opportunity that shouldn't be passed up, I won't.

Turning to Cristian, I give him the nod. He returns the sentiment.

He knows me.

He knows my word is gold.

He knows I never go back on it.

And in that way, I am honorable.

Without a backward glance at the man still sitting naked in a chair, tied up and bleeding from his leg, I walk out of the warehouse and toward the car.

Gunfire rings through the air as soon as I open the door.

It's done.

Now to catch a bird.

# CHAPTER SEVEN

## Phoenix

THE RAPID BEAT OF MY HEART SHOULD BE ENOUGH TO MAKE me wonder if I'm in a bit over my head.

The thing is, stubbornness is a trait of mine, so regardless of my body trying to warn me, I refuse to let it. Even though my brain screams at me to pick up the phone and call this entire thing off, I don't.

I'm sure George is in place by now—and even if I want to, it's probably too late to turn back. I just need to put my big girl panties on and walk out the door.

One more glance, and then it's time.

I head over to the mirror in the foyer of my hotel suite.

Everything is as it should be.

All the pieces of my façade are in place.

My dark brown hair is pulled up in a messy bun with slight wisps framing my face to give me a sexy beach vibe. My dress has a plunging neckline that dips almost to my naval. I'm not one for jewelry, but today, I have a diamond pendant that falls low in the valley of my breasts.

Nothing is left to the imagination in this crisp white form-fitting dress. If this doesn't distract him, I don't know what will.

According to what George said, the guns we're looking for are imperative to my father's survival. He will not have enough inventory to give his client without this shipment. Not only has the client paid in full, but he's also one who's not to be trifled with.

No. This could be my father's last chance. He saved me when I was nine. This is my chance to return the favor.

To save him.

I'll find the guns, then he'll give them to the client, and everything will be okay.

It's a solid plan with a bonus that maybe when I'm in Alaric's office, I'll be able to find something else incriminating to use against him in the future.

This can kill two birds with one stone.

This *Phoenix* can at least hope.

After I double- and triple-check that my outfit and face are to my liking, I head out the door. My hotel is close to the pier, so instead of getting a ride, I walk. Yeah, my heels are probably too high for the trek, but it's an excellent way to expend some of my nervous energy.

Throughout my walk, I check my phone. George hasn't called, and neither has my father. I didn't expect them to, but still, it doesn't settle my stomach not knowing whether everything is going to go as planned.

The air, although warm, isn't unpleasant, and a gentle breeze picks up as I get closer to the docks.

There's a chill in the night air once there.

Small goosebumps form on my arms from the breeze coming off the ocean. But even as cold as it is, it's not cold enough to ruin my outfit by wearing a coat, however it appears my nipples have a different opinion as they have pebbled into hard peaks beneath my white dress. It probably will add to my allure, or at least that's what I hope as I approach the boat.

His boat isn't a boat, but rather an enormous yacht. The thing of beauty gleams against the night sky.

It's much bigger than I had imagined, but from what I have heard, Alaric Prince lives on his yacht.

When I'm standing close enough, I can see on the side of the boat is the name that makes me cringe. *Empire.*

It makes me want to turn back. I don't need a reminder he is the king here, but he's about to find out, unlike his little soldiers, I'm no peasant.

There is no turning back now, so with my head held high and my shoulders pulled back, I make my last approach, tearing down walls that I never knew I had inside me until I embarked on this mission.

Soon I'm standing in front of one of his men. The man is tall and jacked. He looks like he spends half his life in the gym and the other half probably torturing people for fun.

As he looks at me, I wonder if I'm his next victim, but before I can turn around, he's stepping aside and allowing me to pass.

The party isn't in full swing yet; only a few people milling around the deck. They are all drinking and laughing, but that's why I'm here early. I plan to slip in and mingle, and when more guests arrive, I'll sneak beneath the party deck and look around.

If what George says is true, and Alaric Prince does live here, the guns could be on this boat, or maybe at least an address or something.

I keep walking as I allow my eyes to take in my surroundings.

I don't see George, but if he said he'd be here backing me, then he will. And knowing George, I won't see him unless I need him.

I'm on the deck when I see Alaric from the corner of my eye. Tiny goosebumps form on my exposed skin as he makes his way over to me.

He looks dashing as always, dressed in black pants and a crisp white button-down with the sleeves rolled to his elbows.

The worst part is the way he looks at me. The way his full lips tip up slightly on the right side of his face into a perfect smirk is downright sinful.

One that says he knows just how perfect he is.

Too bad he's the enemy. If he wasn't, I might allow myself to get lost in him for a moment.

He's not the man you fall in love with.

He's not the type you hang your hopes and dreams on.

He's the man who uses you and then spits you out.

It's a good thing he's the enemy. I can't afford to let myself get lost in anyone, especially someone so deadly.

The closer he gets, the more unnerved I get. His eyes trail over me, starting on my legs and moving to the valley between my breasts until our gaze locks.

His blue eyes are stormy.

Full of emotions I can't place.

I see lust.

I feel it. It exudes through the strained muscles in his face and neck.

I feel the lust too. It's thick in the air, making my skin heat. My cheeks flush at the way he looks me up and down.

His gaze slithers over me seductively.

He's so damn enticing, but I need to remind myself why I'm here. I'm not here for that. And as much as he warms my body with his stare, I can't get lost in the fire he stokes within me.

"What would you like to drink?" he asks as he places his hand on the small of my back and walks me toward the bar. A few people are already standing there, but I know he won't wait. Alaric doesn't wait. The crowd parts for us as we walk past them.

Like the Red Sea. Like a king.

Well, technically a prince, but something tells me his name is not enough for the man that he is.

"Glass of champagne," I respond.

The bubbles will loosen my nerves. I'll need all the help I can get if I'm going to sneak around this place.

He's quick to get me my glass, and I'm even quicker to drink it.

Just as I suspected, it calms me. It helps me believe that maybe I can pull this off.

After a long sip, I lower my glass to smile at him, batting my eyelashes like a seductive temptress.

"This is beautiful," I say.

"Thank you." He turns from me briefly, looking around the open deck, and gives a nod to someone. The man looks vaguely familiar. I think it's one of his henchmen who was with him at the club. Once he seems satisfied with whatever silent message he is trying to convey, he turns his attention back to me. "Now that I have you here"—cue grin—"and we can hear each other, what brings you to the Bahamas?"

"Probably the same as you." I run my fingers up and down the stem of the champagne flute as I lift my shoulders.

"And what would that be?" The deep timbre of his voice has my insides growing warm. Not a good thing when I'm supposed to hate this man. At least there is a chance he might fall for my act since I'm so obviously affected by him.

"Relaxation, of course." *I wish.*

My life right now is anything but relaxing. It takes everything in me not to allow myself to shake like a leaf blowing in the wind as I try to manipulate this man into giving me the ammunition to help my father take him down.

"And you're all alone …"

I allow my lip to tip up into a playful smile. "What makes you think that?"

"The fact that you aren't here with anyone," he deadpans dryly.

"I'm in the Bahamas with friends." *Lie.* My voice stays leveled. Hopefully, I don't give myself away.

"Is that so?"

"It is."

"You could have brought your magical friends over."

*I did, and his name is George.* "They had other plans." The inside of my chest feels like it will burst from the deception, but I keep my breathing steady and throw myself into the mission.

"And you didn't want to join them instead? I'm flattered."

*Snake.* The longer we talk about this, the better the chance I give myself away. Time to up the sexy.

"You should be." I bite my lip. "Turning you down was hard to do."

To that, he gives me a large smile, gleaming white teeth and all.

"Their loss is my gain." He lifts his drink to his mouth and takes a sip, all while watching me. Or appraising me is more like it. By the way his blue eyes trail over my body, I feel naked, and the worst part, I like the way he looks at me. It makes my stomach churn, that even though I know he's at war with my father, I can find him attractive. What kind of person does it make me? "Tell me about yourself." The deep baritone of his voice pulls me from my inner ramblings. Lifting my glass to my mouth, I use the time it takes me to take a sip to calm my racing heart before I can answer.

"I just graduated." I once heard if you are going to lie to keep it as close to the truth as you can, so that's what I do. I allow myself another taste of the crisp and refreshing champagne and let the bubbles loosen my tongue.

His eyes never leave me. Instead, he stares at me like the words leaving my mouth are the most interesting things ever said. "What did you get a degree in?"

"History."

My answer makes his eyes taper. "Interesting."

"How so?"

"I never met a history major. Now that you're done, what do you plan to do with it?"

His comment is hard to believe, seeing as it's a very popular subject to study, but I don't let on my thoughts on the matter.

"Isn't that the age-old question? Probably nothing, I guess. Maybe become a historian," I answer truthfully, or at least my truth before my father called me back. Funny how one phone call can change your life. A part of me always wanted to talk to my father about the business he was in, but I never had the guts until that fateful day in the office. It seems like forever ago, but it's only been a week. Before that I chose to be ignorant, my life was simple, and now … Now it's anything but, as I stand here, batting my eyelashes at a man dangerous enough that I should be scared, but instead, I'm wondering if my plan is working.

"I'd like to see that." His blue eyes sparkle with mischief.

"What do you mean?"

"You. Behind a desk." He parts his lips, and his mouth spreads into a smile, but not just any smile. No, this one is deadly. This smile could suck all the oxygen in the room. *Good thing we are outside.* "Maybe a pair of glasses."

"I said historian, not librarian. And you? What is it that you do?" I step closer to him, feigning interest.

"Import and exports," he answers with a straight face.

*Not a lie, but not necessarily the truth.* It seems Alaric Prince follows the same rules as I do when it comes to false truths.

"What do you import?"

He shrugs at my question, his gaze leaving mine, and looking across the deck.

"A little of this. A little of that."

"And export?"

"Same."

"A man of many words." He doesn't answer that with a sarcastic rebuttal, and I wonder if I took it too far. Did I ruin my chances? Blood pounds in my ears at the thought of failing my father. I owe him everything, and I might have lost the game before it even started. But then Alaric lifts his hand and gestures to the small crowd starting to form.

"Before more people come, would you like me to give you a tour?"

My heart hammers hard behind my breastbone. This is exactly what I need. A tour to determine the lay of the land. This is perfect.

I take another sip before placing my glass on the bar.

"Lead the way."

He takes my hand in his and then links our fingers together. It's intimate, and I have to will myself to stop the butterflies swarming in my stomach.

Damn. Maybe I shouldn't have had the champagne because the farther I walk with him and the longer he touches me, the harder I find it to keep my body from shaking with nerves.

I suck in a slight breath, praying he doesn't notice, but if he does, at least he's courteous enough not to mention it.

One point for the villain.

I almost chuckle at my endless mental commentary, but I don't. I can't fuck this up. As we walk together, he points at the galley. The kitchen. The bar. We take another step, and he smiles. I want to ask why, but he just walks up the stairs.

"This way. It's not too many."

I follow him up. There's a parlor, and at the end of the room is another door.

"What's that?" I ask.

"Just my office," he says as he leads me back toward the stairs.

"You aren't going to show me?"

"Do you want to see my office?"

He raises a brow, and I realize I'm about to step into a problem if I keep this up, so instead, I lean in toward him.

"Not really."

"Then what is it you want?"

I bite my lip and meet his gaze. He steps forward, and I step back, hitting the wall. He's so close I can feel the fabric of his shirt grazing my exposed skin.

His hand drops from mine and trails up my arm and across my collarbone.

I lean in closer, and now, his mouth is almost touching mine. I can smell the earthy hints of scotch on his lips.

"You want me to kiss you," he states, his warm breath tickling my flesh.

His fingers cradle my face, and when he pulls back, I get lost in his gaze.

It feels like I'm on fire, ablaze with a desire I need to extinguish. But will one kiss change anything?

I don't have time to think about it before his lips find mine. His mouth opens, asking me to let him in.

I do. I let him kiss me.

Allowing our tongues to dance to a seductive rhythm.

Becoming lost in the sensation.

Lost to this man.

He tastes like everything I knew he would.

Sins and lies.

His tongue runs across my bottom lip. Mouth hungry, his lips leaving a searing kiss. It's as if he wants to give me everything. Demand everything.

But as soon as the kiss starts, he pulls back, his vibrating phone breaking through the haze of lust between us.

He scoffs at the disturbance, pulling out his phone and reading the message.

Then he shakes his head. He steps back, and I miss his

warmth, but at the same time, relief hits me like a ton of bricks. Five minutes more and I don't know what I would have done. By the way I was just kissing him, I probably would have abandoned the mission like a love-sick teenager.

Thankfully, that doesn't happen because I'd never forgive myself if my dad lost everything.

"Everything okay?" I whisper, still not one hundred percent over the kiss.

"I have to go back down."

This is my shot. I'm a mere two feet from his office, so maybe I can sneak in without him being the wiser.

"Where's the little ladies' room? This lipstick is not going to fix itself." I make myself sound coy and even blush when he looks at my lips. "Next to the office. You can find your way down?"

"Yes."

He pulls me closer, sealing his lips to mine one more time. My legs are like putty as he worships my mouth and then pushes away.

"What was that?"

"I figure you won't let me do that later." I cock my head at his statement. "After you fix your lipstick," he clarifies.

"True."

"See you downstairs."

As soon as he heads down the stairs, I jet off to the office.

The door is locked, which I expected. It's a good thing I can pick a lock—another little thing I picked up in boarding school. I'm sure my father would love to know what his money paid for. Sneaking around and not getting caught.

I lift my hand and grab the extra bobby pin in my hair. It's now or never.

The door creaks open, and I step inside. I close it behind me and make my way toward the desk, pin still in hand. Something tells me I'll have more locks to pick.

I begin to search the desk by opening each drawer. I need to be quick so he won't look for me, but I also need to be thorough.

Once I pull the drawers open, I rummage through each one, my fingers flipping through papers. The boat dips slightly, and my hand slips.

A boat must be docking next to us, making the yacht rock from its wake.

I look through more papers. Something has to be here. I'm in the bottom drawer when I knock on it and hear the echo—a false bottom. My fingers feel around, and I can feel a tiny protruding piece of wood. I carefully lift it, and the wood pops off.

*Bingo.*

I found it.

It might not be about the guns, but it has to be reliable intel my father can use.

With the false bottom exposed, I find a lockbox large enough to hold folders.

Grabbing the pin, I attempt to open it up when I fly backward.

What the hell? I grip the desk to keep my balance.

We are moving.

And not just from another boat. No, this boat ... Alaric's yacht is really moving. It's as if we are no longer docked, and instead, we are taking a joyride.

With a deep inhale, I try to remain rational. It wouldn't be so far-fetched to believe he was taking his guests out for a spin. The night is gorgeous. Maybe he wants to show everyone what his toy can do.

I wouldn't put it past him. Maybe some bimbo asked him to.

But how long will this ride last, and will it affect my plans?

Shit. I need to get this open, find George, and then we need to abandon ship.

I head back to the desk and continue my pursuit. I'm sure we'll dock again soon, and I need to make sure I'm down below when that happens.

It pops open, and I don't even bother looking. I just grab my phone and start clicking the camera, taking pictures of the documents Alaric has hidden in the desk.

The boat turns again and starts to pick up speed.

Something isn't right. It's one thing to show off, but not like this.

I need to get out of here. I put the papers back in the box and close it then place it back in its spot, leaving everything the way it was.

Then I head toward the door.

It feels like my heart is beating out of my chest at the sight in front of me. There's no knob. No door. It's locked completely from the inside. I'm stuck, and I can't get out.

I grab my phone to call George for help, but I have no service.

I don't know what to do.

I bang on the wall, hoping a guest will hear and find me. I'll explain I thought it was the bathroom and the door shut before I realized.

I continue to bang and bang, but no one comes.

Time stands still as I start attacking the door. No one is coming. The party music is too loud, and with my luck, they are probably driving around to light off some fireworks.

I'll just have to wait until Alaric realizes I'm gone.

I feel sick to my stomach, but since the bathroom is next door, he might believe my story. I sit down on the couch, my feet starting to hurt from my shoes.

I flip through the pictures I took on my phone when I was in a rush to gather any evidence from the documents in his desk. It's too small to read the text on the papers, so I enlarge the words on the first image I took.

What I see makes my fingers flick faster and faster.

It's not a document. No, not at all.

It's the same words typed over and over again. It feels like I'm living in a horror movie and I'm the star of the film.

*We think caged birds sing when indeed, they cry.*

John Webster? Why is there a quote from John Webster here? I keep reading, and the wind is knocked out of me with what I see next.

*How do you like your cage, little dove?*

My body trembles as my phone slips from my hand and crashes to the floor.

He knows.

# CHAPTER EIGHT

## Phoenix

THIS IS BAD.

Way worse than anything I had mentally plotted out in my head.

The boat is still moving, and I'm still locked in this room. There is no way this isn't intentional.

They are driving out to sea to dump me overboard. The worst part, my phone is still not working, which leads me to believe they have something blocking the signal.

My father will never know what happened to me.

It won't take a rocket scientist to know I'm dead, but he'll never get the closure he deserves.

Now what do I? And another question is, where's George? If I can get out of here and find him on the boat, we might have a chance.

If I was caught, there's a good chance he was too. Maybe if I can get out of here and search the boat, I'll find him, and we can come up with a plan.

The only problem is, I'll have to wait until someone opens this damn door. Resigned to my fate, I flop back on the couch in the office.

I could search for something, but let's be honest. It's pointless.

I'm stuck here. Probably in the middle of nowhere and the worst part ...

All that planning on using the bathroom as my excuse for being here now makes me have to pee.

*Don't think of water.*

*Don't think of water.*

Easier said than done when I'm on a boat surrounded by water. I sit for what seems like forever before I stand and start pacing.

The boat rocks, hitting a wave.

Come to think of it, the boat has been getting rockier with each minute that passes.

Oh God.

There's only one reason that would happen.

He's taking us out to sea. No matter what happens now, I'm royally screwed, because if the roll of the boat is any indication, we are nowhere near land.

This is bad. Really, really bad.

What the hell am I going to do?

When we do finally stop, will I be able to get off? As if summoned by my thoughts, I can hear the door opening from the outside. I glance around the room, looking for anything that I can use as a weapon. It's probably not a smart idea. There is no getting off this boat. But at least I can fight. The door opens just as I'm grabbing the lamp.

"Well. Well. Well. What do we have here? A stowaway." Our gazes lock before he's dropping his to look at my hands. "I wouldn't do that." His voice cuts through the stale air, loud and sinister. "Drop the lamp."

"You lock me in here, and you don't expect me to fight back?" My hand is still reaching out, but without the element of surprise, I have no hope to get past him, even with a giant lamp as a weapon.

"There would be no fun if you didn't try. But let me tell you something, little dove, there's no getting off this boat until you tell me what I want to know."

"Little dove?" I grit, not liking what the nickname is implying.

"It's more fitting than Phoenix," he says with a wicked and large smirk, confirming my fear that he knows exactly who I am. "A dove is easily caught."

"I won't talk." I flatten my lips into a straight line.

"Everyone talks. It's all about finding the right incentive. I'll find yours or …"

"Or?"

He ignores my question and opens the door farther. That's when I see he's not alone. A freaking team waits for me in the hallway. Four men, to be exact. They surround him in the room as he catches me by my arm. I kick and punch, but it's no use.

Before I can even think about what to do next, he wraps a zip tie around my wrists.

Bound and now helpless, he steps back, admiring his handiwork. "Now let's go up top. It's quite a beautiful sunrise. No need to waste it inside."

Sunrise. What the hell does he mean by sunrise? How long was I locked in this room?

He pulls my hands.

"Wait—"

He exhales a breath. "What now?"

"I have to go to the bathroom," I answer through gritted teeth. Not a lie. I've had to go for hours.

His brow lifts. "Isn't that what got you into this mess in the first place?" I don't answer his silly comment, so he continues. "Very well, I'd hate for you to make a mess on the new rug they just installed prior to this trip."

He leads us out of the office, and once we're back in the main room, he points at the door I know to be the bathroom.

"Don't even think of doing anything fucking stupid. There's no escaping. Soon you will see, your options are limited, so trying to defy me is futile."

Not wanting to hear another word he says, I gesture to the bathroom. "Are you going to at least open it for me? Seeing as my hands are tied," I deadpan. My attitude probably won't get me anywhere, but I refuse to give in that easily.

"And what will you do for me if I do?" He chuckles, and I grind my teeth together. As much as I want to tell him to go to hell, I know that what he says is true. My options are limited; mouthing off to him won't help. The only option I have is to look for George, and then I need to get hold of the radio. Every boat has a radio. I should be able to call the Coast Guard.

It's a solid plan. *As solid as the last plan you had.*

God, this is bad.

I step into the bathroom then use my feet to kick it closed.

To get out of this bathroom, I'm going to have to do some fancy maneuvers with my hands, but I don't want to ask for his help.

The need to pee was so bad that I was desperate, but once I'm done, it will be fine.

I make my way over to the toilet, and using my fingers, I lift it. Hard but manageable. It doesn't take me long before I'm done, and I thank my lucky stars I'm wearing a dress because pants would've been difficult at this moment. I wash my hands and then go to the door. My fingers are just about to start to turn the knob again when it opens. Alaric is standing there.

"I thought you could use a hand." I step past him, and he chuckles. He probably thinks I should say thank you, but nope, that will not happen. No thank you will ever leave my mouth.

Now, a colossal fuck you? That I can do.

With my head held high, I walk toward the door to the deck on this level.

The sticky salty air hits my face, lashing my skin with the disheveled wisps from last night.

We are going very fast for a yacht.

He's trying to get as far away from land as possible. Seeing as we have been on the water for at least six hours, who knows where we are. This is bad. Terrible.

"I can see the wheels turning," he says as he stands beside me. "Trying to figure out where we are. Well, I hate to be the bearer of bad news, but there's no hope for you unless I decide to be a gentleman and let you go."

"Yeah? How are my chances looking?" I bite out. No point in playing coy anymore.

That makes him laugh. A hardy laugh that bounces around inside me and warms my stomach from the sound. I hate how my body responds to him. I hate that I gave him liberties to kiss me yesterday because now as he laughs, I can imagine the feel of his lips on mine.

When his laughter dries up, he advances toward me. I step back, hitting the cold metal of a safety rail.

I turn over my shoulder, glancing at the water below. The way it shines and sparkles as the sun dances on its surface reminds me of an explosion of diamonds.

How far is the drop? Would I survive? I look out at a horizon of endless blue with no land in sight.

"To answer your question …" he starts, and I turn back to face him. "No. Also, don't jump. I'd hate to jump in after you. That's right, little dove, I won't let you die. Death would be too easy for what he deserves."

# CHAPTER NINE

## Alaric

SHE TRULY IS A SIGHT TO BEHOLD. HER HAIR IS DISHEVELED, whipping against her face. Her skintight white dress hides little of her small and petite frame, and its hem is a little too high, but with her hands tied, she can't do anything about it.

She's feisty, I'll give her that much. And gorgeous.

It's a shame she's Michael's daughter. I'd fuck her to get her out of my system, but the way she snarls at me, that will not happen.

But now I know what she tastes like, so not wanting to fuck her will be a problem.

I won't go there, and neither will she, but when I see her struggle against the bonds, I can't help but imagine what she would look like tied to my bed, begging me.

I shake my head. There's no place for that. "Come on," I say, wrapping my hand around her bicep and turning her. "You must be hungry, and we have to talk."

She refuses to speak. Instead, her lips are impassive, and it's actually a cute look on her.

She's acting like a petulant child, throwing a tantrum and refusing to speak, but she makes it look good. Much better than most would fair under the circumstances.

I would expect tears and begging, yet I find neither with

this one. She's resolved in her mind that she won't talk, and to be honest, I kind of respect her for it.

She may be a worthy opponent.

Leading us to the deck, I pull a chair out for her when we reach the table setup.

"Sit," I growl, not at all liking how much I enjoy staring at her. I can't have any distractions now. George, Michael's henchman, had no useful intel for me. I hadn't questioned him really, but the daughter of my enemy? Yes, I could use her as bait. I could finally get the revenge I have desired all these years.

Ever since her father killed the only family I had left.

My brother.

A casualty of a war he should never have been a part of.

The guilt I feel in my chest is a weight that makes it hard to breathe some days. Today, looking at her makes me clench my fist. I'm better than this. Yes, I'll kill Michael, and yes, I'll use his daughter in my plan, but I won't hurt her. Not truly.

When she doesn't sit right away, I push her shoulder down, forcing the movement.

Although she's frail like a small dove, she's no porcelain doll.

Anyone who did what she intended to do can face the consequences of their actions.

"I said sit," I bark out, aggravation heavy in my voice.

"I'm not a dog that you can command." Her comment makes me chuckle.

"No, you're a caged bird."

"Great metaphor," she hisses. "Very lyrical. Now tell me why I'm here."

"Is that really how you're going to play it? I catch you snooping in my office, and this is how you're going to act?" She leans forward in her chair, resting her elbow on the surface.

Cocking her head to the side, she smiles. A coy smile filled with the innocence of a child who found her presents on Christmas Eve but is pretending she didn't.

"I have no idea what you're talking about. I had to go to the bathroom, and I opened the wrong door. By the time I stepped inside, the door had closed, but there was no doorknob."

Now it's my time to lean forward. Mimicking her position, I lift my brow in question.

"You really expect me to believe that?" I ask.

"Well." Cue a broad saccharine smile. "Of course."

My fist pounds the glass, making the table wobble under the pressure. "Cut the shit."

Her eyes widen, and the silly smirk is now gone. She thought she had one more shot to pull one over on me.

She doesn't. She won't.

"Phoenix. Adoptive daughter of Michael Lawrence."

Sitting across the table from me, she tries hard to appear unaffected by my revelation. Her face is stoic. She shows no emotion whatsoever.

But that is for the unobservant person. I have made it my lifelong mission to be able to read people. I don't even know her, but I can tell knowing all of this secret information scares her. I watch as a little vein in her neck throbs, and her jaw tightens. At my news, I watch as her breasts heave on the inhale she takes. Again most people wouldn't notice, but I see *everything*.

"So, what are we going to do with you?"

"I don't suppose dropping me off at the next port would do." She shrugs.

"No. I don't think that's in the cards right now."

"Why don't you tell me then?" She leans back in her chair, trying to look uninterested.

"Here's what we'll do. We are going to talk about you."

She chuckles. "As if I'll tell you anything about me."

"You will." There is no room for objection in my voice, but she just smiles.

"Oh, is big bad Alaric Prince going to torture me?" Her words drip with sarcasm.

"I won't need to," I respond coolly.

"I'm not going to speak."

"Probably not." I smile. But I don't say another word. Instead, I reach for the glass of water in front of me.

As if on cue, one of my staff members brings out plates of fresh food. I didn't know what she liked, so I had my chef make one of everything.

"Enough food here?" she says.

"I don't think so, actually. Shall I order more?"

She shakes her head at my quip.

"How do you expect me to eat this?"

"With your mouth, obviously."

She lifts her hands and puckers her lips. "With what hands?" she deadpans.

"From where I'm sitting, I see two perfectly good hands."

"Tied hands," she interjects.

"As you're a rather resourceful girl, I don't expect this to be a problem for you."

She glares at me from across the table. "And how am I supposed to cut it?"

"Again, you're resourceful. You did sneak into my office, after all."

"A fat lot of good that did me," she murmurs under her breath.

"You get an A for effort."

She rolls her eyes before lowering her bound hands to the plate, and then she does something I don't expect. She bypasses the fork altogether. Instead, she grabs the piece of French toast between her fingers and lifts it to her mouth. She pretends she doesn't like it. Hell, she pretends she's not starving, but I know she is. She eats the piece without ever lowering her hands, and once she's done, she looks back up at me.

"Is this necessary?" She wiggles her arm around.

"No. It's not," I admit on a chuckle.

"Then why are you doing this?"

"Because I like to play before I go in for the kill." Her face blanches at my words, but she's quick to pull herself together.

"You plan on killing me?"

She stops eating now, and all her attention is focused on me, on what my answer will be. It's impressive how calm Phoenix pretends to be. If it weren't for the sound of a knee bouncing, I would think she's unaffected by my threat.

"Still on the fence. It all depends."

"Is this the part where you try to make a deal? Because if it is, you can hold your breath. I'm not going to tell you anything. I'm certainly not gonna tell you where my father is. And I'm not gonna be used as bait."

"But that's where you're wrong." Lifting my fork, I take a bite of the French toast in front of me.

Her eyes narrow, and then she opens her mouth. "How do you figure?"

The fork clangs against the table as I place it down and then stare into her eyes. "You already are bait. Already strung up and hooked by the fishing line. The only question is, are you a catch and release?"

# CHAPTER TEN

## Phoenix

HOLY CRAP.

I am in way over my head. My stomach flip-flops as his words bounce around in my head.

There has to be a way off this boat.

It takes all my effort to appear unaffected, but it's pretty much a lost cause. Because no matter how hard I try, what he said sits heavy in my belly, and all the food I've just shoved in my mouth is not making me feel any better. I can feel bile rising up my throat. I try to swallow, but it's hard.

Slowly, and with careful precision, I reach my hands to grab the glass of water in front of me.

Eating and drinking, pretty much doing anything, is nearly impossible with your hands tied. Each move I make hurts more than the next. The plastic bites at my skin, but I don't show that I'm in pain. I refuse for him to see that it's hurting me.

The only thing I should be thankful for is that he didn't secure my hands behind my back. Lord, that would suck.

I lift it to my mouth and guzzle it down. Yeah, this is much easier in the movies.

"Having a problem?" the bastard asks from across the table. It's probably a good thing I'm in this predicament right now because a very large part of me wants to throw this glass across the table at his head. That move would one hundred percent get me a one-way ticket into the ocean. Life vest not included.

Nope. Dying is not part of the plan. It's obvious I have to abandon my mission, and now my only plan is getting off this boat alive and not allowing this asshole to use me as "bait."

"How about I take those off?" Alaric says as he continues to look at me. I wish he would stop because it's unnerving.

"Why do I feel like there's a catch?"

"There's no catch."

Not one part of me believes him.

"There always is. Spit it out, and I'll decide."

"You don't try to kill me. That's the catch," he says nonchalantly, and my mouth drops open. "I'll keep you alive. I won't kill you. I'll even promise once your part is played in all this, I'll let you go."

The bargain doesn't sit well, but I know I have no choice. "Fine."

I'll think of another plan. I always do. I'll pretend to play nice, then I'll search the boat for George. Together, I'm sure we can think of something.

Alaric abruptly stands and prowls over. With me sitting and him standing, he towers above me.

Tall and domineering.

He's quick to reach under his shirt, to his hip, and pulls out a knife.

This isn't some small pocketknife. This is a large hunting knife.

Seriously, Phoenix, what the hell have you gotten yourself involved in?

Who carries a knife that big? Someone who probably has a gun there too. Why am I surprised? The man employs an entourage of villains all on standby. He's an arms dealer for crying out loud. Yep. I'm in way over my head.

The plastic pulls at my wrist, but then with a slice of his knife, I'm released.

I shake out my wrists. Once the blood begins to circulate properly, I rub at them. A small groove is present from the plastic. Luckily for me, it didn't chafe.

After he banded my hands, I didn't bother fighting because I didn't want to tear my skin. With my free hands now at my disposal, I look at the table, my gaze lingering on the knife.

"Easy there, killer. We had a deal."

"I know."

"Then stop eyeing the butter knife. One, it won't kill me, and two … it will just piss me off."

"Good to know."

I grab my fork and continue eating. With what I have planned, I'll need my strength.

---

After the meal, Alaric escorts me to my stateroom.

It's different than what I imagined. Luxurious and decadent. An enormous queen-sized bed sits in the middle of the room, and there are pillows for days, which makes me yawn.

But I don't step inside.

"Is it not to your liking?" he asks, his voice dripping sarcasm.

"It's not what I expected."

"Did you expect a dungeon in the boat's bow?"

"Basically," I mutter.

He moves toward me, and I back away from him.

"You are not my prisoner."

"Could have fooled me."

"Go to bed. You haven't slept yet, so you must be exhausted."

I hesitate before stepping farther into the room.

"This isn't a trick or a trap. You are safe here."

*For now.* He might not have said the words, but they hang in the air, heavy and thick with a warning.

"No one will disturb you." He doesn't wait for me to step in, nor does he say goodbye. Instead, I'm left standing in the door's threshold. The choice is mine.

I don't know if I believe him that I'm safe for the time being, but I have no choice but to accept that I'm here now, and I have no place to go.

I'll need my strength and my wits, and I won't be able to think if I'm delirious. I decide to walk inside, close the door, and throw myself onto the bed. I don't bother looking for clothes or stripping. Instead, I close my eyes and let sleep find me.

When I wake sometime later, the boat is no longer moving. Or if it is, it's moving very slow.

Pulling the shades back from the window above my bed, all I see is darkness. It's the middle of the night.

Now is the perfect time.

I can sneak around …

Maybe I'll find George.

My bare feet hit the carpeted floor, and I wonder if I should put on shoes, but then I shake that thought away. If I do, I won't be able to creep around.

I'm still dressed in my clothes from before, but I don't have anything else to change into, so it will have to do.

Heading for the door, I slowly open it, not wanting to make too much noise. The door is heavy. Much heavier than a normal door. The urge to use all my weight to swing it open is strong, but I can't. Instead, I try to be as quiet as I can when I open it. When it does finally open, I realize my attempts were in vain.

Standing outside my door is one of his men.

Without a word, I slam the door shut, not caring how loud it echoes, and flop back on my bed.

So much for that.

# CHAPTER ELEVEN

## Phoenix

FALLING.

It feels like the ground is rocking underneath me, and I'm about to lose purchase just as my eyelids jolt open.

A dream. It was only a dream. But as I rub the sleep from my eyes, I realize that's not the case. My nightmare, as it turned out, is also my reality. I am stuck on Alaric's boat. I look around the plush and beautifully decorated stateroom Alaric led me to. When was that? How long have I slept? I feel groggy, not refreshed. Sitting up in the bed, I look around the room. There's no clock, which makes sense.

Time is irrelevant. It drips between my fingers, almost tauntingly.

The drapes are still pulled back from my earlier attempt to leave, and again, I am met with darkness. The moonlight reflecting in the distance is the only visible light.

How can it still be night?

Should I go outside? Should I try again? Although I slept, I'm not in the mood to bump into him, so instead, I walk into the bathroom inside my room and turn on the shower. Before I strip out of my clothes I have been wearing for days, I look around for something to put on, and that's when I see a robe hanging behind the door. Later, I'll look to see if there're any clothes, but for now, I need to wash off the past forty-something hours. I don't know how long it's been, but it makes no difference. I still feel dirty, tired, and disgusted with myself.

Once the water is on and my clothes are on the floor, I step into the scorching water and let it beat down on me, cleansing away the grime and salty air that clings to my body.

It doesn't take me long to feel like a new person. I shut the off water and dry myself with a towel. Then I wrap the robe around my body and feel ready to search the boat. The only problem is my lack of clothing. I have a choice, but the idea of putting on that little dress again makes my skin crawl. I notice a pair of slippers, put them on, and head out the door. The first thing I notice is that my guard is missing. The next is how quiet the boat is, leading me to believe that it's well past midnight. If it's the wee hours of the morning, this might be the perfect time to look for the radio. The boat isn't moving right now—or if it is, it's moving slow, which could bode well in my favor. Maybe the captain is sleeping. I kick off my slippers, realizing the sound they make slapping against the floor is too loud.

I make it up the stairs and toward the front of the boat. When I push open the door to where the captain should be, I see a light glimmer in the corner.

I'm not alone in here. Fear wraps around me like a tight belt. Each step I take farther into the room tightens the belt another notch.

"Look what the cat dragged in," the voice that has haunted my dreams purrs from the shadows.

I turn my head in his direction, but there's not much I can see. Even with the lamp, he is bathed in darkness, but the whites of his eyes shine in the dim light.

"Are you here to play, little dove?"

That made me step closer, teeth bared and ready to fight. "My name is Phoenix."

"I'm well aware of your name. But it doesn't fit or work under the circumstances, so I've changed it."

"You can't change it on me. I have a say. I'm not frail or weak."

"No. You are just a pawn I will use to my advantage."

I place my hands on my hips in defiance. "You think so little of my father that you can lure him into a trap?"

"Not little," he says, but he doesn't clarify his meaning.

"Then what?"

"He loves you. He will do anything to get you back. I will use this to my advantage."

"Will you kill him?"

He leans forward in his chair, the light now hitting the sharp lines of his face. The way he looks at me makes my insides tremble. The usual smirk is long gone, and the playfulness in his eyes has disappeared.

Only malice and hatred stare back at me.

He is every bit the killer right now that the rumors spoke of.

"Killing him would be too easy."

I charge forward, not knowing what I'm doing, but as soon as I do, I realize my mistake because he grabs my arms, twisting and pulling, until he's on top of me.

My back hits the couch, my hands drawn together in his grasp above my head.

He's too damn close, his rock-hard body against mine. "Do not test me," he hisses as I try to break free. "I don't like to be tested."

"Let me go." The pressure of his body against mine has me going into fight-or-flight mode. I try to move my hands to push him off me.

It's useless.

"Not until you calm down. I don't want to lock you up. I don't want to hurt you. But if you don't put your claws away, I will."

I can't move. Completely immobilized. My chest heaves with each attempt, but it's no use. We stay in this position for too long. His warm breath fans my face, my body pliant beneath his. He could try to take me, and the thought makes me tense.

"You don't have to fear that," he says as if he has a window into my soul, like he can hear my nightmares as they replay in my head.

"Sure."

"I don't need to force anyone." His voice is cocky, and I know he's not lying. There's no hint of anything but arrogance. He doesn't need to take because women must throw themselves at him. Beg him.

Not me. I'll never beg. Nor would I ever want this man.

No matter how beautiful he is from the outside, the inside is rotten to the core. Time crawls slowly as I inhale and exhale, trying to calm the anger inside me.

When it finally subsides, he stands and releases my hands.

"Let me go."

"You chose to be a stowaway. It's not my fault you ended up stuck on my yacht." The bastard smirks.

"I didn't know you were going to leave the port."

"I made an announcement. You must have been busy searching my office. Did you find anything?"

"Fuck you."

"You don't want to be my enemy, dove. Now be a good little bird and go back to bed. We have much to discuss tomorrow."

I stand, fixing my now disheveled robe. "I won't stop until I burn you to the ground."

"You can try."

# CHAPTER TWELVE

## Alaric

"SHE'S SLEEPING?" CRISTIAN ASKS AS HE STEPS OUT INTO THE warm air. I've been here for the past hour—ever since I walked Phoenix to her room. I brought out a glass and a tumbler of scotch.

"Can't you hear it's quiet?" I gesture to the seat across from me. "Grab a glass and have a drink with me."

"Should I gather the men?"

"That would probably be an excellent idea," I say, lifting the drink to my mouth. It doesn't take long. Soon, five of my best men surround me at the table. A few light cigars, and everyone drinks.

When my glass is empty, I lean forward. "What have you heard from Michael? Has he put two and two together yet?"

"He's been quiet. No one has seen or heard from him. But seeing as Peter dropped George's body in the middle of the square, wrapped up like a Christmas present, we have to assume he got the message. It's been two days since he's probably spoken to her. He must know we have her."

"So, then what the fuck is he waiting for? He needs to crawl out of the hole he's hiding in."

That's the thing about Michael. Ever since our war began, no one has seen him. He was like a fog, hovering close but just out of reach.

Cristian leans forward. "Cut her finger off."

My hands hit the table. "No. She won't be harmed. We don't have to harm her to get what we want. Her father will leave his rock if we give him enough rope to hang himself."

"You want to let him know where we are." His brown eyes are wide in shock.

"Yes."

"But—"

"No buts. We won't hurt her; he will come. And because it involves his feelings, he won't risk her. No war has to bring him to us. It's almost too easy. He can trade himself for her."

"Think he will?" Cristian asks.

I think about that for a minute. To ask that question would imply he didn't love her, but to keep her hidden so well for all these years means my plan will work.

I won't need to hunt for him. He will come to me willingly.

---

The next day comes before I know it. I spent most of the night not sleeping but talking logistics. We have a fairly large shipment of guns on the boat. We need to transport them to Caracas and make a pickup. Then I can handle Phoenix. The problem being, however, what to do with her.

She's a slippery little thing, one who will use the opportunity to attempt escape. We won't be there for a week, though, which will give us plenty of time to get her father to come.

Once on land, we can make the trade—one feisty little bird for a dead man.

That's what he will be. I've already taken his guns. This last shipment I plan to intercept will be the nail in his coffin. He owes money to corrupt men as is. But I'm fair. Although I should torture him for my brother, I've grown tired of this war.

We've been on the boat for two days now, and the waters are choppy as we cross over toward South America.

As I walk down the hall, I hear a noise coming from Phoenix's room. The first thing I notice as I make my way into her dark stateroom is the bed is unmade, the second being that it's empty. Scanning the room, I hear the grumbling again. It's coming from the bathroom.

"Dove." I walk toward the door. Lifting my hand, I knock. She doesn't answer, so I push it open.

The sight before makes me inhale deeply.

She looks so pathetic curled over the toilet. Since she wasn't sick yesterday, I thought she would be okay, but the waters are rocky even for me, and I live here.

I move closer. Her hair hangs in her face as she gets sick all over again.

I step up behind her and reach my hand out as she continues to be ill.

A part of me can't believe I'm doing this, that I'm holding her hair back. But seeing her like this touches a place in my heart. I don't want to care, and I don't. But one thing I enjoy most about Phoenix is her attitude, her spirit, and now she has neither. It's not fun when we don't spar.

"Why are you being so nice to me?" she asks, lifting her head to look me in the eyes.

"I can't have my bait dying before I use her?" I respond, ever the asshole.

Phoenix scoffs into the toilet. She must be done because she gets up quickly, and my hands slip out of her hair.

"Where are you going?" I ask, standing up as well.

"To bed."

"I'll get you some medicine. Don't stay inside when you're sick."

"Leave me alone. I don't need your advice." She walks away

from me but doesn't make it far before the boat hits a wave and rocks abruptly. She groans loudly as her hands reach out to steady herself on the wall.

"Go upstairs. Can't you just listen to me. What the fuck are you thinking?"

"I'm thinking you trying to help me is rich."

"I might be an asshole, but I'm not that big of one."

"Only a murderer."

"Yep. Only a murderer. Go up to the sundeck. Fresh air and the horizon will make you feel better. I'll grab you some medicine. It'll take about thirty minutes to kick in, but as long as you take it for the next few days, you won't get sick, and you'll get your sea legs."

"Where are we going? Why can't you just let me go?"

"Unfortunately, that's not in the cards for you right now."

"My presence is still needed?" She groans.

"It is."

"Whatever." She scoffs as she wipes her mouth and walks past me.

Even sick, she's stronger than most, an interesting and somewhat upsetting notion. Because to do what I'm going to do, I can't feel anything for her at all, and every second I stay with her, I'm finding it harder and harder not to like her.

She's the enemy.

I shake my head. Even as sick as she is, I can't let my guard down.

She's the girl who could knock on death's door and still find the strength for one last stand.

That's why she's dangerous.

She's the female version of me.

# CHAPTER THIRTEEN

## Phoenix

A NOTHER DAY.
The endless loop of waiting and not knowing what my future will bring makes me restless.

I know Alaric has a plan.

And I'm well versed with one aspect of said plan.

That being my role in this whole mess.

At least I am no longer sick.

That's a miracle.

Now that I feel better, I really have to search this yacht. There is no time left to wait.

In my nightmares, the ones that plague me while I toss and turn in my bed at night, George is tied to some strange contraption in the engine room. When I wake, covered in sweat, I tell myself maybe he never got on this godforsaken yacht.

Maybe he's okay, and maybe he told my dad when the boat left the dock.

My father will find me.

The waters haven't calmed; we still cross deep, dangerous waves that make the boat roll like a ball in a pinball machine.

I wonder where we are.

I know nothing about sailing, but if I had to guess, we are crossing between continents. Today, I found the men on the deck. They were deep in conversation, and I know without a measure of a doubt that they were talking about their plan for me.

Without waiting to be announced, I take a seat beside Alaric. No one speaks.

"Boys, what's the plan today?"

"Are you bored?"

"I am."

"Would you like me to entertain you?" His words drip with innuendo. Decadent and sweet. Like a strawberry freshly dipped in chocolate, oozing on your lips as you lick it off. His voice is so damn husky that the words leaving Alaric's lips explode inside me like little butterflies let loose.

"Not with you," I hiss before standing abruptly and walking away from him.

A few days ago, I finally noticed the clothing Alaric had bought for me. Everything I would need for a long trip at sea. I realized then that I had walked into a well-thought-out plan. He had thought of everything. There were short dresses, bathing suits, and the worst part—the part that made me squeamish, that made me feel sick to my stomach—was when I found the tampons. Because yes, that meant I would be here for a long time.

I'm not stupid.

I know that my stay will be at least a few weeks. Hopefully, since I just had it, I won't need to worry, but it doesn't matter.

I'm trapped here indefinitely, all because I was stupid enough to walk into a damn trap.

I make my way to the front sundeck. This deck is larger than the one I usually find Alaric sitting at. This deck has lounge chairs and a hot tub.

I strip off my clothes, until I'm only in my bikini, and walk toward the beckoning warm water. The footsteps behind me don't deter my progress.

"Going for a swim?" he asks, his voice like warm honey dripping all over me. I shake the thought of the sexy way he sounds out of my head.

"If I'm stuck here, I might as well work on my tan."

"Let me help you with your sunblock."

I turn around to find him smiling at me—smirking is more like it. "I would rather burn than have you touch my skin."

Instead of going in the water, I lie down on the nearest lounge chair. Maybe if I fall asleep, he will stop bothering me.

*No such luck.*

He steps in, and I look up from where I'm lying on the chair. The shadow his large frame casts blocks the sun, and I peer up at him.

"Do you mind?"

"This is my boat, and there are rules."

"Is there something else you wanted me to do … Prince, or should I call you king?" I roll my eyes.

"I like that."

"What, the nickname?"

"Your attitude. Makes me want to show you who's in charge."

My teeth grind, and I sit up, pivoting my body toward his. I narrow my eyes in defiance. "You wouldn't dare."

He steps closer. A predator stalking his prey.

"Wouldn't I?" His eyes gleam. "I have you at my mercy. Maybe I would."

A snarl leaves my mouth. "What do you want me to do, then? If I can't sunbathe, then what?"

"Ask next time."

I flip my hair and turn back around, dismissing him. "Fine."

"You still haven't asked permission."

Air leaves my mouth. "May I please relax on your deck?"

"Why, yes, you can. See. Was that so hard?"

"Asshole," I mutter under my breath.

"Did you say something?"

"Nope. Nothing here."

I close my eyes and go back to enjoying the beautiful day. I have realized there is no getting off this boat now, so I might as well get a good tan and piss him off in the meantime.

"Dinner is at seven. Be dressed by then and meet me in the dining room."

"I'm good."

"If you know what's good for you, you will be there."

I don't acknowledge the threat in his words. They ring very clearly in the afternoon air.

I'm done with him.

I'll be dressed and ready. And I'll bide my time because although I might be stuck on this boat, I'll make sure to find a way to tell my father not to fall for the trick. Let me die, but don't come for me.

No matter what.

---

I spent hours outside. At some point, one of his men brings me a bottle of water and something to eat. It's almost like being on vacation. Well, unless you consider that we are probably doing a gun run right now.

Who knows where we are going? All I know is as I sit in my towel with my damp hair falling down my back, I have to get ready to eat dinner with the enemy.

Normally, if I was somewhere else, I wouldn't mind so much. At least he's easy on the eyes.

Too easy if you ask me.

Personality-wise, he sucks. Sure, I see him and his men laugh every so often, so maybe he's not bad with them, but with me, he's my captor. Someone I have no interest in spending more time with.

Oh well, no use crying over spilled milk. I have no other choice, so I might as well put on my big girl panties. I look at the tiny scrap of lace Alaric has provided for me and chuckle. It's certainly not what I think anyone had in mind when they came up with that sentence.

Once I finish putting on my makeup and blowing dry my hair, I stand from the vanity and put the underwear on and look for a dress.

He was spot-on in the size department.

A chill runs up my spine over that fact.

How long was he planning this? I had only been planning for a few days before I got stuck on this yacht.

As I stare at my reflection in the mirror, another idea pops into my brain.

Seduction.

It's the one thing I haven't tried yet.

It's the only thing that can work.

I need to seduce Alaric.

Once I do, I'll be able to look for George, maybe even find a way to get help.

But how?

If I come on too strong, he'll know. But if I'm drunk …

That could work.

Squaring my shoulders in the scrap of a dress I'm wearing, I head toward the door that will lead me up to the main deck.

This has to work.

When I make it out of my room, I can hear the men speaking in the distance. I follow their voices. They are sitting in a different spot than usual. Now they are at the aft deck.

Stars illuminate the dark night sky. Alaric has scattered a few lights in the space for added ambiance.

Not for my sake, I'm sure.

These lights are probably left over from the party.

The party that set my fate in motion.

"Dove, to what do we owe this honor?" His tone is mocking.

Keep your cool. The plan won't work if you blow up and throw something at him.

"I was bored," I respond in my best nonchalant voice, hoping that I do nothing to give myself away.

"Then, by all means, let me and the boys entertain you." A small smile tips his lips. It's meant to be playful, but I can read through Alaric. This smile is anything but playful. This one is deadly.

I'm about to walk into hell, and the devil wants to play.

I square my shoulders and take the seat next to him. He lifts a brow. "You really must be bored if you want my company."

"There are only so many ways I can keep myself entertained in my room every night." I bite my lip; it's a seductive move, but I play it off as coy. Then to seal the deal, I part my mouth and then roll my tongue over the now puffy skin.

His pupils widen as he watches the movement, and then he must think better of it, because he shakes his head, places his hand on the table, and stands. I know it hit its mark when he clears his throat. "What are you drinking?" he asks as he walks over to the bar.

"Vodka on the rocks."

I watch his movements as he starts to make my drink. This is probably a bad idea, but in order for me to make a pass at him later, I need him to see me looking.

The problem is that's he's beautiful, dark, and elusive. A deadly combination, if I can't keep my wits about me.

The tattoos on his forearms are on display. Again lethal. Those tattoos should come with a warning label. The desire to look away and stop gawking at him is intense, but I don't. Instead, I've thrown myself into the ruse.

I keep watching as he walks back over to me, takes a seat beside me, and then hands me my drink.

The taste of the vodka is a welcome distraction.

It courses down my throat, burning a wake in its path. I enjoy the burn. It makes me feel like I can do this.

I'll need all the strength in the world for this.

"It's a nice night," I say, even though I sound like an idiot. Because what else do you say when you're drinking with a bunch of guys, and one happens to be your father's biggest enemy.

"You really must be hard up for entertainment, if you're leading with that."

Telling him he's a jerk sits heavy on my lips, but I refrain. Instead, I give him a false smile.

"Then what do you guys normally talk about?"

"Pussy," one says.

Alaric shoots him a look that puts the drunk idiot back in his place. I don't know his name or what he even does for Alaric. I do remember him at the club, stone-cold and serious. Obviously, they don't perceive me as a threat here on the boat, wherever we are. This will work to my advantage.

"What Tom meant to say is we talk about …" He lets out a chuckle. "Fuck it. I can't think of anything."

"Women it is."

He shrugs.

"And when you aren't talking about women …"

"We sure as shit aren't talking about the weather."

"Touché." I lift my glass and down the rest of the clear liquid. "Then let's talk about women. Or sex or whatever you guys talk about. But first another."

Alaric's mouth parts, and he smiles broadly before standing. This time he doesn't take my glass. He takes the whole bottle. He holds it up to me.

"Glass or do you just want to drink straight from here?" He winks.

I grab the bottle from his hand and take a large swig, causing the boys to cheer and give me a round of applause.

"Careful. I don't want you getting sick."

His meaning comes in loud and clear, hinting at the night he played nurse when I had seasickness. What he doesn't know is, I might be small, but I'm no lightweight.

Back in school, my roommate Hannah and I drank a lot. I'm no stranger to drinking heavily. I can hold my own. But he's doesn't need to know that, and he won't.

"I'll be fine," I say and then giggle.

I see the look that passes between Alaric and his boys. The look that says *she's yours to take care of if she gets sick.*

Good. Take the bait.

As we continue to drink, everyone around me loosens up.

Somehow, we venture into a conversation about sexual positions.

Now, I'm no prude or anything, but sitting around the room talking sex with a man who looks like Alaric has my cheeks feeling hot.

The man who I now know as Tom laughs about the last woman he slept with.

I listen with feigned interest, watching Alaric the whole time to see what he adds to the conversation.

"And you …" Tom asks, and I realize I was so enthralled with my father's enemy, I didn't realize what he asked. I look up at Alaric with confused eyes, and a wicked smirk lines his face.

"Position? Tom was just telling us he likes it when he doesn't have to do any work. Now, he wanted to know your favorite."

If my cheeks could get any warmer, they would be on fire, but I don't let it stop me. Instead, I continue to look at the man whose attention I need. I lift my right index finger and start to trail it across my lips as I think.

"For me …" I can see the lust in his eyes and the way his gaze traces over my lips. I part my mouth, and his jaw twitches, his Adam's apple bobs as he swallows, watching me. "Well, boys … That I'm not going to tell." I wink at Alaric, and he rewards me with a smile. A heart-stopping smile. "On that note …" I move to stand and purposely stumble. Alaric is fast, and before I know it, I'm in his lap, his arms wrapped around me.

A slight breath escapes my lips at the contact. His fingers splay across my ribs. The position is intimate, and I tilt my head up to look at him.

He looks down at me, ready to meet my stare but not before an unspoken command is issued. The next thing I know, it's only us.

The salty air feels warmer now. Or maybe it's the proximity of our bodies.

With our eyes now locked, he pulls me closer. Close enough that my chest now touches his. I can feel him breathe. Can feel his heart as it beats against my own. The feeling is intoxicating. Regardless of why I'm here, or why I'm doing this, I can't deny this pull between us right now. Despite the heat, goosebumps break out across my exposed skin. His fingers decadently trail up my arm as if he's tracing them. He moves to my shoulder, across my collarbone, until his journey takes him to my jaw.

He cups my chin. His eyes are dark and hungry as they pull away from my gaze and travel down to my mouth.

My heart beats rapidly in my chest, heady and desperate for him to kiss me. Maybe it's the vodka that courses through my veins, but I desperately need to feel his lips on mine right now.

"Dove," he says, and our breath mingles together when he does. The faint hint of an earthy wood dances on my lips. His scotch. The desire to lick the peppery taste of him has a small moan leaving my lips.

The sudden force of his lips slamming against my own makes me quiver. Or whimper. I'm not even sure.

All I know is that his kiss is firm and demanding. It commands me to open to him and give him everything I have.

A part of me screams not to, that this is part of the ruse. But as my mouth opens to his, and his tongue sweeps inside, all those thoughts are brushed away. Instead, I find my hands sliding up his chest.

This isn't real.

It shouldn't feel this good.

But it does.

I push away my thoughts and all the things I know I should be thinking right now, and instead, I give in to the kiss.

Allowing him to deepen it.

Allowing myself to become lost in it.

Our tongues collide. His arms wrap around my back.

There is no space separating us now.

This kiss is different than the last one. Yes, it's still under false pretense, but it feels different. It feels real. Too real.

The notion has me pulling away, panting.

Alaric dips his head down and looks at me.

"Show me your boat," I whisper.

"No." His words take me by surprise. A smile curls up his lips. "Little dove, what are you looking for on my boat?"

"Nothing," I respond, my voice quick and shaky.

"As much as I liked the kiss, do you think I'm an idiot?"

I push my hand off his chest and stand.

"Little dove," he muses.

"Phoenix. Repeat after me. Phoenix. *P. H. O. E. N. I. X.* That's my name!" I scream. Clearly, the booze has gotten to me because this is not a part of my master plan of seduction. Which has failed, apparently.

"What's in a name? That which we call a rose by any other name would smell as sweet," he chides.

"We are not Romeo and Juliet." I step back from where he's sitting as he moves to stand.

"We could be." He approaches me, and it feels like I'm trapped in a tight space with nowhere to go.

"Never going to happen."

"But didn't it almost …"

He steps toward me, his hand reaching out. It starts to run down my arm until it's enclosed around my wrist.

"We could fuck," he mocks. I step back, but he follows. It's a wicked dance.

"No. We can't," I hiss. "I don't want you."

Lies. My attraction to him is painfully obvious, from every whimper to every moan. The evidence screams of my lie, but I keep my back straight and tell the lie anyway.

"Then why does your skin heat when I touch it? Why do you tremble beneath my fingers?" Again, he lifts his hand, and this time I swat it away. Anger fuels me.

"Don't touch me," I hiss like a viper ready to snap.

"Are you sure?"

His brow lifts in a mocking gesture, and I grind my teeth at his question. "Yes."

"If you say so. I guess that means you're not hungry for dinner." With a large self-satisfied smile on his face that I so desperately want to smack off him, he starts to walk away.

"Wait." He stops and turns to look back at me. "Let me and George go." My hands move to the side of my hips as I prepare for a showdown.

"But what message would that send?"

"That you're not a monster."

"But that's where you're wrong, dove. I am, and your father made me one." My mouth opens and shuts because I don't know what to say to his comment.

"Then keep me. Don't do this to George. He doesn't deserve it." My words come out as a plea, desperate to save this man my father calls a friend.

"You don't have to worry about George," he retorts in cold sarcasm, and I bite down hard on my lower lip at his blank and empty stare. "He's not on this boat."

By the time I make it back into my stateroom, I can barely control the pain I'm feeling. When the door slams shut behind me, I allow the tears to cascade down my cheeks. I'm all alone here. There's no one to help me.

*You can help yourself. You aren't helpless.*

I just have to remember the plan. No more kissing. No more forgetting that Alaric Prince is not a good man.

He is the villain in this story. He will pay.

I'll make him.

My hand reaches up, and I swipe at the wetness under my eyes.

Tonight was a misstep. But the plan can still work. I need to play nice. The idea doesn't sit well in my stomach, but I'm a survivor. There is nothing I can't do.

When I was young, cold, and hurt, Michael Lawrence took me in.

Now it's my turn to do what I need to for him.

No matter the consequences.

I'll do whatever I have to so I can save him and protect him, even if that means ending my own life.

# CHAPTER FOURTEEN

## Alaric

WE'RE GETTING CLOSER. THERE'S ONLY ANOTHER DAY OR so before we will hit port. I know Michael knows we have a guest on our boat. It's only a matter of time before he'll try to contact us.

We are still too far out to make a concrete plan, but as of now, when we call him, we expect the exchange to go smoothly.

We'll suggest a simple trade.

Her for him.

My men on the island have already secured his guns. The information will spread fast, and he will know I have him exactly where I need him—royally screwed.

There has never been a moment in the last four years that Michael Lawrence hasn't had a hit on him. He's been smart, though. He rarely leaves his compound. When he does, he has an armed guard with him. He's like me in that way. That's why seeking my revenge has been unfruitful. But now I have him.

Now, he'll be lured out of the hole he's been hiding.

He is a dead man walking the moment the Camerino family finds out they had paid to secure guns, and he has no product.

Maybe he can figure out a way to get out of this mess and pay back the money. But I have already fucked him there too.

The money from the deal is gone. I don't just want revenge

for my brother's death; I want him to suffer for the innocent life he took. That's where he and I differ; I have never killed someone who hasn't deserved it. Take George for example, he was plotting against me with Michael, but my brother …

Michael Lawrence deserves what's coming to him, and he's soon going to pay for his crimes against me.

Without the guns, he has no choice left but to make this easy on himself. Striking a deal with me will have the same result. Him dead. But this way, in the offer I gave him, his precious child will be safe.

I'll make the call tonight. But first, I have to find the little minx.

It's been hard to keep my distance, even with a boat as large as this is, she's always there. Always barely dressed.

It's as if she's doing it on purpose, which I wouldn't put past her, to be honest.

She knows she is gorgeous, and she is wielding her beauty like a weapon.

Too bad for her, I appear to be immune. Even if it's not true, and the idea that I'm not pisses me the fuck off, she'll never know the truth. She thinks I am, and that's all that matters.

My men, on the other hand, aren't so lucky. She's been laying it on thick by batting her eyelashes at them.

But I know my men. I've saved them from too many wars to have them turn their back on me.

That's the thing a girl like her will never understand. When you lie in the trenches with someone, when you bring them back to life, they owe you a life debt.

My men owe that to me, and I owe my life to them. There is no coming between us. Not now. Not ever.

I find her right where I expect her to be, in the scrap of a bathing suit I bought her. I should have thought this through better.

If she's going to be flaunting her beauty, I might as well watch as she slathers sunblock on her legs. Legs that go on for days.

I step forward. Like yesterday, I purposely block out the sunlight, giving her no choice but to stare up at me with a hand covering her face against the glare.

"What do you want?" she hisses.

I'm used to the attitude. The sugary sweet voice she has is only ever aimed at my men. No, for me, she reserves the lethal one, a voice dripping with venom.

"We need to talk."

That makes her sit up, and her hand reaches out to grab a towel. She knows what I'm about to say is real, and she doesn't want to be vulnerable when I do.

Not naked like she is now.

Once the towel is wrapped around her body tightly, she looks at me.

"Speak."

"Such an attitude. Have I harmed you in any way to have you talk to me with such disdain?"

"I'm here—somewhere I don't want to be—alone. I'm thinking that yes, you have."

"But see, that's where I must have gotten mistaken. You came on my boat. You chose to look around … If anything, this is your fault."

Her face turns pale as my words hit her, making her jaw tremble, but she must catch herself because she clenches her teeth to stop the chattering as she faces me head-on.

"That wasn't an invitation to move," she seethes. "I thought you would be docked."

I nod. "Yes, you thought you could just sneak into my office and what …? Find your father's guns? Hate to break it to you, dove, but those guns, they are long gone. And the ones my men just seized? Gone too."

Her mouth drops open, her shoulders going rigid at the same time.

"You-You ..."

"Stole his next shipment." I beam as I fill in her missing words.

"But ..." She can't even speak because she is shaking so badly.

"This was all for nothing. You sneaking on my boat. You looking. I was always one step ahead of you."

"Why don't you just stop and tell me what you want."

"Tonight, we call your father."

Her eyes go wide. "And say what?"

"Inform him of the trade I want to make."

Her head shakes back and forth, already coming to understand what that means. "No."

"Yes."

My one-word answers for most would make them shut up. But she's not most.

"I will not have you use me as bait." Before I know what she's doing, she's flinging her towel off and running to the railing.

"Stop!" I shout.

She's already jumping by the time I spring into action.

Everything stands still for a second, an endless second as I'm screaming for my men.

Running to the end, I see her surface from below. She's kicking and swimming, but there is no place for her to go. She would rather die than let me use her as bait.

Too bad I'm not merciful.

Without another thought, I'm jumping in after her. My body hits the water, and then I'm kicking up to the surface. The water is much rougher, and I can see the fear in her eyes. She wanted to die, but until you look death in the eye, you don't really know what that means.

And I wonder if this is it. If this is the way to win.

Let her die.

Don't save her.

My brother's words ring in my ear as I kick my legs out to grab her. Her movements are choppy, her strength waning on the onslaught of the battering waves. "Only the dead have seen the end of war."

She will be a casualty regardless, but this way, if she dies, she won't have to see the bloodshed.

I look at her, our eyes catching. She implores me without words to let her go.

If I was a better man, I would.

But I'm not.

# CHAPTER FIFTEEN

## Phoenix

IT FEELS LIKE A WEIGHT IS PULLING ME. HEAVY. SO HEAVY I can't breathe.

I know I need to kick, but I can't.

After everything my father—a man who was never supposed to be my father—did for me, I can't allow myself to be used to hurt him. So I jumped. As much as my lungs scream, I won't fight.

I will let the dark abyss have me. Let it seal my fate.

Darkness comes fast. Followed by what I can only imagine death must feel like.

Drowning. Drowning.

Hands reach for me, and a choke breaks through my mouth. My eyes flutter open.

What the hell happened? The world around me is still blurry, but with each inhale, it comes into focus.

I'm on the boat.

"No," I scream, thrashing my arms, trying to break free. I can't let him use me to hurt my father. "No!"

"Shh," he coos. For some reason, it calms me. It shouldn't, but it does.

My breathing regulates, and I take in everything. From my wet bathing suit to the water still clinging to my body, but the big thing I notice is Alaric sitting beside me.

Wet as well.

He saved me.

And in doing so, he's condemned my father to death.

His hand reaches out.

"Don't." I push back. "Don't touch me."

"Touch you. I fucking saved you." His voice would make the arctic melt. There's a fire I've never heard before in his tone. It's scary, but it also lights me up—something I don't want to think about.

"I didn't ask you to. I didn't *want* you to."

"What would your death cause? Nothing. Your father will die regardless. His crime is too great not to, but with your death, nothing changes. I'm offering him more. I will pay off his debt for his life, and in turn, you will live. No one will collect his debt off your flesh."

The meaning behind his words sinks in. My body shivers at the thought.

My father owes dangerous men their guns. They would use me. No different from Alaric.

No. That's not true. Even though he's killed, when I look at Alaric, I know he's not lying. He would never use me like that. Not unwillingly.

But even though I know it, I can't help but fire back. "They are taking a play out of your book."

A very angry Alaric stands from where he was perched on my seat.

He paces back and forth then turns to me. "I never hurt you. I never raped you. Do not compare me to those animals."

"But you want to kill my only family. My father." My voice is barely a whisper. I look down to the ground and swallow before meeting his eyes again.

"I am giving him mercy. I won't let them harm you. I will take my pound of flesh, and in return, I will guarantee your safety, which is more than he deserves."

"Why would you save me?"

But he doesn't answer my question. He just stalks off, leaving me with his men.

I look up at the one called Cristian. His right hand. "Aren't you going to chase after him?"

"You should count yourself lucky that he is fair. If it was up to me, I would let you both die." And with that, he stalks off too. One thing is abundantly clear. I can't die. Jumping is not an option.

No matter what, my father's fate has been written if I die, but if I live … if I fight, if I get the chance to warn him …

Yes, maybe there's still hope. Tonight, we call my father. I can warn him tonight. Tell him our location, something, anything, and it will all be okay.

It's hard to keep myself busy and entertained. The truth is, I'm nervous. Another truth: I'm disappointed with myself. In the end, no matter how hard I try, I keep messing up.

I only have one more way to deal with this.

As soon as Alaric and his men are confident I won't fling myself off the boat again, I'm allowed to head back down to my stateroom.

I refuse to give them the satisfaction of losing my shit, so I catch my breath, throw up my walls and pretend not to care.

It works.

They know I am no longer a threat.

That I'm safe and will play their game.

Once I get out of the shower, I go to look for Alaric. I want to see if I can pinpoint our location.

Anything to help tip off my father. I find him on the bridge.

He's sitting at a small table with Cristian.

I don't know what I expected. Maybe a map that will tell me where we are going. But since that's not the case, I plop down in the chair next to him and lean forward until my elbows rest on the cold metal of the table.

"Since I have nothing better to do …"

"You might as well annoy me?" Alaric finishes for me.

"Exactly." I can hear the groan emanating from Cristian's mouth, but he doesn't say anything. "Where are we going?"

"Caracas."

The little composure I've held since the other night when I lost it is starting to evaporate when he tells me the location. What concerns me isn't the distance, I haven't been back to South America since my parents died.

A strange feeling worms its way into my soul, like this trip will be the end for me. I was ready to jump, but now that I know what's in store for my father, regardless of my life, I can't give up without a fight.

"Why there?" I ask with as little emotions as possible, trying my best not to give anything away.

"So many questions."

"I don't understand what the secrets are all about. There's nothing I can do. I'm stuck on this boat. I haven't seen another boat. It's not like I have magical powers where I can mentally tell him your plan."

Alaric's brows pinch, and he leans forward. "Very well," he says before standing and walking to a desk in the corner.

He comes back a second later. This time, a map is in his hands. He must not think I'm a threat at all if he's prepared to show me the location. The thought is sobering, but I don't allow myself to get burdened by it. Instead, I welcome any information I can get. I'm not good at maps or at least nautical maps, so I cut my head to the side and then look up into his crystal blues.

"What's the plan?" I ask.

"You see this island over here?"

His long arm stretches across the map.

"We are about seventy nautical miles from it."

His lips tip up into a wicked smile.

"Basically, what you're trying to say is had I swum, I would've died because there's no place to go."

"Yes, basically."

"And where are we headed?" I asked.

"Right here." I look back to where the map is and where his finger sits. Between the two points—where we are now and where we need to go—there is vast blue, so at least a day at sea.

I do notice a sprinkling of islands, and he must catch me.

"You won't find any help there. And again, it's too far to swim. Most of those islands are uninhabitable."

"How do you know that?"

"Because I know everything about the ocean."

I wonder how much of that is true. Does he really know everything? It would appear so, since he lives on this boat, spending his time going from port to port. I imagine it's so he can transport guns under the radar—a small private yacht under the guise of being some sort of rich playboy. I wonder if he pays off the government at each location.

"So now that you've told me where we are and where we're going, why don't you just tell me what your actual plan is?"

"You'd like that, wouldn't you?"

"I think it's only fair for you to tell me if I am to be used as bait."

"Here's the thing you need to learn: life is not fair. You'll be granted life, but unfortunately, to do so, I must take your father's. He wronged me. There is always a price to pay. Now, it's his turn, and no, I won't give you leverage to try to stop that."

His words feel like tiny shards of glass cutting me. Even though I knew this was the case, it still hurts to know he wants to use me to kill my father, and there is nothing I can do to stop it. Maybe I can try to convince him that my father played no part in his brother's death. I've been working to try to stop his plan, but maybe I just need to talk to him.

"Talk to me. Maybe I can help mend this—"

"That is between him and me."

I slam my hands down on the table. "That's horseshit, and you know it. You want to kill him because you think he murdered your brother. He didn't."

"You don't know shit. You think this is your war, but this started when you were still ignorant, nestled in your private school. Let the adults handle matters. This is no game for a little girl."

"Little girl? I'm twenty-two."

He moves closer to me, his hand reaching out to brush a loose strand of hair from my forehead.

"Still just a little dove. Not strong enough to fly."

"And how old are you?" I sneer.

"Thirty-four."

With that, he stands and walks out the door, leaving me with the map and nothing more.

This afternoon was a complete waste of time.

I found out nothing.

He took my father's shipment. Not once but twice. The men who paid my father still don't have the guns, and Alaric did something with the money, making it impossible for my father to even pay them back. This shipment, the one Alaric has intercepted, was a shipment of goodwill, coming out of my father's pocket. Yet again, it was taken.

Nothing I can say will change the fact that there are two prices on my father's head. The question is which one is worse.

Will my father come willingly to the slaughter in order to save me? Maybe there is still hope. Maybe the guns are on the boat, and maybe my father's men can take the boat, kill my captor, and everything will be okay.

Tonight, we call him. Tonight, Alaric will tell him of the proposed swap. I'll tell him our location. I'll make sure he knows where we are. And I'll trust my father to do what is needed to survive, even if I'm a casualty.

My days have been numbered for a long time. The sand in the hourglass should have run out when I was ten, but I was given another chance. So maybe it's time.

# CHAPTER SIXTEEN

## Alaric

S HE IS UNUSUALLY QUIET TODAY. I'M NOT SURE WHAT I expected. More pushback, I guess. Which is why I'm sure she will do something to sabotage the call to her father.

We're sitting on the deck when I pull out my phone. Phoenix's eyes go wide at my movement. Her skin, which normally sports a healthy tan, seems to whiten in fear.

"Yes?" I ask in a teasing tone. Its only purpose is to play up her fear.

"I thought ... I thought phones don't work here?" She's wondering if this whole time she could have done more to escape. More to warn him.

"They don't usually." I smile wickedly. "Not unless I allow them to."

Her mouth opens and shuts at my admission. "I thought you would be using the radio thing?"

"Were you hoping you could call for help?"

She scowls at me. All traces of fear are now gone, replaced by the anger I have grown to like in her.

"Unfortunately for you, calling the Coast Guard is not an option. Now come over here," I pat the seat beside me, "and speak to your father."

She shakes her head.

"No. Interesting. And I assumed you would want to warn him of my trap." I smirk as her eyes narrow at me. "No need. I'll tell him point-blank that it is a trap."

I grab my phone from the table and then dial. It rings one time before he picks up.

The phone is on speaker when he answers.

"Give me back my daughter." His anger echoes through the air, and I laugh.

"Work on your manners. That is no way to say hello."

"Cut the shit and tell me what you want. I'll give you anything."

I lean forward in my chair. "Here is the thing, Michael, you don't get to make suggestions on how we handle things. Phoenix is in no danger." He scoffs on the phone, obviously not believing me.

"She got on my boat," I remind him.

"What do you want?"

"Here's what you don't understand. I have everything I want already. I have your guns. Both shipments. I have your money. And best of all … your daughter. The most important person in your life is on my boat as my guest, so there is nothing you can give me other than yourself."

I'm dangling the hook. Let's see if he bites.

"Fine."

Hook. Line. Sinker.

"No." Phoenix stands, rushing over to where I am and grabbing the phone from my hand. I let her have it, loving the fire that plays in her eyes as she thinks she can pull one over on me yet again. "Don't do it. I'm not worth it," she pleads.

"You are." His voice is soft, pleading with her to let him do what he needs to do. "Take me off speaker, Alaric."

Standing from where I'm sitting, I make my way over to her. She's nibbling her bottom lip. The movement calls attention to how her mouth trembles. "Phone." My hand reaches out, and she looks into my eyes. Her big blue eyes beg and plead for me to reconsider. That ship has sailed already. There is no going back. Unless I give him back his money or his guns, he's dead. Truth. He's dead regardless, and he knows it. This is his best option.

"Please," she mutters as I take the phone. "Please don't do this." She's speaking to both of us.

To her father for offering himself on a platter and to me for doing this in the first place.

I grab the phone from her hand and place it on my ear.

"We'll meet at The Port of La Guaira. You will come alone."

"You won't harm her?" His voice is broken. He loves her. I should care, but I don't. He deserves what's coming to him.

"You have my word."

"And you'll make sure they don't."

"As soon as you are with me, I will have the guns dropped off for the Camerinos."

He's silent as he considers this. He is probably trying to find a way around this, which would require him to find the guns first.

Would he risk his daughter for one last Hail Mary?

"You have a deal. How long until you're there?"

"One day. You have one day to get your life in order." He understands my meaning. He has one day to make sure his affairs are in order to make sure Phoenix is forever taken care of. With the guns and money returned to him after the exchange, he will have to transfer everything into her name. A lot of work to do in one day, but that's his problem, not mine.

"Very well." He pauses, and for a moment, I wonder if he hung up. "Will I see her?"

"Yes."

It's the least I can do. I can grant him that little mercy, although he never granted me the same. Had I known that day four years ago would be the last time I spoke to my brother, I might have said something different or done something different.

But unlike this man, I won't do the same.

With nothing more to say, I hang up the phone. My gaze slides toward Phoenix, who is now sitting in the chair across the table from where I was sitting.

Tears stream down her face.

I take the seat across from her, staring at her as she cries. She's mesmerizing as she lets her walls crumble.

I shouldn't enjoy her crying.

Normally, watching a woman cry would put me on edge, annoy me.

But the love she feels for him, it's real. Genuine. He is her world.

The two sides of this man don't reconcile with me.

He killed my brother. No remorse. He killed him because he thought he was me. Unforgivable.

"Don't do this." She hiccups as she sobs.

"I am offering him an option the Camerino won't. I will give him a swift death and make sure you are safe."

"You did this to him. He's only in this position because of you."

"Your father started this war, dove. I'm only finishing it."

I stand and grab a box of tissues, placing them in front of her.

"Clean yourself off and pack."

"There is nothing here I want," she fires back, tears now dry from her rage. It simmers beneath the surface, the red flames peeking out from behind her eyes. They remind me of burning coals full of fire and heat.

"Then don't pack. This is our last night together. Join me for dinner."

"No."

I shrug. "Very well."

Turning from her, I stroll out of the room, ready to make the final provisions for the exchange.

By this time tomorrow, vengeance will finally be mine.

# CHAPTER SEVENTEEN

## Phoenix

Time is running out, and there is absolutely no way out of this situation.

It's late. Probably around midnight, maybe later. I still don't have a clock, but seeing as the boat is quiet, I have to imagine the time to be after everyone has fallen asleep.

With so much nervous energy jumping in my veins, I decide to go for a walk.

I'm too cooped up in this stateroom. I throw on a pair of yoga pants, a tank, and sneakers.

I don't get very far before I hear a crash at the same time the boat lurches forward.

What the hell?

Screams pierce through the air.

Did we crash? How is that possible?

Then I hear footsteps running.

*Pop. Pop. Pop.*

The noises echoing through the boat makes my blood run cold.

Those were gunshots. Someone is shooting on the boat.

It feels as though my legs are stuck in quicksand. I can't move. I don't know who is firing or where to go.

The sound of steps has me shaking out of my fog as I dash

for the staircase. The one place I don't want to be is caught without a chance to escape. If I'm at the back of the boat, I can …

What?

Jump?

There is no place to go.

*The extra boat.*

Although I've never seen it, there must be something. Isn't it mandatory to have a lifeboat, raft, something?

I'm running now, as fast as I can, but the gunshots get louder. My heart pounds in my chest as I make my way toward the back of the ship.

What if that's where they are?

I'm not sure what's happening, but soon I will as I swing open the door and make my way out in the warm summer air.

"Phoenix." My movements stop, and I turn to see Alaric. He looks disheveled, like he's been fighting. Dressed in gray sweats and a white T-shirt, he looks like he could have been working out. But I know better, and if I need any more evidence to prove he wasn't, he has a gun in his hand.

My brow furrows. Maybe he was firing at his own men, but as he lifts his free hand to his mouth, I know that's not the case.

He's being hunted too.

"Follow me," he whispers as we move toward the passage that will lead us to the back.

"What's happening?" My voice is low enough that I don't think he can hear me.

"Pirates."

My feet stop short, and he turns around to look at me, imploring I move.

"Nice try, Captain Sparrow. Pirates don't exist. This isn't a Disney movie," I deadpan. "Tell me the truth!"

"Not that we have the time to argue, but there are, in fact, pirates in the Caribbean, and as funny as that sounds, it's no joke.

They are ruthless, out for blood, and they are about to board this ship."

"What are they after?" I whisper, hoping they don't hear me.

"*You.*"

Before I can ask more questions, he grabs my arm and is pulling me.

Why would someone want me? Unless …

"My father?" I whisper. That's the only thing that makes sense. But does it? They are shooting and firing—

Crash.

Our bodies fling in the air as an explosion rocks the ground.

A bomb.

"They're trying to blow up the ship."

"It can't be my father." *Could it?*

Why would he have bombs on a boat? Especially a boat I'm on.

"I don't know. Maybe he decided you weren't worth the hassle. Now, let's go unless you want to die on this boat."

He pulls me around, and I allow it. The air is filled with smoke. Fire engulfs the space behind us.

Panic fills my veins.

I always knew that death was a possibility, but now that I'm looking at it in the face, fire and smoke billowing from behind me, I know I don't want it.

I need to fight. My brain becomes more alert, and I see where we are going.

"Come on. We are headed toward the Zodiac. If we get on it, we can escape," he says, his words giving me the strength to push on.

Another series of gunshots ring out through the air. My arms pump harder.

The sound of footsteps approaching.

"They boarded," he whispers, and I wonder if he's worried

about his men. "I can't let them get you." His words sting. If it really is my father behind this, wouldn't it just be easier to give him what he wants?

It makes little sense. "It can't be him."

"We won't be here long enough to find out. As much as I should fight, I can't let anything happen to you."

Heavy footsteps are gaining on us as we get to where the large Zodiac tender is. There's no way we will make it out of here, though. Not without them hearing us open the back of the boat to escape. If they hear, they will just come after us.

"We won't have time."

"What should we do?"

He pulls me out of the room then starts to guide me farther away. I follow him blindly in the dark as we keep moving through the yacht until we are finally outside. The warm air hits my face once we are on the stern of the boat.

"Help me grab the raft."

"Seriously? You want to take a raft out into the ocean instead of the boat?"

"One, we would never have had enough time to get the tender in the water before they found us. Two, even if we were able to, there is no quiet way to do it. The sound alone will have them firing at this."

"Fine, I guess we are taking the raft. Where is it?" It might be dark, but there is enough visibility out here, and I don't see anything at all resembling a raft.

"It's on the transom."

"Do you have that in English?"

He points at a large white canister that's attached to the horizontal wall of the boat right above the waterline in front of us.

"What the hell is that?" I whisper-shout.

"That's the raft." My eyes go wide at his words. "Once I throw it in the ocean, and pull the painter out, it will inflate."

"And then what? We get on a raft and pray?"

"Pretty much."

"There's no way whatever is in that box will have enough room for both of us."

"It's built for six. This isn't *Titanic*. I have no intention of letting you push me off."

He moves away from me and grabs something, then he throws the white canister into the water before pulling on a rope, which I guess from his earlier description is called a painter. It starts to inflate before my eyes. The bottom looks like a large black inflatable tube, and on top is a red canopy.

My eyes are wide, and Alaric must see my distress because his hand reaches out and reassuringly squeezes my own. "It's not fully inflated. It will be okay; we just have to wait a few more seconds."

The sound of air seeping out has my nerves on edge that someone will hear, but Alaric doesn't seem worried. I have to assume that with the gunshots sounding in the distance, no one will hear.

Once it's full size, Alaric pulls it close until it's hovering right by the boat in the blackness of the water below.

It reminds me of the type of life raft the Coast Guard uses in movies I've seen. I can't imagine he ever thought he would have to use it, but here it is inflated. He probably uses it for fun. It's probably nothing more than a toy for him to play with.

"This is crazy. We are going to die," I mumble.

"Probably, but at least we won't die by their hands."

"I can't do this." My head shakes back and forth. No way am I jumping into that little thing that can probably pop if a wave is too big.

"You can, and you will. Cristian will find us. If anyone is going to live through this, it's him. We just need to get you off the boat now until he kills them all." He pulls me along to where the back of the boat is open. Water batters against the ladder.

"I'm not jumping in."

"Then I'll push you in. But either way, you are getting on this raft."

The water is choppy, and no part of me wants to jump in. Just as I'm about to step off, the boat pitches again, and another explosion sounds in the distance.

"Step in. Can you reach?"

"You want me to step into that? How?"

"Step through the canopy entrance. Come on, we don't have any time. Get in!" he screams, getting impatient with my fear.

With a deep breath, I jump, angling myself through the entryway until I'm landing in the middle of the raft.

Once I'm inside, Alaric looks down at me. "Catch."

He throws something at me—a very heavy bag—and then he's jumping in after me. We are engulfed in pitch-black from where we are in the back of the boat.

"Do not say a word. Not a sound. They can't see us back here. As long as we're quiet, we will be okay."

"But for how long?"

"There are hundreds of islands out here. We'll be fine."

"But who will fin—" He places his hand on my mouth.

I'm not sure if it's from the chilly water or the fear that's rushing through my veins, but as we drift off into the darkness of the night with guns firing behind us, I can't help but shake.

I have no idea what's in store for us, or how we'll make it through the night. The only thing I'm sure of is my fear.

# CHAPTER EIGHTEEN

## Alaric

We watch the yacht become smaller and smaller in complete silence. I haven't closed up the canopy yet. Instead, I watch as the lights flicker from on board, and I know without a measure of doubt that my men are dead.

There is no way they could have survived that fight. It's only a matter of time before my yacht sinks. But I don't care about the damn boat. An empty feeling spreads through my chest as I realize despite my best efforts to never mix business with pleasure, I fucked up. I did.

They do mean something to me. I care.

The men with me might be evil to some, but to me, they are my brothers.

A heavy, somber feeling weighs me down, and the desire to scream into the night overwhelms me.

But there would be no point. Instead, I turn toward Phoenix to make sure she is okay.

Her knees are pulled into her chest, arms wrapped around them. She shakes beside me. A part of me wants to comfort her, but I'm not even sure how to do it.

She blames me for everything.

If only she knew how wrong she was. None of this was my doing. The boat is just a casualty from actions a long time coming.

"It will be okay," I say to her, but it's as if she's in shock and can't hear me because she says nothing, just clutches her knees tighter and looks out at the ocean ahead of us.

It's a cloudless night tonight, which is the only saving grace. If a storm hits, we probably won't live.

But if the water remains calm, there is a good chance we will come upon another boat tomorrow.

We are too small, and with the proximity to my enemies, I won't risk the flares today, but tomorrow, when the morning sun hits us, we should be able to find someone to help us.

Both of us settle into a tense quiet. She's too afraid to speak, and I'm too angry.

Once they find us, I will send word to my men who weren't with me on the boat. After that, a painless death will no longer be on the table for Michael.

No, the time for mercy is over. He will pay. Repeatedly.

Stars are the only light around the raft, the sound of the water crashing the only music.

I will myself not to sleep and stay vigil during the night.

But as each wave hits us, and as the energy that had once coursed through my body fades, I find it harder and harder to keep that promise to myself.

Instead, darkness beckons to me.

Vivid nightmares full of screams and death lull me to sleep.

# CHAPTER NINETEEN

## Phoenix

WATER SPLASHES AGAINST MY FACE. A BRIGHT BLINDING light makes my eyes squint.

I lift my hand to wipe the sleep out of my eyes.

It feels like I'm blind when my eyes flutter open.

Where the hell am I? What happened? With a jolt, I fling my body forward as everything that happened comes back to me at breakneck speed. Guns. Explosions. Escaping into the night on a raft.

The bright red canopy is pulled back from the raft that I see I'm still sitting in. I look around, trying to take in where I am.

Blue water surrounds me, but I'm not moving. It splashes over the side of the boat …

I look behind me and see that we're actually on sand.

Alaric?

Where's Alaric?

Frantically, I look for him. He's a few feet away on the sand with his hand lifted toward the sky to block the bright rays of the sun.

He must see me sitting up because he walks in my direction. "You're up."

I blink a few times. "Where are we?" I ask, my voice cracking from how parched I am.

"Beats the fuck out of me."

His answer makes my belly feel like it's dropping.

"What do you mean?" I ask.

He lowers his hand for me to grab it, and as much as I want to feign that I don't need his help, I'm not stupid. I do.

The nausea and dizziness make me feel as though I spent the night in the middle of the ocean.

Which I did.

His hand encompasses mine, and then he's pulling me up.

Once on the sand, I look around. "Do you really not know where we are?" I ask.

He shakes his head. "No. I can guess a general location, but we were in that raft for hours."

"How many islands can there really be?"

"You'd be surprised. Remember the map I showed you?"

I think back to that moment, to what now seems like a million years ago.

The map. The location. The cluster of hundreds of small islands.

Deserted islands, he'd said.

We could be on any of them.

As if reading my mind, he shrugs. "Yep."

"This isn't good."

"Thanks, Captain Obvious."

I have seen many sides of him since I stowed away on his yacht, but never have I seen the expression he has on his face now as he looks across the vast beach and at the trees behind him.

"We'll be okay," he finally says, but I'm not sure who he is trying to convince, him or me.

The first thing I notice is nothing.

Lots and lots of nothing.

White sand that stretches for miles. Turquoise blue sea that spans even further.

"Have you looked around yet?" I ask.

"Not yet. I didn't want to leave until you were up."

"And now that I am?"

"I'll go, and you'll stay here."

My eyes flare. "You want me to stay here alone?"

He steps closer to me, his face hard. "You will be safer here. Fuck knows what I'll find in there." He gestures to the woods. Tall trees block whatever is in the center of the island.

"There could be people."

"Or animals. Until I know what's there, I can't have you slowing me down."

My mouth flies open to say something, but I'm at a loss for words.

"Also, what if a boat passes by? If we are both in the middle of God knows what in there, who will signal to them?"

I know he's right. However, the need not to agree makes me scowl at him. It's deep-seated, and I can't back down. I refuse to be weak, so I plop myself on the sand and turn toward the ocean.

"And how do you expect me to get their attention if they come?"

He steps up behind me, his sizeable frame casting a shadow in front of me. I look up, squinting into the sun as he hands me an enormous flare gun. My eyes go wide, I can't use that.

*It's not a real gun.*

It feels heavy in my hand, but nothing like—I stop the train of thought that threatens to put me in a dark place.

Instead, I openly gawk at him, as I realize he just gave me a weapon. One I could use to hurt him. What does that mean? That he thinks me weak, or is it something else? Does he trust me?

"You fire this in the air."

"Can I just shoot you with it?" I mutter under my breath, low enough that he probably doesn't hear.

However, his chuckle as he walks away tells me he heard.

Great. Just great.

Stuck on an island with him.

How can things get any worse?

Hunger. That's how. Because the moment Alaric leaves, my stomach growls loudly. Embarrassingly so.

Lucky for me, I'm alone.

Unlucky for me, there's nothing to eat.

So instead of thinking about it, I keep my gaze toward the ocean. The water is unlike anything I have ever seen.

A shade of blue that only appears in dreams. It's as if the sky and water blend seamlessly in the distance.

I can't tell where one stops and one begins. I lose myself in the horizon, staring and wondering how this all came to pass.

The last week filters through my brain.

It's all his fault.

Everything that happened.

One might say I'm to blame for my circumstances. A stowaway locked in a room deserves what she will get.

But this feud has been brewing and festering for a long time. Eventually, it would have come to a head.

It's my fault I stepped in and tried to play a game I was grossly unprepared for, but this man doesn't fight fair. I had no choice.

I'm not sure how long I sit, staring out at the endless seas.

How long I squint to see if that's a boat or just a mirage.

It's the latter.

Each time, I'm sure.

Placing my hand on the flare gun, I aim toward the sky, and each time my finger goes to press down, as I feel the weight and pressure forming, I realize it's just my eyes playing tricks on me.

No one is here to save us.

A thought pops into my head …

How can they save us if they can't see us?

I remember watching a documentary about a group of sailors. Their boat lost fuel, leaving them stranded on a remote Pacific island. A military team found them alive three days later. The sailors had written SOS in the sand. Lucky for them, a helicopter spotted the message.

I wonder if we could do something like that. Would it work for us? Never know until you try.

Standing from my spot on the beach, I place the flare gun down and walk toward the tree line, looking for anything I can use to build my SOS. Unfortunately, I come up empty-handed.

There are no large rocks, nor nearly enough twigs to do anything.

Instead, I head back over to the sand and get on my hands and knees. How big does this have to be? Large enough that someone in a helicopter can see it. On an exhale, I place my hands in the coarse sand and begin to dig. Instantly, I realize this will not be as easy as I thought.

My nails are full of sand and I only just started. I used to love playing on the beach as a child.

When I was around five, a few years before my parents died, they brought me with them on a trip to the Dominican Republic. I spent hours burying myself in the sand. The coarse grains were everywhere. Even places that later I wished they weren't. The memory makes me smile. For a second, I pretend I'm that person again. Young, innocent, untainted by life.

But the feeling of happiness doesn't last long.

This isn't paradise. This is hell.

With a shake of my head, I go back to what I'm doing, dragging my hands through the sand.

Time passes.

I've scraped my knees, and my hands are dried out, but I've carved out the letters SOS. Took me way longer than it should have. Also, a shovel would have been nice, but I guess in the end it doesn't matter because I did it. Without Alaric's help.

# CHAPTER TWENTY

## Phoenix

HOURS PASS, AND BY THE TIME THE SUN IS HIGH IN THE SKY, I'm no longer sitting on the sand. Now my back leans up against a palm tree that faces the beach.

I hear the sound before I see who's coming. The faint slapping of shoes hitting the ground behind me. I turn swiftly and then rise to a standing position. My hands cross in front of my chest, all while gazing around to determine if there's a weapon I can use to defend myself. But my breath releases in a puff of oxygen when I realize it's only Alaric.

"You changed locations?" he says, taking long strides toward me.

"I can still look from here," I tell him before lifting my arm to block the sun rays. "It was getting hot over there. Not that this location is much better."

He nods to himself, walking closer, until he stops short, noticing the beach. "What the hell is that?"

"An SOS. I thought it was rather obvious," I deadpan.

"I hate to burst your bubble, but that's useless." He points to the letters I spent hours digging in the sand.

"You're just jealous that I thought of it first."

"Though I appreciate the effort, you realize all your work was for nothing."

The look on Alaric's face is one of faint amusement. It makes my teeth grind together as I ask my next question, "How so?"

"See that?" He points to where the sand meets the tree line. "The water comes *all* the way up to there. As soon as the tide comes in, your message will disappear."

"You're an asshole."

"We've established this. It's not new. But on that note ... Are you hungry?"

"I'm fine." I'm not sure why I'm being so difficult, but after the past week and everything that has transpired, including him crushing my dream of an easy rescue, I can't let him be my savior.

His lip tips up. "So, that means you don't want food ...?"

"I'm not hungry." *I'm starving*, I think to myself, but I stand and start walking in the direction that will take me far away from him. "If you're back, I'm going to go look around." He walks up behind me. I can feel his presence catching up with each step I take.

"I wouldn't do that. If you want to go looking, I'll come with you."

"Fine," I huff. "I'll stay here."

I plop myself back on the ground as he walks to the life raft. He rummages through it, and I'm shocked when he pulls out some things that must have been packed away inside.

He places them back and pulls the whole raft out of the water and up the beach until it's sitting right in front of me.

"While I search the other side of those trees, you can look through and see what we have. I threw in a few of the packs from the Zodiac, and there should be water." I lean forward to look as he continues to talk. "Don't eat or drink until I get back. Don't know how long we will be here and what is on this island, so rationing is important for now."

"Whatever you say," I mumble under my breath, trying my hardest not to look up at him. If he notices my attitude, he doesn't say because, without another word, Alaric walks off in the opposite direction. This time I notice what he took from the boat and what he's still holding in his hand.

A large knife.

This one is even bigger than the knife he used on the boat. This is like a freaking machete. I wouldn't want to be the one he is hunting. However, from what I can see, that won't be a problem.

Other than the sound of the water crashing against the sand, there are no noises on the island at all. Okay, that's not true. There are birds. Bugs. But nothing that implies any life.

Absolutely no sign that this island has any people on it. It's deserted. Or maybe no one has ever been here?

Which is not good if we hope to survive.

No one knows to look for us.

Everyone from the boat is probably dead, and even if my father knows what happened, he wouldn't know where to search. I never got around to telling him our location.

The only chance we have is if some random boat passes by, but seeing as I sat and stared at the water for hours and there was nothing, I doubt that is in the cards for us.

The future is looking bleak.

Despite the beauty of this location that I now might call my final resting spot, it's not looking like we will get out of here.

Wait, maybe there is a radio in the raft?

Leaning forward, I reach my hands into the side compartment, where I noticed that Alaric had pulled out the flare gun earlier today.

I'm met with nothing but sand.

There has to be more. No way is there only one storage space in this thing. I move into a standing position, and then I'm stepping into the life raft to look around. There are actually a few places for things. I remember Alaric placing stuff inside before we left last night, so I move to see what it was.

My hand touches a soft bag, I pull it out and find that Alaric had the presence of mind to pack a first-aid kit. A bottle of water.

That won't get us very far. Next, I find some kind of straw, but I've seen it before; it filters water. Unless we find a stream or lake, it won't help.

He took the gun and the knife.

I find another pack, and this one weighs a lot more. I recognize it right away. It's the bag he grabbed from the Zodiac before we jumped into the ocean.

Holy hell.

We might be stuck here on this island, but at least we won't die on day one.

Alaric had at least packed an emergency survival bag with everything you would need to survive on a deserted island for a few days. If we're conservative, probably for a week.

A flashlight, batteries, pocketknife, water, food. It even has one blanket. I keep searching, pulling out more and more stuff. My mouth drops open when I see toilet paper. This bag really does have everything. Well, that's not true. There is one thing I don't find. It's missing a radio, but this is better than nothing. I hear his footsteps before I'm done taking everything out.

"I see you found the ditch bag."

I look over my shoulder to see him walking toward me. He's taken his shirt off and tied it around his head. It's hot on the beach where the breeze is strong, so I can't imagine how it must feel in the center of the island. I let my gaze linger too long on his face, on the tiny beads of sweat dripping down his brow. I need to pull my gaze away, but when I do, I regret the decision right away.

I have seen him every day for the last week, but I have never seen him without a shirt on.

His tattoos are on full display.

I knew from the first day I met him that he had tatts up and down his forearms, but this is something else. I find no ink marring his chest, just rock-hard abs and a V that makes drool pool in my mouth.

I hear the faint sound of a chuckle, and I know I've been caught gawking.

Not wanting to hear anything more from him, I swiftly turn my face and go back to pulling out all the supplies we have.

He moves closer, and then once he approaches, he steps into the raft.

The last thing I expect is for him to sit next to me while I search, but here he is, only a few inches away as I pull out more items.

"We have enough here to last us for seventy-two hours." His low voice cuts through the air, weighing me down with the implication of what that means.

"And then what?"

"Then we hope someone comes."

"Do you think they will?" I ask, my voice cracking.

It's rare that I'm afraid, but knowing we might die here has my body shaking.

His hand reaches out and lands on top of my trembling one. The warmth is a balm to my troubled soul ... until he opens his mouth.

"Your father sent fucking pirates after my ship. There is a bounty on both of us. I'm sure they will come."

I stand abruptly, his hand falling from where it was perched.

"It wasn't my father," I spit.

"You can't possibly believe that."

"I do. The people on the boat wanted us dead."

He lifts his brow. "It would solve all his problems," he responds.

"It wasn't him. What part of that do you not understand? He will find me. George will find me. They are both looking for me." Red fiery anger boils inside me. I start walking away from him.

"That's where you're wrong."

My pace halts. "What do you mean?"

I can hear him as he steps closer.

"George is dead."

My stomach hollows at his words. My legs drop from beneath me.

Alaric is quick to try to lift me from the ground, but I swat at his arms.

"What did you do?" I cry.

Tears pour down my face at the revelation he has just made.

"I was protecting my empire." His voice makes my body shiver in fear, but I push down that feeling, standing up tall in front of him.

"Your empire!" I scream. "He meant more than that. He meant more than your tarnished empire."

"George was a casualty of war, and that war is between Michael and me. He knew what he was risking when he got involved."

"You're a monster." As the words leave my mouth, I feel the familiar feeling of moisture starting to collect in my eyes, but I push them back.

I won't let him see my tears.

George and I weren't close, but he's been with my father since the day he took me in. I can't believe he's gone. I can't believe that Alaric—

I stop myself. Of course, I can believe it. As I said, he is a monster. A certifiable monster. If I thought there was a way off this island without him, I would kill him myself for what he's done.

I feel helpless.

Nothing I do will change what's happened, but it's the feeling of the walls inside me closing up and no solution that makes the oxygen in my lungs feel depleted. Ever since I was a child, I have hated this feeling. I have tried everything to prevent it, and this man has stranded me in it.

"Where do you think you're going?"

"Away from you." It takes everything in me to hold back my sob as I hiss at him.

"Yeah, and where is that? We're on a deserted island."

"Anywhere but where you are sounds promising."

Walking a few feet in the opposite direction, I head toward where the trees part, leading farther inland.

"I wouldn't go that way if I were you. It's about to get dark out. Who knows what lives in there. And seeing as I have the knife and you have no weapons, it wouldn't be smart."

I scoff at his comment and continue walking. I don't go in, though. Instead, I find another palm tree to plop myself in front of, and in silence, I let my tears fall. Like wax slowly dripping down a candle until there is nothing left, I, too, fall apart.

# CHAPTER TWENTY-ONE

## Phoenix

MY STOMACH WON'T STOP GROWLING. IT'S AS IF AN ANIMAL is living inside me. Unfortunately, food isn't an option. But as much as I know I can't eat, it doesn't stop the gnawing feeling of hunger from spreading inside me. My vision is spotty, and my limbs shake. But I'm too stubborn to do anything about it; even if I'm so dizzy, I'm afraid I'll fall over if I move too quickly.

Maybe if Alaric wasn't a murdering asshole, I could bite my tongue and ask him for one of the protein bars in the safety pack he grabbed before we left.

But, alas, that won't happen. I'd rather starve to death than speak to him now.

Which very well might happen.

Instead of eating, I stare out at the ocean.

The bastard was right. My SOS is no longer written on the beach. It's long gone. Battered by the water.

The waves are stronger now than they were earlier in the day.

They crash against the shore like a storm might come. That would be just our luck: stranded on an island with no shelter when a hurricane hits. Behind me, I hear hammering. Alaric is building something, but I refuse to turn around and acknowledge whatever he's doing.

The sea blurs after a time, and the sunlight fades into the horizon as night beckons.

My stomach screams at me to grow up, and I'm thankful he left a bottle of water with me.

At least I have that.

From across the sand, I can hear the crackling first, and then the smell hits me.

Fire. The bastard started a fire on the beach.

Great. Just freaking great.

Here I am freezing, and he's probably roasting marshmallows.

No, not marshmallows, as those weren't in his survival pack.

My eyes roll of their own accord. If I could gag over how annoying he is, I would. But seeing as I have no food in my stomach, vomiting won't happen.

"Are you going to sulk over there all night?" he asks, and I'm still angry and hurt over what he told me earlier, so I respond, "Yes."

"Suit yourself." He goes back to whatever he's doing.

"I will," I mutter under my breath before I look up to the night sky and pretend I'm on this beach alone.

With the silence descending yet again, it grows nearly impossible not to look, so I do. I turn my body and glance at where he is sitting.

With his back against a palm tree, he's tied the raft to a tree to keep it from moving. In front of him is a makeshift firepit. He's even using the damn blanket.

From this angle, it looks like Alaric Prince is living his best life. Must be nice. He's on vacation, relaxing, the only thing he needs is a drink with a little tiny umbrella in it. I turn away so he doesn't catch me staring. Instead of looking at the endless ocean, I turn my gaze to the sky.

I have never seen a sky like this. Millions of stars twinkle in the darkness.

I feel so small, looking up at the vastness above me.

Leaning my back against the tree, I will my breathing to slow.

Inhale.

Exhale.

Praying that sleep finds me.

---

I'm woken the next morning to the sound of buzzing by my face.

The mosquitos are in full effect this morning.

My stomach revolts from the lack of food, and sharp pains stab my insides.

Reaching my arm up, I wipe the sleep from my eyes.

It's hard to pry them open today. As much as I slept, I still feel groggy and sleep-deprived. A tree apparently does not make a suitable bed. I wonder how he fared with his tree, his fire, and probably his turndown bed. I stretch my arms and look over to where he set up camp. It's empty.

The fire long since put out. Where did he go?

Now awake, I move to stand, and that's when I realize one of the protein bars is sitting on my lap. In my mind, I think I am better than to tear into the wrapper like I'm starving even though I am.

Unfortunately, any semblance of restraint was apparently set adrift because I want to be calm, but I'm not.

Nope. Instead, my actions resemble that of a rabid animal feasting on a meal after months of starvation.

I'm pathetic.

But as I rip into the wrapper and stuff a piece in my mouth, I let out a sigh of relief.

"I wouldn't eat that so fast. Take small bites and have a sip of water with each bite."

My chewing stops when I see Alaric standing directly in front of me.

He looks as disheveled as I feel, but I probably look like I have a bird's nest in my hair, whereas on him …

Well, he just looks freaking amazing, and it's not right for anyone to look this good when stranded on an island without a bathroom or shower. It's not fair. No one should sleep in the sand and look as good as he does.

I pull my gaze away from him quickly, and even though I don't want to listen to his pearls of wisdom, I do. Something tells me he knows a lot more about living than I do.

This time, I take a feeble bite. The texture is chalky, so I grab the bottle of water from yesterday and take a small sip to wash it down.

"Try to wait a minute between bites. Not only will it help you feel fuller, but it will keep the nausea at bay."

I give him a nod. My way of saying thank you before I continue to eat.

Standing, it feels too close on this big, open beach, as I wait for him to speak, but it appears he's not going to. He's content just watching me.

"Is there something you need?" I ask.

"I'm going to go explore some more today. You should join me."

"Thought it wasn't safe?" I say, my annoyance from before obvious.

"I checked it out a little, and there seems to be a clearing. There might be animals, but nothing we can't handle." He lifts the knife for emphasis.

"What about keeping an eye out for a boat?"

"That's why I tied up the boat."

"I thought you did that … oh, never mind," I say, not really knowing what I'm trying to say. I'm tired and delusional, apparently.

"For a shelter?"

I nod at his question.

"Hardly. Although we could actually use it as a bed. That way, if a storm comes, we can put the top up."

I cock my head. "What is this? A convertible. Put it on, take it off?" I roll my eyes.

"Yep." Why does he always have to sound so damn sarcastic? It drives me crazy.

"Oh."

"The only problem is it will get rather small if the two of us are in it with the top on. It's fine on the ocean, but here, we can make a better option so we don't feel claustrophobic. Maybe if I can find wider leaves, I can build something in case it rains. But another reason I tied the raft in this location is because there is reflective tape on it. Maybe a boat can see it."

"Smart," I mutter.

"I try." He shrugs. "Let me know when you're done doing everything you need, and we can go."

"Everything I need?" I question, but as if my body understands, the need to pee hits me and hits me hard.

My mouth opens and shuts like a fish out of water.

"Where should I go?"

Yesterday, when I was alone, I did my business in the sand. It wasn't my finer moment, but at least Alaric wasn't here to see it. Now he is, and my faces warms with embarrassment at the thought.

"Two choices. Behind that tree. But we have very little toilet paper, so we probably shouldn't waste it this early on. Or in the ocean. But we have no towels." He smirks.

"Either I'm a little wet or a lot wet."

"Wet dove is not a sight I'm opposed to seeing."

That makes him smile even wider, and now I huff.

I choose option one, sexual innuendo be damned.

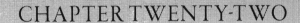

# CHAPTER TWENTY-TWO

### Alaric

SHE IS A LOT MORE STUBBORN THAN I GAVE HER CREDIT for.

No question.

Here we are alone on an island with no food source, no water, and no shelter, yet she refuses to play nice.

I get it, she hates me. I killed someone she cares about, but the simple truth is, she needs to get over it.

I might have been her enemy on the boat, but here on the rugged terrain, I can be her ally.

Not that she'll do it.

That girl would rather eat worms than talk to me.

I watch as she stands from where she slept last night.

Her body probably aches. I'd offer to give her a hand or maybe a massage, but something tells me she'll reject my offer.

Pity.

She really is something else.

In a different place and different world, I'd like nothing more than to have her naked in my bed.

I really need to stop checking out her ass, but the smirk still comes even as I'm shaking my head while she walks behind the trees to do her morning business.

Today is another gorgeous day in paradise. It's hot, but the breeze from the ocean makes it bearable.

Where we are going, however, might be different. The options for rescue are slim.

I didn't tell her that, but it's the truth. I can't imagine my men are still alive, and if her father was behind this, he wouldn't know where to look.

It's not good.

Without another water source, I estimate we will run out of what we have in three days.

By then, even with rationing, we will already be severally dehydrated.

I know most of these islands. They're close together. It might be worth trying our luck in the open seas.

The first thing we need to do is see what else is here.

From a few feet away, I can hear Phoenix cursing.

Not happy at all about the fact that she has to pop a squat behind a tree.

But at least I'm giving her privacy.

After a long string of swear words, she steps back into the clearing of the beach.

"Here." I throw her a container of toothpaste that was in the pack. "You still have water?"

"Yes."

"What crawled up your ass?" I ask as I hear her gargling and swishing toothpaste in her mouth.

After she spits, she wipes her mouth with her hand and then walks back over to me to hand it back.

"Other than the fact that we will probably die here?"

"We won't die here."

"How do you know?" she asks, stepping away from me and walking to the pack.

She moves to a kneeling position, but I can't see what she's looking at.

"I just do. Listen, I won't sugarcoat it. It's bad. We have two choices. We can wait here and see if anyone comes. Or …"

"Or what?" Her eyes are wide. Large and blue like the ocean backdrop behind her.

"Or we can chance it."

"What does that even mean?"

I lift my hand and point at the raft. "We can take it out and see if we can find help."

Her mouth opens and shuts, probably trying to figure out a question to ask.

"The problem with that is, I'm not sure it's worth the risk."

"Either way, there is a chance we will die."

I think about how to respond to her comment. My jaw tightens as different things to say play in my head. "Yes, but before we can decide, we need to know what we are dealing with. The island might not be a death trap. The sea might not be one either."

"Do you think anyone is looking for us?"

"Yes. But depending on the supplies on this island, we might not last long enough to find us. There are hundreds of islands in the vicinity."

"What would we have to do if we left?"

"We would have to gather supplies, food, and water. And then I guess we have to hope."

"What do you suggest?"

Without realizing, I've begun to pace. I take a deep breath and then blow it out. I turn to face her, our eyes locking.

"I suggest that we search the island for food sources and a water source and collect everything we can find. We give it a few days, and then if no one comes, we chance it."

Her brow furrows. "We'll die if we leave," she whispers, more to herself then to me.

"Maybe."

"We'll die if we stay."

"Maybe."

She nods, resigned to the fact that, in both cases, we are living on borrowed time.

"Are you ready?" I ask, needing to change the topic.

"Yep. Lead the way."

I reach into my pocket and pull out a folding knife. "Here." I hand it to her.

"Aren't you scared I might stab you with that?"

"No."

"Why not? Maybe I want you dead." She smiles coolly at me.

"That might be so, but I'm your best chance at survival. Kill me now, and you might as well slit your wrists right after."

She stands there quietly for a moment and then moves farther into the brush. "Are you coming?"

I walk after her. She stops a few steps in, gesturing her hands in front of her. "Lead the way." I do.

Together, we walk into the unknown. We will go farther than I have in the past. I have a gun, my knife, and enough food for a day trip. I mark the trees as we walk, leaving a trail of bread crumbs back to the beach if need be. Hopefully, we'll be back before dark, but just in case, I packed the flashlight as well. The palm trees near the beach didn't have coconuts, but a little farther inland, they might. This is a tropical island, after all, so I'm sure I'll find fruit. We walk for some time on the trek, and I stop every so often to check for food.

Unfortunately, everything I have found thus far is inedible.

Which only means we have to go deeper into the island.

Who knows what that will bring.

# CHAPTER TWENTY-THREE

## Phoenix

WﾞITH EACH STEP WE TAKE, THE TREES GET THICKER AND thicker. Branches snap at my skin, cutting into the flesh, but I don't allow them to stop my moves. Even with a minor gash forming on my right arm and a slow trickle of blood escaping, I press on. I have no intention of allowing Alaric to think I can't keep up.

As I huff and puff to keep his pace, I can feel the strain burning in my limbs. We walk for what seems like hours. He's ahead of me, pushing the vegetation back to make a path. I can't even imagine how cut up he must be.

If he is, it doesn't show.

A part of me expected that this being a deserted island would be a lie, but this walk is proving otherwise.

"Need to take a break?" Alaric asks from ahead of me.

"Nope. I'm good."

I'm not good. I'm far from it. Though that thought will never be spoken aloud.

I'd rather die than tell him.

Nothing of value is found during our whole walk. Sure, there are trees, and lots of bugs too, but where is the fruit?

Animals.

Anything.

"Thank fuck," I hear him say, but I have no idea what he's talking about.

I push through the branch he holds back, and I see what has him excited.

There in front of us, in the distance, is a large waterfall and clearing and lake. It's straight out of a movie like *The Blue Lagoon*.

They don't die in that one. They lived there for years.

As soon as that thought pops in my head, I groan. Yes, they lived there for years, but would I really want to live on the island for that long with him?

As if the wool has been pulled from my eyes, I suddenly realize how grimy I feel. The water looks so refreshing, and I just want to jump in. I could. But then my clothes would get wet. As if he could hear my inner rambling, he turns to me. His face is sun-kissed. I hadn't noticed it before, but during his walk yesterday, he must've gotten more sun than I thought.

"We should go in. Wash off."

"I—"

"I won't watch you if you want to get undressed."

I can feel the heat rising to my face.

"Um. Okay."

Normally, I'm no blushing schoolgirl, but for some reason, the idea of being naked with this man has my cheeks on fire.

"Turn around," I say, and when he does, I remove my T-shirt and leggings. I don't have a towel, so I have to put them back on while I'm still wet, but at least I'll feel clean.

Once my clothes are off, I make my way into the water. I'm not sure how deep it is, so I carefully walk in. When the water finally covers my breasts, I turn around. Alaric is still not looking, and I'm thankful for that.

"All clear," I say.

I expect him to say the same to me, to tell me to close my eyes, but as he strips out of his shirt and pulls down his pants, my eyes grow wide. I should look away. I really need to, but it's as if I'm stuck in quicksand and can't move. My eyes have been glued open instead of shut.

I physically can't look away. Instead, I watch him as he strips naked and walks toward the water. He stops, and I'm surprised, but then he reaches into the bag and pulls something out. I don't want to ask him what it is because then he would know that I'm staring at him.

I pretend not to watch him as he makes his approach. The water shifts and I know he's moving closer.

My eyes are still closed, and I'm scared to open them.

"Scared, little dove?"

My eyelids jolt open. "Don't call me that."

"But it's what you are." He smirks.

"You're annoying. You know that?"

"I might be annoying, but I'm also the guy who has soap."

He lifts his hand out of the water, and a bar of soap sits in his hand.

"Seriously, is that soap on a rope?"

"What else did you expect in a survival kit?"

"I am in prison, so it makes sense," I gripe.

He motions his hand around us. "I would hardly call this prison."

"Speak for yourself."

"Look around you. I have been to prison, and this is not it. This is paradise. Maybe you wouldn't choose to be here with me, but …"

I lift my brow. "You think."

"I'm not that bad."

I shake my head adamantly. "You most certainly are."

"Admit it, I'm at least easy on the eyes." Cue the smirk. That damn smirk.

The first time I saw it, I knew it would be a problem, but

now? Now, I realize just how big a problem it will be. He's smirking at me like that when we're both naked underneath the water. How easy would it be to just cross the divide and lose myself for a bit? To pretend I'm here on vacation with someone I want and desire. Unfortunately, that's not the case, and he is not that person for me. No matter how good-looking he is.

"See? Case in point, the arrogance."

"At least I'll keep things interesting on this island."

"Just give me the soap."

"Say please."

This man. If I didn't want the soap so badly, I'd splash him. Or drown him or something. But, alas, I do need that soap. "You're intolerable."

"But at least I'm clean." He chuckles, and just as I'm about to close the distance and throttle him, he reaches his hand out.

I take the soap before he can change his mind.

Then I wipe off the past few days. With each pass, I feel cleaner.

But as he stares at me, hair slicked back, tattoos showing, I fight the urge to bite my lip.

There is no amount of soap to wash away the impure thoughts running through my mind right now.

And that will be a problem.

It isn't long until we are back at the beach. I'm not sure if we'll camp out here again, or if we'll set up camp further inland.

Alaric must read my mind because he unties the raft.

"It's too heavy to drag it."

"What are you doing?" I ask.

"If you help me, we can drag it further away."

"To do what?"

"Sleep on it."

"You want us to sleep in that … together?"

"I know I should have thought of it last night, but I was too tired. But seeing as we don't have any other option, I figured there's no reason for us to sleep on the sand again."

I look at him and then at the tree where I rested yesterday.

But as much I want to say okay, I can't. My damn pride is still getting the best of me.

"I'm okay over here."

He lifts a brow. "You sure? The wind is picking up. You might get cold."

"And I'll be warmed by you?"

His lip tips up. "Body heat. Plus, I do have the blanket," he teases.

"I'm sure that's what you tell all the girls you want to lie with on a tiny raft."

"It's hardly tiny. It can comfortably fit six."

"Whatever you say, dude."

"If you aren't going to sit with me, then at least take this." He throws a protein bar at me. By my calculations, we will run out of these bad boys by tomorrow.

As if reading my mind, he opens his mouth. "I'm going to fish tomorrow."

"You know how to fish?"

He gives me a look that says, *Are you kidding me?*

"Of course, you know how to fish. Is there anything you can't do?"

"I can't get you to shut up."

"Ass."

At that insult, I turn from him and eat the protein bar. This time, I take tiny bites while drinking the remaining water to get fuller faster.

It's not long before I hear the familiar sound of a fire crackling and the smell filters around me. I wrap my arms tighter around myself. He was right; the temperature is dipping and rather fast. It will be fine. Sooner rather than later, I'll fall asleep, and I won't notice the cold. Or at least that's what I hope as I close my eyes and will myself to bed.

Time must pass, but I'm having no such luck on the sleeping front. I'm still wide-awake and freezing my ass off. I turn toward Alaric, the still roaring fire a foot from where he's lying on the raft. He wasn't lying when he said it wasn't tiny. It's actually pretty big, and I'm not sure why I hadn't thought to sleep in it. If I went over there, he'd probably never know. Maybe I could just sit there long enough to get warm, and then once I am, I can find another tree, maybe one a little closer to sleep under.

I watch him for a minute. The way his chest rises and falls, I'm sure he's asleep. If I go there, he'll never know. I just have to move before he gets up.

That won't be hard. I just won't close my eyes. Making sure I don't make a sound, I stand from where I'm sitting and head over. I step over it, redistributing my weight so as not to wake him, and take a seat closest to the fire. It feels so good. Much better than the other location. My teeth stop chattering, and I want to inhale deeply, but don't dare.

That's when I hear it.

A chuckle.

A chuckle coming from what I thought was a sleeping Alaric. Goddammit, he tricked me.

I go to stand, but then I feel it. His hand touching my skin. The pads of his fingers warm on my flesh.

"Don't," he says, and I look down to where he touches me, a million goosebumps erupting at the contact. "Just sleep."

I should move, but with the warmth emanating, I can't help but obey.

# CHAPTER TWENTY-FOUR

## Alaric

IT'S OFFICIAL. SHE IS THE MOST STUBBORN WOMAN I HAVE ever met in my life. Without a doubt, she is probably the most stubborn person in the world. Which, if you really think about it, is kind of admirable. To be the best at something. *Even if it's the most annoying thing in the world.*

When I opened my eyes this morning, she had moved from her spot on the opposite side of the raft to right beside me. She had curled up next to me. While asleep, her body must have sought my heat. I watch as she dreams, her breathing soft and peaceful.

She looks gorgeous in the morning. Not that she's not always beautiful, but now, in a deep sleep, her face is peaceful. There are no frowns and scowls present.

When I look at her, I don't see hate, anger, and the many ways she wants to kill me.

I see a girl I have never seen before. A girl in another life. If we were different people, I might be interested in getting to know her.

Unfortunately, that's not the case. She's my enemy's daughter, sent in to infiltrate my life.

Not a woman I can mess around with.

But as my eyes skate across the distance, I realize I can't think of her as that here on this island. Here, we have to be allies. If we ever collect enough supplies to leave, we have to work together.

I'm still hopeful someone will find us, but with each day that passes, that hope diminishes more and more. There is no denying the reality of our situation.

Revenge doesn't seem nearly as important as it once did.

Instead of waking her, I decide to slowly move from where our bodies are touching to start my day.

I'll let her rest.

My movements, however, have the opposite effect because she jumps up, eyes wild as she takes in her proximity to me.

Leg still entwined with mine, she sits up and moves away.

"Morning," I say. She scowls at me, but it just makes me chuckle. Sleeping, her body found mine, but now with her mind awake, she's backpedaling.

"Comfy?" I jest. "You slept well, wrapped in my arms."

I'm not sure why teasing her is so entertaining, but when there's not much else to do, I guess we have to get our excitement somewhere.

She stands abruptly and leaves our makeshift raft bed. I watch as a furious Phoenix rifles through the bag to get the toothpaste, all while glaring at me.

I want to laugh at how absurd this is, but something tells me she will throw that container in my face. Literally.

"Brush your teeth and do your business. We leave once you're done."

"What's on the agenda today? Fancy lunch?" she mocks.

"One, we hunt for food. Two, we are going to look for anything edible."

As it is, we won't last much longer without an alternative food source.

"What about the raft?" she asks, her cheeks pinched in.

"In order for us to get on the raft, we need to have at least enough food and water to last a week. We also need to find wood to make oars. Without a way to push past the tide, we will get nowhere fast."

She takes a deep, lengthy breath. "Do we really have any chance?"

"There's always a chance. But we need to get ahead of it while we still have the protein bars. Right now, that's our only source of energy. We won't be able to hunt and gather once it's gone."

"Then let's get to it," I hear her say, and then she's behind a tree doing what she needs to do.

Unlike her, I don't need to hide behind a tree to do my business. Instead, like the asshole I am, I whip my shit out and pee on the palm tree.

"Wow. Seriously?"

She sounds annoyed. Which I kind of understand, since I did pee on her tree. "You couldn't hide that shit."

"It would take too long." Once I put myself back in my pants, she walks over to me, reaching her hand out with the toothpaste.

"Here. You stink."

"I don't stink. And even if I did, you stink just as bad, so you wouldn't smell me."

"Real nice, asshole."

"Just keeping it real." I shrug.

I take the container from her and place a small amount on my finger and clean my mouth and gargle and spit. With that out of the way, I point in the direction we will go today. It's relatively close to the water but in the right direction of the lake, which means there's a chance some fruit will be there. Together, we walk and don't go more than a few feet before I notice a few palm trees that might have a coconut.

"Look." I point up. "This might be our lucky day."

"Yeah, but how are we going to get them down?"

"Well, that's easy. I'll climb."

She raises her brow. "You can climb a tree?"

"You can't?" I deadpan.

"Can you ever be nice to me?"

"Oh, that's rich. Here I am, offering to climb a tree so you don't starve to death, and you're saying I'm mean."

She lets out a long sigh. "Fine. You might be right."

"What do you suggest?"

She swallows and then bites her lip. "A truce."

Knowing that it took all her strength to make that suggestion, I push down my need to make an arrogant, sarcastic remark, instead opting for a different approach. "For how long?"

"As long as it takes to get off this island."

"Deal."

"Let's shake on it."

I reach my hand out, and she hesitates.

"If you want me to climb the tree …"

Reluctantly, she reaches out her hand.

I take hers in mine, and when I do, I see the way she stares down. My finger gently strokes the skin on her palm, and she shivers, her pupils dilating.

She shakes her head and pulls away. But not before I realize that Phoenix is one hundred percent affected by me.

Good.

Because she affects me too.

Now what to do with that is the real question.

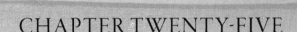

# CHAPTER TWENTY-FIVE

Phoenix

N O MATTER HOW HARD I TRY, I CAN'T TAKE MY EYES OFF him.

It's annoying.

No man should be able to do that with his body. He's limber in ways that make my imagination go wild.

The worst part? Before he started this ridiculous tree-climbing, he removed his shirt.

So yep.

Here I am, six feet beneath him, watching his heavily tatted arms flex as he lifts himself up. If that isn't bad enough, his back muscles are in full effect.

I can barely breathe. Not just because I'm fairly certain he will fall, but also because he looks like he's a freaking god up there.

Turn around and stop looking.

But as much as I try to pull my attention from him, here I am, just staring.

"Fire in the hole," he shouts, and I'm not quite sure what he says, but then a coconut hits the ground a few feet away from me.

"That could have hit me," I grit out. He lowers his head, and I can see his big blue eyes dancing with mischief.

"I warned you."

"You warned me as it was falling. That hardly counts." My own eyes narrow.

His lip tips up on one side of his face. "It counts."

I shake my head, but instead of saying anything more, I take a step back. That way, any loose coconuts won't hit me.

One by one, they fall. The sound of heavy breathing is present, but other than that, Alaric doesn't seem to care that he's up in a tree.

I'm happy on the ground.

"How much longer?" I ask.

"One. See that one." He points at one that is way too high for him to get.

"Um, no. Don't you dare get that one!"

"Afraid I might hurt myself?" he chides. "I thought you hated me. This could get me out of the way."

"You better be careful."

"If I fall and die, it would probably make you happy."

I'm ready to respond, but I can't form words as he swings his body to grab the coconut way too far away.

When it's in his hand, I let out a gigantic sigh of relief, but it isn't until he's firmly on the ground, bending down to survey his handiwork, that I realize just how much I didn't want him to get hurt.

I can't do this without him.

Nor would I want to.

"Grab a few, and we can bring them back to camp," Alaric says as he hands me four.

"Then what?"

"Then we do this again."

My mouth drops open. "You are going to climb a tree again today."

"Yep."

148

I must go pale or something because he laughs. "You worried about me?"

"Hardly." I snicker.

"Whatever you say, dove."

"Phoenix," I clarify for what must be the millionth time before turning from him and walking away.

We have eight coconuts, which, according to Alaric, is not nearly enough.

I know he's right, but I have no interest in watching him climb again.

"Can I do something else while you act like Tarzan?"

"Very well, Jane. What are you good at?"

I stare blankly at him.

"Can you hunt?" I shake my head. "Fish?" I continue to shake it. "Can you gather?"

At that question, I nod my head.

"Okay, so gather all the fruit you can find. Eat nothing."

I take a step back and look at him. "Let me get this straight. Not only can you climb a tree but you also know which fruits won't kill us?"

"Yes."

"How is that even possible?"

"Why, because I'm a criminal. Believe it or not, before I became this, my life was quite different." Without another word, he sets off to where the trees are, leaving me to myself on the beach and wondering what I said wrong.

After a few minutes of waiting for him to come back and maybe explain, he doesn't. I have two choices, wait or look for fruit. If I want any chance of ever having the option to get off this island, I need to pull my own weight on this escape mission.

But which way to go …?

The day we found the lake, we went east. Should that be my direction, or should I look west?

I hem and haw over it before I decide to try the path we didn't take.

Hopefully, I'll have better luck that way.

I'm only a few miles in when I realize my mistake. The terrain is rugged, not nearly as smooth as the other direction.

My leg keeps getting scraped, but I need to keep going. There has to be something.

Somewhere.

Anywhere.

My breathing grows choppy from the exertion, and I know I have to take a break. I stop and reach for the bottle of water.

I sure hope Alaric has filtered the lake water because our bottled water is running low.

Add water filtering skills to the lengthy list of things this man can do.

Top it off with being the sexiest man I know, and he's deadly.

It's not fair, to be honest.

No one should have that many talents.

Maybe he sucks in bed?

Dammit.

Why did I let myself think that? Because now, all I'm going to think about is whether he does.

Couple that with the fact that only yesterday I saw what he was packing.

That alone probably means he would rock my world.

Enough.

Head out of the gutter, Phoenix.

You cannot keep thinking about him like that. You're tired, scared, and horny now. You'll probably die in a few days too.

I try to shut off this train of thought by drinking, and as I guzzle the water, I close my eyes. When I open them, I notice something in the distance. Something yellow.

Holy crap.

I set off to check it out, hoping and praying I'm not wrong.

By the time I get to the tree, I might actually cry.

A fruit.

There is freaking fruit here.

This is a dream, right?

I'm not sure what they are, but they must be edible. It looks like an enormous football with pointed ridges. In my head, I try to catalog the fruits I have eaten when I went to the Caribbean. Starfruit? Maybe. Alaric would know.

They're too high for me to grab, but maybe I can be like Alaric.

I should just go get him and bring him back, but my damn stubbornness will be my downfall.

On tiptoes, I raise my body. Not enough.

If I can just put my foot here …

Lifting again, I try to use the trunk for leverage as my fingers grab the fruit and throw it toward the ground.

Unfortunately, only one comes down. I'm going to have to do this all over again. I move a few feet and try to grab it from a different angle.

This time, I'm not so lucky. As my finger grabs the fruit, my leg loses its hold, and I fall with a thud.

---

My ankle screams with each step I take. This is bad. I hope I didn't break something.

Being stuck on an island with a broken leg or foot would be just my luck. I stop my movements and look down. It's not swollen yet, and the color hasn't changed.

No. I didn't break it. I let out a sigh of relief. But it's definitely twisted.

If that's not bad enough, blood leaks from a small gash on my leg.

Alaric will have a field day with this.

I will never hear the end of it.

Why did you climb the tree?

No part of me is interested in listening to a lecture on what I should and shouldn't have done.

I'm just going to tell him I tripped.

Except for the fruit in my hand, he'd probably believe it.

The damn fruit.

A part of me wonders if I should have left them there, so he wouldn't know what I was up to.

But then my stomach growls, and I know I have no choice. I need to bring them back to camp and hope he doesn't tease me too much.

We're on a truce. Maybe he won't be a complete dick about it.

For someone as brooding as he was when I first met him, he certainly has a sarcastic sense of humor.

If it were anyone else, I'd probably like it.

*Who are you kidding? You do.*

I try to shoo the thoughts away. The only problem is without my brain occupied with thoughts of Alaric, the pain radiates more intensely.

Think of something else.

Anything else.

I try to imagine anything, but all I can see is Alaric walking naked toward the water. His body looks like it was cut from marble.

Yep.

I have issues.

Each step is harder than the next, and the feeling of blood trickling down my leg has me taking the steps slower.

Finally, I push through into the clearing of the beach.

Alaric must hear me because he turns in my direction and rushes over to me.

"What happened to you?"

"Would you believe me if I said I fell?"

His right eyebrow lifts, and he gives me a look that says no.

"It was worth a try." I take another step, and now I'm standing directly in front of him.

I lift my hand to show him what I have. "I got fruit, though." I groan.

Before I know what's happening, Alaric has lifted me into his arms, pressing me into his chest, and carries me bridal style.

If this couldn't be any more embarrassing, my body shivers at his warm hands on my skin.

Apparently, my good sense has taken a back seat, and my hormones are driving because I can't seem to keep myself in check.

With each step he takes, I can feel how his muscles flex and his heart beats. I can feel everything, and I need him to put me down.

"You don't have to carry me."

"I do. You looked like you were in pain, and seeing as we are on an island, and I'm not sure how long we will be here, I can't risk you getting more hurt."

He's right—I know he's right—but it doesn't make it any easier to admit.

I don't want him to help me.

But unfortunately, I need him to. Which sucks.

*Someone tell me this is not my life.*

I let out a long, drawn-out sigh. One that tells him I know he's right, and he chuckles.

When we are back to the makeshift raft bed, he sets me down. "Lie down so I can look at it."

"You want me to lie down in there. Where we sleep?"

"Any other suggestions? I have to clean it, and seeing as I don't want any sand getting into the wounds, our locations for this procedure are limited."

Again, he's right. Always the voice of reason. He's freaking perfect and smart, and a giant ass—

"Down," he orders again, and this time, I listen. I get into the raft and recline.

I don't fully lie down; I want to see him when he looks at my ankle.

He steps in and then sits next to me. My breath comes out choppy as he reaches forward and places my leg on his lap.

I swear to God it feels like there is a belt around my chest that tightens with each touch of his fingers.

He lifts my ankle, rotating it slowly. Pain shoots through me, and I cringe.

"What about this?" He does the same movement in the other direction. This time, it doesn't hurt.

"It's just twisted. No breaks. No sprain. But I'm going to wrap it with a bandage for the rest of the day, just in case."

"Can I walk on it?"

"I wouldn't suggest it. Wait until tomorrow."

"Shit."

"Yeah, it sucks, but at least it will heal. I'm not sure what will happen, but we can't afford for it to get worse, so you'll have to take it easy and let me take care of you."

His words shouldn't warm me. They shouldn't make butterflies take flight in my stomach, but they do.

I will them to stop, but they have a mind of their own.

"Now let me clean this off, and then I'll get you something to eat."

He's so gentle as he takes my leg and slowly cleans off the cut. When he places a bandage on my cut and then wraps my ankle, I swear I think I might cry. No one has treated me so delicately in my entire life. Not even my father. Sure, I know he loves me, but he was never like this.

He never treated me like I needed taking care of. Maybe it's because I would never have allowed it. I had to fend for myself for so long.

But I would be lying to myself if I don't admit Alaric is giving me exactly what I need.

My mind is at war with my body as Alaric sits down beside me after he cracks open a coconut.

He hands me one side and takes the other for himself.

Then he hands me a bottle of water, but what's inside isn't water.

"It's the milk from the coconut. I opened and drained it."

"Wow. Okay. Thanks," I say like an idiot.

I don't know how to handle him being nice. I know we had a truce, but this feels different than that.

It feels strangely intimate, our bodies touching, drinking from the same bottle.

"I'll make more tomorrow. I was going to do the rest, but then I saw you."

"It's okay. This is perfect."

We settle into a comfortable silence as we both eat the fleshy part.

I groan on the first bite, and he laughs.

"It's good, right?"

"Not that I want to complain because I'm grateful you had the presence of mind to make the survival kit, but those bars are pretty nasty."

"That they are. They do the trick, though. But yeah, this is much better."

I lean back, getting more comfortable.

Alaric had started a fire, and now its blazes warm around us.

"How do you know how to do all this?" I ask.

"I just do."

"Come on, that's not really an answer. Climbing. Fires, first aid ..." I look up at him, and he's staring intensely at me.

"It's just something I know."

He's holding something back. I know it. He knows it. But it's obvious he's not willing to tell me his secrets. Not that I would fault him for that. Yes, maybe right now, we are on the same team, but I can understand if he's still wary.

"If you don't want to talk about that, then what do you want to talk about?"

"Who says I want to talk at all?" His gaze is penetrating. It's unnerving.

"What then?"

"We can enjoy the silence together."

"Oh."

"It's not that I don't want to talk to you, but do you ever feel like it might be nice just to enjoy nothing with someone?"

I cock my head but continue to look at him.

"Yeah," I whisper back, understanding exactly what he means.

He settles next to me, our bodies still close but not quite touching, with both of our heads tipped back to look at the sky.

I'm not sure how long we stay like this, but it's exactly what I need right now.

Silence. A moment to calm down, calm my mind, and just stare at the stars.

Tomorrow, I'll go back to analyzing everything and probably hating him too. But tonight, I'll just be.

Whatever that means.

---

Bright sunlight streams down, making my lids flutter. For a brief second, I forget where I am. Then it all comes crashing down, like an early morning wave beating against the rocks. I'm still here.

I'm living my own version of groundhog's day. Waking the

same way each morning, hoping the outcome will be different, or that maybe none of this is real.

But none of this is a dream.

No one is coming to look for us.

My heart races, and I sit up from where I was lying. Alaric is nowhere to be seen.

I have gotten used to him being missing in the morning, but after the temporary reprieve from our hatred yesterday, I assumed maybe he'd be here.

How ridiculous am I?

Just because we didn't kill each other yesterday, and he was kind to me, does not wash away the past.

I'm not sure how to move forward from here.

A part of me wants to put the past behind us for now, revisit it once we are off this island. Another part can't.

We might never get off here. Can I live the rest of my life holding onto this in my chest?

The idea of being stuck here forever has me feeling suffocated. I move to stand, but then I remember how tight my ankle is. Removing the bandage, I look at it.

Normal.

There's no swelling. I just need to figure out a way to work out the muscle without hurting myself more.

What would I do if I was back home?

Water.

I remember when Hannah hurt herself back at school, her physical therapist had her do exercises in the water to loosen her tight muscles.

That's what I'll do.

Today, I opt to swim in my bra and panties, not wanting to chance Alaric coming back early and seeing me naked.

I'm surprised how much better my body already feels today. Yes, it's still tight, but I'm sure it will be better soon.

My toes are the first to hit the water. Even though it's summer and the water's warm, it still takes a minute to adjust to the temperature.

Slowly, I walk farther in. Once I'm submerged to my chest, I lift my injured leg up and move my ankle around.

In the water, I don't feel pain. The movements are fluid and easy, and I can feel the muscles loosening.

From where I'm swimming, it's almost as if I'm on vacation. The tropical landscape a picturesque backdrop that one would pay good money to relax in.

It's not the case for us.

No matter how beautiful and lush the palm trees are, there isn't enough food to make this island sustainable for long.

Someone could build here and make it livable, but it feels like a waste.

How do you destroy something so beautiful?

For some unknown reason, Alaric's blue eyes come to mind. The way he laughs, but his gaze always seems so far away.

Beautiful, but broken.

There's more to the story there with him.

I can tell, and although I shouldn't want to hear it, I'm desperate to understand him.

From a distance, a noise startles me. My eyes scan the beach in front of me until I catch Alaric running toward the ocean. His arms are waving in the air, and he's shouting, but I can't make out what he's trying to say.

He looks frantic.

Instantly, I'm on edge and looking around me to what has him scared.

Then I see it. In the distance, a fin. A dark-gray fin peeks ominously out from the choppy waters.

I can't breathe. It feels like hands are wrapped around my neck, and someone is choking me.

Adrenaline flows through my veins, making my heart ping pong around in my chest.

The horror of the situation has me paralyzed as my limbs fail to get the memo that I need to swim.

"Get out of the water," I hear him shout, but still, I can't.

It's getting closer, and I can't move.

The sound of Alaric's screams gets closer and closer, and the next thing I know, his arms wrap around me and are pulling me toward the beach.

We flop onto the sand, our chests both heaving as I glance back to where I was previously swimming.

The fin is there now, circling, but then it pops out more, and a giggle escapes my chest.

"That's not a shark." I laugh with the nervous energy that's pouring out of me. "It's a dolphin."

Still in Alaric's arms, my head turns to face him. The look on his face is scary. His jaw is set tight enough that it could crack. "You were lucky this time," he mutters through gritted teeth. "Next time you won't be. Do not go into the ocean alone." Abruptly, he stands, letting me go and causing me to drop onto the sand. That went well.

# CHAPTER TWENTY-SIX

## Alaric

AFTER THE INCIDENT IN THE WATER, WE DON'T SPEAK. I spend the rest of the day acting like a complete douche, but I couldn't face her. When I thought it was a shark and thought she would die, I thought I had failed her too. Even though I haven't known her long, I feel responsible for her. She might hate me and want me dead, but I can't let anything happen to her.

I fish and cook for us, and then when we finish eating, we both fall asleep.

Now I'm up, and she's not, and I am using my time to fish. *Again.*

As many coconuts as I got, we don't have enough to chance it. As soon as Phoenix is able to, we need to head back to where she fell and collect more fruit. There are probably other things we can eat here. We just have to look.

With the sun low in the sky, I'm hoping to catch something. I'm happy she's asleep. I don't want to leave her when she's awake to do this.

I'm on the beach with a makeshift net. The sun beats down on my head and shoulders.

As I wait for a fish to swim by, I turn to watch her. She's really something. All fire and equal measures of bite.

*What's her story?*

She's been hidden for a long time. Michael never even said he had a daughter. Hell, I didn't even know he had children at all until recently.

I'm interested in finding out, but she's a nosy one. If I ask, she will want answers of her own. Am I willing to part with my own story to fulfill this crazy desire to know more about hers?

Maybe.

I'm torn.

On the one hand, who knows how long we will be here, so what harm is it?

On the other, I don't like to let people in.

But would I have to?

I could tell her a little about me without telling her anything her father could use against me … if we ever get out of this mess.

As if she can hear me thinking about her, she moves in her sleep. She inches toward where I was. As if her body is seeking me out.

She would hate to know that she's doing it. A part of me wants to tease her for it, but another part doesn't want to do that at all.

That part finds her fascinating.

That part finds her beautiful. The part that wishes things could be easier, and I could lose myself in her body briefly.

I shake my head and realize I haven't been paying attention to the fish. I need to do that if we are going to eat.

Time has no relevance on this island. But from what I can tell from where the sun sits in the sky, I have been at this for at least an hour, with only one fish to show for it.

Better than nothing, I guess.

Deciding to call it a day, I lift my net and head back to the campsite.

Phoenix is stirring when I finally arrive.

Her hands reach up to wipe the sleep from her eyes.

"What do you have there?" she asks.

"Lunch and maybe dinner." I laugh.

"You can cook too?"

I nod, and she chuckles. "Of course you can. There is nothing you can't do."

"I can't build a radio out of a coconut," I respond flatly.

"Few can."

I place the fish down and then move to sit back next to her.

"How does the ankle feel?" Without waiting for her to speak, I reach my hand out and take her leg in my hands. My fingers trace circles on her skin as I wait for her to answer.

As I make the motion, her cheeks flush.

"I—I don't know. Fine. I guess."

"Does this hurt?" I move her ankle, and she shakes her head. "What about this?"

"Nope."

"Okay, good. I'm sure you'll be fine. Today, I want you to stay here, though. Do not go into the ocean."

"But—"

"No buts. One more day of rest and then tomorrow you can go back to whatever you were doing when this happened. But no swimming without me." I lift my brow. "And I highly discourage you from climbing a tree."

"I didn't climb a tree."

I give her a look that tells her I wasn't born yesterday and that I know she did.

"Fine." She rolls her eyes. "I climbed a tree. But did you see what I brought back?"

"Yes, and that's why I won't yell at you. But you have to be more careful."

"Sorry, not everyone can be perfect like you."

I wink at her before standing. "I am pretty amazing."

"Where are you going?" she asks as I stride in the other direction.

"I'm going to the lake to see if I can catch more fish."

"And you are just going to leave me here?"

"Yes." My one-word answer probably pisses her off, and that thought has me smirking.

"But I feel fine."

I turn to face her. "That may be the case, but I would feel a lot better if we didn't press our luck."

She makes a brief sound of disappointment.

"I'll be back before you know it." She pouts her perfect little lips, and I leave.

I need to get away. With the little sounds she makes and the way her lips look, I can't help but imagine her beneath me. Since that will not happen, I know I have to go, maybe relieve myself too.

That or I'll probably end up attacking her, which is something I can't and won't do.

When I finally make it to the lake, I'm rock hard.

Phoenix will be a problem.

My dick will be a problem.

Before I can think twice, I'm stripping off my clothes and grasping my cock in my hand.

I just need to take the edge off. Then I can fish and go about my business of trying to prepare for us to leave. I imagine Phoenix's legs wrapped around me. I imagine what it will feel like to slide into her and pound into her flesh.

I stroke myself up and down, climbing toward my release. It doesn't take me long. Much less time than normal, but this girl has me wound tight.

I come hard into my palm, grunting, "Fuck," as I do. My eyes open, and I'm not alone. At the edge of the clearing, watching me come, is Phoenix.

Eyes wide, cheeks flushed, she's watching. She can't pull her gaze away. She's not even swallowing as I tug one last time and milk it out completely. Finally, when every last drop is spent, I let my lips tip up.

Silently asking if she enjoyed the show.

Saying nothing after that, I head toward the water and fully submerge myself. I expect when I resurface, she will be gone. That she will have turned tail to hide from me.

But instead, I find her exactly where I left her, still staring in my direction, still breathless from what she saw.

# CHAPTER TWENTY-SEVEN

## Phoenix

I NEED TO LOOK AWAY.

I need to look anywhere but at him.

But as he touches himself, eyes closed, I can't. I can't seem to budge at all.

Something about this man is completely mesmerizing. Looking at him is like watching a car accident unfold. You know there is a very good chance you can get hurt in the crossfire, yet you can't seem to pull away.

That's Alaric Prince.

Deadly.

Corrupt.

Yet tarnished in all the right ways.

I can't stop myself from watching him. I'm silently enthralled by the scene playing out and even more secretly wishing I was the one touching him.

With my mouth dropped open and my eyes wide, I watch as he strokes himself, and I'm rooted in place.

Finally, I shake myself out of my haze, and I'm about to move when his eyes open.

Shit.

Shit. Shit. Shit.

He's staring right at me, still stroking himself.

The lust that fills the space between us is heady and makes me warm. The sight makes my body flush, my core growing wet with need.

It would be so easy to walk up to him and put on the façade I gave him at the club only a few weeks ago.

Pretend I'm that girl. The one who takes what she wants.

And what I want right now is him.

So badly it aches.

I want him to touch me. Stroke me. Fill me.

My cheeks warm even more, and I'm sure my face is beet red. I'm probably the color of a cherry tomato by now.

The way his damn lip tips up lets me know that he knows. Yet even with him smirking at me, a tease heavy on his tongue, I don't move. I still can't.

I wait for him to make a witty comment.

For him to say anything, but he heads into the water and dives below.

Now is the moment that I need to leave, yet I can't.

Instead, like the drunk-on-lust idiot I am, I wait with bated breath for him to pop back up so I can see him again.

I'm pathetic.

When he surfaces, I can see the look of surprise on his face. He expected me to be gone, yet here I still stand. Not knowing what to do or say.

Thankfully, he's the one who breaks the silence.

"I thought you were going to take it easy?"

"I got bored," I admit. I don't tell him I missed his company—and that I chanced re-injuring myself to be with him.

I don't need to say those words. They are heavy in the air, regardless.

"Do you want to come in?" His husky voice cuts through the air, making my nipples pebble with the weight of his words.

*Do I?*

I don't even know anymore. Rather than speak, I stare at him like an idiot.

His words bounce around in my brain until I'm not sure what to do. His stupid chuckle is what finally snaps me out of my lust-filled thoughts.

"It's a natural thing, dove."

There must be marbles or glue in my mouth because even though I will myself to respond to his ridiculous comment, I can't.

I can't even find it in me to yell at him. I'm flushed. So damn hot, I'm on fire.

But hell no am I getting in that lake. Even if it's what my body wants, there is no way he will get the satisfaction of me admitting it to him.

This isn't me wanting him. I'm just the product of my environment. What woman could be stranded on an island with that man and not want to jump his bones?

It wouldn't matter if I was a nun at this point. Looking at a naked Adonis wears on me.

Finding space, lots and lots of space, to calm my libido is imperative right now. Before I do something I will regret.

Without a second thought, I turn from him, his laughter fading into the distance the farther I walk.

"Where are you going?" he asks in a playful and not welcome tone.

Nope. Not answering.

"I don't bite. Unless you ask, but you'd have to ask very nicely, and use the word *Sir*."

Ignore.

Each step I take makes his voice fade more and more until I no longer hear him.

I need to cool down.

The blue water in front of me calls my name.

I know Alaric said not to go in, but he's being ridiculous. It was a dolphin, not a shark. He's not my boss. I'll do what I want to do.

Streams of sunlight brush the surface of the water. It's beautiful.

It's the perfect weather for me to take a dip. *Cool off from the erotic show he gave me.*

I strip down completely.

With Alaric in the lake, he won't bother me.

I'm all alone, so I might as well.

Also, this way, my clothes won't get wet.

Stepping onto the sand, I curl my toes in bliss.

Yesterday, I hadn't allowed myself the luxury of relaxing, but right now, that's what I do. Right now, I'm on a tropical island, relaxing. *That's what I tell myself, at least.*

If I let the rest settle in, my anxiety will flare, so I shake it off and give myself these brief moments. My feet are now bathed in the warm water. Not as warm as a bath, but not frigid enough to make it uncomfortable.

With each step I take, I submerge my body deeper and deeper.

My head tilts back as I'm fully engulfed, and I look up at the sky.

Here and now, it feels like a dream.

Blue as far as I can see.

It's perfect.

If only the company was … Nope, not going there. Instead, I think of nothing. Inhaling deeply, I silence my brain.

My chest rises and falling as I relax.

I'm not sure how long I stay there, but soon, the water is pulling harder, and the once blue sky is turning a different shade.

In the distance, the sky is turning gray now, and the waves are growing larger and more vicious.

Is a storm coming?

I turn my attention back toward the beach.

Icy tendrils of fear fill my body as I realize I'm much farther away than I imagined.

The water has been pulling me out to sea.

In my haste to get away, I have done just that.

I start to swim, kicking strongly, but no matter how much I kick, it doesn't seem to make a difference.

I kick harder and harder. But no matter how much I do, it's as if I'm stuck.

Adrenaline floods through my veins at the precarious situation I've placed myself in.

What am I going to do?

As my arms work to push me forward, an endless stream of what ifs plague my brain, making me panic.

*I can't freak out.*

I have to push these morbid thoughts away.

They won't help me now.

I could call for Alaric, scream for help, but it's no use. He's too far.

*He's not here to save you this time.*

No, I'll need to save myself.

It wasn't that long ago that I had found myself in a similar position, but a world of change has happened since then.

I don't want to give up.

I don't want to die.

With all the strength I can muster, I push past the riptide. I kick and thrash, and soon, the shore is approaching. By the time my feet hit the sand, I'm done.

My breath comes out in sharp bursts, chest rising frantically to inflate.

I hear the sound of his screams first, but my eyes are closed from the exertion. My naked body now lies on the sand. Strong arms lift me, cradle me to a firm, warm chest.

I should be cold, but the hands touching me set me ablaze.

"What the hell were you doing out there? Are you insane? I told you yesterday not to go into the ocean alone."

I don't answer, too tired from the fight to make it back to shore.

I know I should tell him to put me down, but I don't. I allow him to hold me. To keep me warm and safe.

He sits by the fire, and I'm happy it's still lit from before.

My teeth chatter, more from nerves than anything.

When he starts to rock me, I can feel the tears forming behind my eyelids.

He's comforting me. This strange and beautiful man, who I should hate and who should hate me in return, is picking up the pieces I broke on the beach and putting them back together.

"You're okay," he says, and I let out the sob lodged in my throat. "Everything is going to be okay. You're safe."

More tears pour out of me. This isn't about the water or the riptide. It's about the island, the fear. I haven't allowed myself to stop. Pushing to find food. Pushing to survive. But when it all sinks in, I feel like I'm drowning in my own grief.

"I have you."

"But who's got you?" I ask, tipping my head up for our eyes to meet.

"I was hoping you," he responds, but this time, there is no humor in his tone. I continue to look at him, searching for something, but all I see is loneliness. Fear. Feelings that mirror my own.

Neither one of us speaks as my body dries. Not even when it becomes painfully obvious that I'm naked in his arms.

Not when he places a soft and gentle kiss on my forehead and then on the lids of my eyes that have now closed.

"Rest. I have you."

# CHAPTER TWENTY-EIGHT

## Alaric

ONCE SHE'S ASLEEP, I CONTINUE TO HOLD HER IN MY ARMS. I wait for her breathing to level out, so I know she won't wake up.

With careful precision, I lay her flat on the raft before I stand to get her clothes from the grass beside the sand. When I make my way back over to her, I realize just how hard dressing her will be. Instead of even trying, I lift my own shirt over my head and move to place that on her body. Because of the size and how tiny she is in comparison, it's easy to maneuver it on her. Then I place the blanket on top of her. She's been difficult about using my blanket, but now, deep in slumber, she has no choice. She can no longer be stubborn.

With her body covered, I take the spot beside her. I spend the next few hours staring out into the horizon and thinking. My thoughts are of the past and what the future will bring. If I'll even have a future.

Before long the sun sets, and when the sky turns dark, I recline back and look up to the stars.

When I saw her, I thought she was hurt again.

But unlike the previous time, my heart stopped.

I don't know when she did it, but Phoenix flew right into my chest, making a nest for herself.

I'm not sure when that happened, but I care about her. It would be easy to say it's just lust. Because let's be honest, she's gorgeous, but it's more than that.

She's been a pain in my ass since the moment I met her, but I think that's what I like about her the most.

She challenges me.

She calls me on my shit.

She's a little spitfire, and yes, it doesn't hurt that she's stunning.

She's an untamable fire. Like a Phoenix, she falls, but every time she gets back up.

I have no doubt that by tomorrow, she'll do just the same, but for now, she nuzzles against me, seeking my warmth, so I pull her closer.

---

Early morning sunlight streams down, forcing my eyes to open.

As the world around me comes into focus, I see yet again that Phoenix is asleep, nestled against my chest.

Unlike before, I don't rush to move.

Every day since we've been here, I've pushed myself from dusk till dawn to find a way off this island.

Even I deserve to sleep in.

Don't I?

I close my eyes against the glare and will myself back to bed.

But my companion seems to have other plans as she rolls almost completely on top of my body.

She's still asleep.

That much I can tell from the way she breathes.

Now, I'm not sure what to do.

Which is wholly unlike me.

I've never given a shit before about what this girl wants or needs, but now I do.

And the notion doesn't sit well inside me.

I need to squash these feelings.

I can't let myself grow attached to her.

Again, she starts to move, her leg draping over me. If she keeps rubbing up against me like that, she's going to wake something else inside me. I can't cross that line.

Something tells me if I do, one time won't be enough to get this girl out of my system, and I can't go there with her.

My inner debate is cut short when she starts to speak in incoherent sentences, and then as if she got struck by lightning, she bolts up into a sitting position.

"What-What happened?"

Her eyes are wide and crazy from sleep, and it takes everything in me not to burst into laughter.

But something tells me if I do, I'll end up with a black eye.

"You were exhausted and fell asleep."

She looks down and lifts the blanket, then her hand reaches for my shirt that covers her.

"How?" She doesn't finish the question, but there is no need, seeing as I can already tell what it's going to be.

*How did I get dressed? Did you do this?*

"You were naked." Her cheeks turn a bright red. "I didn't want to wake you, so my shirt seemed an easier task."

She's quiet as she takes in my answer, but eventually, she nods to herself.

"We should get up," I finally say, breaking the silence between us.

"What's the plan for today?" she asks.

"Other than make coconut phones?" My lip tips up into a smirk, and she shakes her head at my joke.

"Yes, other than that, Gilligan."

"Gather fruit and fish."

"Okay."

"We'll do it together."

Her brows knit together as if she is going to react. Maybe she's perfectly capable of doing it herself, but she must think better of it.

"You can get most of the fruit. I'll be focusing on seeing if there are any animals for us to catch."

"How will you do that?"

"Bait." But the moment I say the word, I realize my mistake. Her body tightens, and she's up before I can speak, marching off behind the trees.

I would say she has to use the bathroom, but I know better.

If what I said bothered her, she doesn't act on it, instead opting for a time-out. Hopefully, it's long enough for her to be okay. A few minutes later, my question is answered when she steps out of the trees with a smile. I'm not sure if she is being serious or merely mocking me, but I don't really care. Either way, no matter her mood, we are doing this.

"What has you so happy today?" I ask. Her smile brightens, and she points toward where she found the fruit.

"I'm excited to be getting closer to getting off this island."

Now that I have heard her answer, the excitement she portrays doesn't sit well with me. It's not that I want to stay on this island, but the moment I get off, I'll have to figure out who attacked me and why, and there will be a price to pay. As much as this isn't a vacation, I'm not looking forward to the idea of having to do all that.

I turn toward Phoenix. "Do you need anything?" I ask before we head off for the day.

"Seeing as there's really nothing to bring ..." she gestures to the ditch bag and the raft "... no."

"Make sure you bring the knives." After I say this, she turns her gaze to meet mine, and then her blue eyes look at me, wide with confusion. "Are you expecting to fight something? Or kill for that matter?"

"Never can tell what we'll find on our walk."

I wait for her to object, or say something, but today she's on her best behavior. She must really want to get off this island.

Not that I blame her, but I don't have the heart to remind her it's a long shot. This can't be easy for her. She basically has to rely on someone she hates for everything. The problem is, we could leave here and die on the raft. The plan is we'll find another island, one that's inhabitable, and make our way there. But just in case it takes a while, it's better safe than sorry.

"Be honest. How many days of fishing until we have enough?"

"You want me to be honest?" I ask.

"Obviously." She rolls her eyes before she deadpans, "Honesty is the best policy."

"Ten days."

Her mouth drops open at my words. "Are you serious? We have to do this for another ten days?"

"Well, we don't have to do anything, but if we want the best shot, that's my guess." I shrug.

"Okay, well, either way, I guess we have to look for something to eat, so let's go." She turns and sets off again.

We spend the rest of the day gathering food, and before long, the sky is turning dark. With a fire set, we sit together beside it, letting it warm us.

"How will we know which way to steer?" she asks, picking the conversation back up from hours ago.

I point at my head, tapping on it to show it's all up there. That my brain will be our map.

"Do you know your way around the Caribbean?"

"For the past four years, I have conducted my business on my yacht. I know how to sail a boat. I know how to captain a yacht. I know how to read the stars. I know how to figure out the location on a map, and after all these years of doing this course, I know where the islands are on the map." Leaning forward, I throw another log onto the pile and watch as the fire roars to life. Red embers flicker as the smoke consumes the fresh piece.

Phoenix watches me, a small line forming between her brows. "Then how are we here?"

"The thing is …" What happened that night still pisses me the fuck off, but there is no place for lies on this island. "I fell asleep. I hate myself for it because had I not, even in the black ocean, I would've been able to figure out our direction. But I did, and because of that, I might have killed us." My words come out low, and I can't believe I said them out loud.

Phoenix does something I don't expect. She moves to sit closer.

"Tell me about the stars," she says.

"That can take all night," I respond, head tilted toward her. She turns toward me with fascination and curiosity written all over her face.

"Where else do I have to be?" She chuckles, and she's right. There is no place to be and no one else to talk to. Her options for entertainment are limited.

"I might bore you."

With amusement flashing in her eyes, she shakes her head. "I doubt you could ever bore anyone."

"You'd be surprised." I lean back so my head tilts up to the sky, and she follows my lead.

"Do you see that star right over there?"

"The bright one?"

"Yeah, that's Polaris. The North Star. Sailors use it to guide them home. All I need is that, and I'll be able to guide us."

"So why don't you?"

"I need to know where we started. I have a general understanding of our location, enough I feel confident that eventually we will find help, but we just need—"

"Enough food, just in case it takes longer?" She leans forward to get closer to the fire.

"Exactly. Now you're learning." My arm reaches out and grabs another log. I cut enough to last us until we fall asleep. Though we're on a tropical island, the temperature does drop at night. From where she's sitting, I hear her giggle, and I turn to see what's so funny.

"Why are you giggling over there?" I ask.

"Learning from you ... now that's an interesting concept," she clarifies.

"How so?"

She cocks her head to the side and gives me a pointed look. "I don't see you as much of a teacher."

"You don't know me very well. Don't doubt what you can't see."

A part of me expects my clipped answer to be ignored, but then I remember this is Phoenix, and my little dove loves conflict.

"Very well. Starting now, I won't. Tell me more."

It's not exactly what I had in mind when I thought of her response, but I can still work with it. "Oh, I will, but not now."

"Then when?"

"We have at least ten more days together ... might as well make it last before you hate me again."

She lifts her shoulders. "Maybe I won't."

That makes me chuckle. "You most definitely will."

"If there's no more lesson ... good night, Alaric."

"Good night, dove."

"With this new truce, you can call me Phoenix," she states.

"But what fun would that be?"

# CHAPTER TWENTY-NINE

## Phoenix

I'M SHOCKED BY HOW RELAXED ALARIC SEEMS. PLAYFUL, EVEN. This is a different side to him.

Without his men around, he's lighter. Funnier. He was always sarcastic, but before, he had a huge chip on his shoulders.

And now, with each day that passes on this tropical paradise, he seems to change.

I wonder if this is the real him. If this is who Alaric Prince truly is and the rest is a front.

Or maybe the actual world is so bad that he had no choice to be any different.

I guess as the saying goes, *Only time will tell.*

For now, we're stuck here. I can't even try to unravel or understand how much I like this unlikely alliance between Alaric and me. But what will happen if we live long enough to be free of this life?

What happens if we make it back home? Will he go after my father again?

I shouldn't think about it. Right now, the chances of us even … my mind starts to go dark, and then I'm biting down hard on my lower lip.

Maybe I'll think about it later.

Just not now, when we have finally found a level of peace between us.

I lift a berry I found. "What about this one?" I ask.

"Unless we are planning on a joint suicide, that's a no." His words and grim joke have me staring down at the berries in my hand, the ones that look yummy and delicious right now.

The perfect killer. Like Alaric—beautiful to look at but lethal if you take a bite.

But like the glutton for punishment that I am, why do I still want to know this?

"Yeah, I'll pass on that. How do you know so much?" There is a sick need inside me to find out everything about this man.

"Now, that is a long story."

I lift my hand and gesture around us. "Does it look like I have anything better to do?"

"Pick berries." He dismisses my comment with a shrug.

"Since I'm doing such an awful job, you might as well tell me."

He looks up and to the left as if thumbing through files in his memory before his gaze drops back down and into my eyes.

"I guess."

He's quiet for a bit, and when he kneels before another bush, I think he's not going to tell me, but then I hear his voice.

His low timbre.

I should probably continue to look for food, but when he speaks, I'm too enthralled to do anything but listen.

"My knowledge for the great outdoors is all my father's doing. To be a man, he believed you needed to be able to survive on nothing." He looks up, and his eyes scan the surrounding area. "This isn't my first time stranded on an island," he says, and I can feel my eyes widening at his admission.

"What do you mean?" My voice cracks with confusion.

"My father was a strict man. He thought a man needed to be able to survive anything." He stops talking, and I watch as his Adam's apple bobs. "*Alone.*"

My stomach muscles tighten, and I can't even figure out what to say. "How old were you?" I finally squeak.

"The first time he tested me or the first time he dropped me on an island?"

"Both?"

"When I was ten, he left me in the woods alone to find my way. By twelve, I was expected to last a few days. Four, to be exact. By fifteen, I was left for seven days on an island."

"But why? I don't understand."

He stands from where he's crouched and paces.

"This business was his. To survive in this world—his world—I had to be indestructible."

"No one is indestructible," I whisper.

"I know," he responds, his voice lower and filled with pain. I want to ask him about that pain. Is this about his brother? The brother he thinks my father killed? But at the same time, he's finally opening up to me, talking to me, and I don't want to go back to him hating me. If I'm going to probably die in ten days, I don't want to spend the rest of my life in a war.

"What was it like?" I ask, still staring at him. I'm still trying to understand this man and what made him who he is today.

"When I had to find my way home, it was horrifying. Again, I was ten. I vaguely knew where I was. I walked for what seemed like hours, and I didn't eat because I didn't know what would kill me." He looks up from the fruit he's picking and begins to list toxic fruit to me. "Like this. At ten, this would have been the first thing I would have eaten. Lucky for me, I hesitated. I fought past the pains in my stomach and didn't. Later, when I sat down to prepare, I learned that the fruit I had seen in the woods in the European forest he left me in that day would have killed me. I later referred to them as beautiful small red pods of death. If I had eaten them, I would have vomited, become dizzy and disoriented, then died."

"Holy fuck," I say, interrupting him.

"Right." He nods, now looking at the ground. Maybe lost in the memory. "I was starving and severely dehydrated when I finally reached the manor my father had rented when he did business in Europe."

"What happened?"

"He was impressed, very much so, but it wasn't enough. I knew it wouldn't be enough. He would mold me into the man he thought I should be. I watched as my older brother worked with him, but I knew my path wouldn't be that easy. I spent my time from that moment on preparing for whatever would come next."

I wait with bated breath for him to continue, and just when I think he won't, he surprises me again. He sits down, no longer looking at plants.

His face is sullen, and his posture is stiff. "Finding my way home was nothing compared to leaving me on an island. But at least then I was prepared. I knew which fruits not to eat. I knew how to fish. I had taught myself how to start a fire with twigs."

"And you know how to pack a kick-ass survival bag," I say, trying to lighten the mood.

"I do. And I keep that bag with me at all times."

"Why no radio in it?" I ask.

"Good question. There was one."

"But?"

"But I had a crazy stowaway on my boat, so I removed it." He looks up at me again, and now the previous gloom is gone, and it's replaced with a smirk. He likes the fighting. He likes the banter. To Alaric Prince, it's foreplay.

For me, well, I don't know what it is. But what I know is I don't enjoy seeing him like he was before. Lost in a sad memory he can't pull himself from.

We aren't so different. When I was nine, I was alone and thought I had no one in the world. But it wasn't by choice that my parents left me. It wasn't their choice. The big difference between Alaric and me is Michael stepped in and saved me.

I will never understand what it's like for your father to abandon you on an island to see if you'll live or die.

The thought is sobering, and it makes me wonder what else has happened to this beautifully broken man to make him the devil I know.

I know I shouldn't try to find out. Everything inside me screams at me not to pursue this.

I just can't help myself.

My need has become so much more, desire, intrigue, fascination? Maybe it's all of it, but I have to know more about Alaric Prince.

---

After his confession, we settle into a comfortable silence. Maybe it's because there is nothing more to talk about, or maybe it's because we both realize what his confession means to us.

He opened up to me.

He showed me there was more to him.

Now the real question is, what do I do with the information?

Before long, we are walking back to the camp. He leads the way, making sure nothing is in our path. I don't need him to coddle me, but I appreciate the thought, nonetheless.

I'm not a porcelain doll, but regardless of that fact, it means something to me that he treats me as such.

By the time we make it back to the campsite alongside the sand, I'm tired and hungry. We've been eating less and less, and my leggings are no longer tight.

Although Alaric is still ripped, he's leaner now. Even with the fish and coconuts, we are both starting to lose weight. We now have enough coconut stored for our rescue attempt, so gathering fruit and fish is next. The fish we bring will have to be freshly cooked. And hopefully, it will stay good because there's no way to preserve it long term. Fruit has been harder to come by; most of what we have found is still inedible.

Collecting water is one more hurdle we must conquer.

Alaric thinks we will be ready to go in ten days.

I think he just isn't ready to set off to our death. There's no question staying here forever is a death sentence, but leaving is one too.

I think the ten days is a way for him to hold on to hope a bit longer.

Maybe someone will find us. Maybe not all his men are dead? They're the only ones who could track us correctly. If they were wounded in the attack, how many days would it take for them to find another ship and look for us?

Maybe that's why we're waiting ten more days because technically, we could scrounge up enough food to leave now. Or we could try to stay here. The thing is, once the two-week mark hits, no one will look for us, and that's why Alaric gave us ten days. It feels as though a weight is pressing down on my chest every time I think of this, so I walk over to where Alaric is gathering sticks and twigs, and I stand beside him.

"For today's lesson," I say.

"Today's lesson?"

"Well, yeah. Yesterday you told me about Polaris, and today, you'll teach me something else to survive. If we're stuck here for another ten days, I might as well learn the tricks of the trade."

"Is that what you want, dove?"

"It is. What else is there to do to pass the time?" I ask, but the moment I do, I realize I have walked right into a trap.

"I can think of better ways to spend our time."

I can feel the warmth spreading across my face, and if I didn't know better, I'd say he lit the fire, but seeing as he hasn't, I know I'm blushing.

I don't respond to his blatant sexual innuendo. Instead, I let my imagination run wild. I have to stop, but I can't. I would swat my hand and shoo them away if that didn't make me look insane. But it would, so I don't. Instead, I take a deep breath and will my heart that is flip-flopping in my chest to stop so I can look straight at him.

Show no fear, Phoenix Michaels. Show no fear.

"I think my time on this island would be better spent learning how to survive."

"Whatever you want."

I continue to stand in place before he motions for me to come closer. I hesitate for a minute before he opens his mouth. "Do you think you can learn all the way from there?"

He's right. As much as it pains me to admit he is right, from where I am perched, I won't be learning anything.

I do what he says and move closer. And just out of spite, to show I don't care, to convince him I'm not affected by him—or maybe to convince myself—I stand so close that I can feel the heat of his body. I want to shiver, but I don't. I stand perfectly still. Stoic. He turns to face me, his eyes playful and his lip tipped up.

"Let's get started. I'll tell you and then demonstrate for you, and then you will try, okay?" he says, and I nod my head.

"Sounds good." Sort of, anyway.

"You need to build friction where you rub, and it will turn the wood into a hot ember. Once that happens, you will quickly transfer the hot ember to your bundle and blow. This will ignite your tinder. Grab the kindling and use the burning tinder bundle to ignite it. Keep adding more dry sticks until you have the fire you want."

I watch as he does just what he said he would. Staring at his fingers, his wrists, and up to his forearms, I'm mesmerized by the flexing of one of his tattoos. I want to ask him what they all mean. I will tonight at the fire, but right now, I need to concentrate.

His fire is blazing when he moves behind me.

My breath lodges in my throat as his arms wrap around me and his front presses against my back. Warm hands wrap around my hands, and once he's secure in his position of my extremities, he starts to turn our hands so the friction builds.

The movement is sensual as he guides me around the wood. It feels like an erotic dance. His breath tickles my skin.

His lips are close enough that I wonder if he'll kiss me.

I wonder if he wants to.

I turn my head toward him to see what he's thinking, but just as I do, he jolts.

"You did it. Look!"

He pulls back, letting me go so I'm the only one holding the sticks.

"Blow," he commands, and although I think the moment is gone, I can see the look of lust heavy in his eyes now.

"Blow," he says again. "Ignite the flames."

He's no longer talking about a stick.

# CHAPTER THIRTY

## Alaric

THE NEXT FEW DAYS FOLLOW THE SAME PATTERN. I TEACH her the skills she will need to survive if she ever finds herself alone without me on a deserted island. Today is a bit different.

Today, I lead her toward the lake to the clearing right by the banks of where the water is.

"What are we doing here? Are you going to teach me how to—what swim? I already know how to do that?" She laughs.

"No. Today, I teach you how to protect yourself. How to never find yourself in a bad position again." The meaning of my words isn't lost on her. She knows I'm talking about how she's stuck here with me. "If you really want to work with your father, which I don't suggest you do, you need to know how to defend yourself and fight back."

She lifts her brow at me. "I don't need to learn to fire a gun. It's not rocket science." Her hands rest on her hip in defiance, but I don't miss the way her fists clench to hide their shaking.

"You need too. But at the very least, you need to learn how to fight. If you remember the day you found yourself alone on my boat, guns aren't always available when we want them."

A swift shadow of anger slips over her soft features, making her jaw appear tight. She's not happy with that memory. "I'll figure it out," she snaps, her voice inflamed with rage.

"Little dove, there's no need to be mad." And this time I mean it. Normally my words drip with sarcasm, but since we have too much time and very little to do, I do want to teach her this. "Let me teach you how to fight."

She stands there for a minute, her expression blank, before she places her hands on her hips, and gives me her signature, yet sexy look of defiance. "Aren't you scared it will give me the upper hand," she draws out, her voice very low, trying to be mischievous.

"Hardly."

That makes her full pink lips turn up into a grin. "Maybe one day I'll get the better of you. What then?"

I step closer to her. I'm close enough that she now needs to crane her neck to see my eyes. "Then I'll count myself lucky to die by the hands of someone so lovely."

The compliment must take her off guard because she swallows. I use the movement and surprise to my advantage, grabbing her by her shoulders. "Defend yourself." I pull her into me, capturing her hands next. "Fight me off."

She tries to squirm, but her movements do the opposite. It's like she stuck in quicksand; the more she moves, the tighter my grip gets.

"With my arms wrapped around you, there is little you can do."

"What's the point, then?" She huffs, still trying to break away.

"Use what you still have at your disposal."

Her movements stop, and I know she's trying to think of a way to defend herself. "Your foot. Stomp down. The movement will make my grip temporarily loosen. Use it to your advantage."

She stomps down.

"Good, but you're still holding back. Let's try some more."

I spend the next few hours running through basic self-defense moves. Moves that one day, with enough practice, could save her life.

I'm not sure what it is about her, but I have a deep-seated desire to protect her. The thought of that, though, makes me laugh. She's not the kind of girl who would ever let me do that for her. Seeing as I know that won't happen, I plan on giving her the tools to protect herself.

We fight for a while. She's a quick study. Again, in my arms, I hold her tightly, my fingers touching her exposed skin. She shivers beneath my touch, and I move in, placing my head closer to the crook of her neck. I breathe out, knowing my breath tickles her skin … then she strikes.

And believe it or not, takes me completely off guard. I stumble back as her elbow connects with my ribs. Then she swivels around, and her fist connects with my jaw.

It's my own fault as I step back and wipe the blood from my lip.

"You're bleeding," she exclaims, walking toward me. "Are you hurt?"

"I thought you wanted me to die." I smirk.

"I never said I wanted you to die, just maimed."

"Big difference." I swipe at my lip again, and there is still a trail of blood dripping off it.

"Let's grab the first-aid kit. I'll clean that for you."

"I'm fine."

Not really. I let this little wisp of a girl get one over on me. Phoenix Michaels is more dangerous to my health than she knows.

Neither of us speaks on the way back, but when we get back, I let her start the fire and then point back to the sky and tell her more about the stars above.

---

The next day comes before I know it.

She pops up from where she is and smiles.

"What's on the agenda today?" she asks from beside me. I'm barely up, but it makes me laugh. Ever since yesterday, she's been in a good mood. Almost like the idea of learning how to survive has given her a purpose here on the island.

I can understand that. At one time in my life, it gave me a purpose too.

"Today, I'll teach you how to shoot a gun."

Her eyes go wide, and her face pales. Then I notice her hand is shaking. Uncontrollably.

"No." Her one-word answer leaves no room for debate.

"How about I teach you how to fish?"

She moves to a sitting position. "Really?" I can hear the gratitude in her voice that I don't press her.

"Yes, it's different here than it would be back home, but I can still teach you."

"How so?" she asks, and I smile.

"Other than the obvious ..."

"Which is?"

"Well, we don't have a fishing rod."

She inclines her head. "You mean there is no portable fishing rod in your handy-dandy travel survival kit?"

"Nope," I respond with a smile.

"What good is this thing"—she motions to the bag—"without a fishing rod?"

I jump up from where I'm lying in the raft and pretend to go to the bag. "You're right. What was I thinking? I should just throw it out."

Her eyes go wide, and I chuckle. I realize I have laughed more with her stranded on this island than I have in years.

Even before I took over the business, I don't ever remember laughing.

"What?" she asks, and her voice pulls me back to the here and now.

I shake my head. "I was just thinking."

"About?" Sincerity drips from the question. She truly wants to know.

In my actual life, I don't talk about my feelings, and I don't answer to anyone. But it's different here on this island. A part of me wants to tell her, but I don't, but I'm still surprised about my desire to open up to her.

Maybe it's because she is my only companion, but—and I won't admit this to her, although I'm sure she knows—there is a very good chance we will die here.

I'm okay with that.

I made my peace with dying a long time ago.

But even if I'm resigned to my fate, that doesn't mean I want my time left to be spent fighting.

Even if she is my enemy's daughter, that has no bearing here and now.

For whatever time we have left, we'll work together. That's really our best shot at survival. Then if we escape, we can cross the next bridge. I'm sure she knows my vendetta won't end because we went fishing together, but there is no point in thinking about that now.

"Let's go. We'll go fishing in the shallow part of the ocean. I usually go over there." I point toward the opposite section of the beach. "It's about a twenty-minute walk."

"Do I need anything?"

"Grab the tape. Also, I have a spear and also a large stick beside that tree."

"Um, okay."

"I'm going to use the spear. I'll stand on the rock over there and try to fish that way."

"You can do that?"

"Yeah, remember? Years spent training for this," I respond.

"And the long stick and tape?" she asks, brow raised in

question. There was actually supposed to be a net and a hook in the raft, but it must have fallen out—but I don't tell her that because it's not important. I can make something for her to fish with.

"That's for you. It takes years of practice and skill to use a spear to catch a fish, but if we tape the large leaf of the palm tree, you can use that to catch smaller fish."

"Seriously? You have to be joking."

I give her a stare that tells her I'm anything but joking. "You said you wanted to learn." My lip tips up. "If you are a good girl, I'll even let you touch my spear."

She rolls her eyes at my blatant attempt at a sexual joke, but I don't miss the way her pupils widen just before she does it.

Interesting.

It seems my little dove isn't against the idea at all.

This I can work with.

That certainly would be a better way of spending our time, at least our nights. Maybe then I won't have to talk about myself anymore.

When it's obvious I'm not going to say more, she walks over to the tree and grabs the gear I told her to.

"All your stuff. Spear included," she mocks.

"It's a big one, right?"

"Lord." She laughs. A loud and contagious laugh. One that makes me laugh too.

Better be careful, Alaric. If you keep laughing like this, you might grow to like her, and that is not a good plan.

Pushing down the thought circling my head, I grab my knife and place it in the back pocket of my pants that I've since cut into shorts.

She walks up to me and reaches out her hand, holding the sticks.

I take my spear, and we both walk.

We're quiet on the trek. When we finally get to the shallow lagoon, I point at a spot a few feet away from where we stand.

"You're going to fish over there. And I'm going to be a little deeper on that rock."

"Am I going to get wet?"

"Where you're standing? No. But I would recommend if you don't want to get your pants wet that you take them off," I say as I remove my shirt and then set it down on the sand,

"You're just saying that 'cause you want to see me naked."

I lift my brow. "Maybe. Maybe not. But you won't even be naked."

"Practically," she counters.

"You'll still have a tank. It will be like you are wearing a bathing suit. And why so modest? I've already seen you naked."

"Fine." Then she pulls down her pants.

The truth is, she shows no more skin than someone on a family trip to the beach would. But there is still something very enticing about the picture she's portraying.

Her skin is sun-kissed. Her dark brown hair flows in the sea breeze. She looks like a sea goddess, a siren luring me toward her. I don't go, though. Instead, I squat down on the sand and tape the leaf to make a net.

Once I'm done, I hand it off to her.

"You go over there. Scream if you catch something."

It's not long until I hear grumbling from where Phoenix stands. She looks flustered. She's screaming at the water. When I hear curses, I can't help but laugh.

"Problem?" I holler across the distance. The look she gives me is so stern I feel like a little child just reprimanded by a parent.

"You can say that."

"Want help?" I ask, but she doesn't answer, so I take it upon myself to go help her.

My foot steps off the rock, and once it's submerged into the warm ocean, I stride toward her. The water is shallow where we are, so only my legs get wet.

When I'm almost upon her, she looks up, an angry grimace still present on her face.

Angry Phoenix is almost as beautiful as a sleeping one. I prefer her peaceful, but this is my second favorite look. Heated eyes.

I wonder what she looks like in the throes of passion.

What her eyes look like as she comes.

I have to use all my strength to stifle a groan as I push back the desire forming inside me. Keep your head in the game, man.

"Let me help you," I say again. This time, I step up behind her.

"You have a spear in your hand. How are you going to help me?" She scoffs.

Wanting to show her I can, I throw the spear like I'm in the Olympics. It flies through the air, landing on the beach.

"Show-off," she mutters, and I have to try everything in my power not to laugh.

"You're right, I am," I say in my most asshole voice yet. "But I sure can throw a stick."

"You are incorrigible," she says over her shoulder.

"That might be the case, but I'm also a damn good fisherman. All jokes aside, let me help you."

"Fine, but I'm telling you, there are no fish here. They must've swum away. You won't have any luck."

"Let me be the judge of that."

"Fine."

With no more resistance from her, I step closer. My arms reach around her, my hands wrapping around her forearms.

Her body shivers at the contact.

That makes me smile. It's not cold enough for her to shiver unless she is affected by my touch. Seeing as I can feel the goose-bumps that form on her arm, I know she is.

Here we are, dancing around an obvious attraction, but

knowing how all this started, I'll need a verbal confirmation before I ever breach the divide between us.

With my arms around her, I position her in the correct position, and then we drop the net I made into the water.

"Now what?" she asks.

I move her body closer to mine. "Now we wait."

She squirms at the contact. "For how long?"

"However long it takes for you to feel the net get heavier."

"Wait, seriously?"

"I rarely joke," I say, even though that's not true anymore. With her, it seems I'm always joking, always laughing. Hell, I'm basically a different man on this island. My father would have never appreciated this new me.

My brother would have laughed at me.

But since neither of them is here, I'm fine.

With our bodies still touching, we wait.

Her inhales make me inhale.

When she exhales, I exhale.

It's very peaceful.

I don't think she realizes when she was doing this on her own, she was moving around too much. You can't move when trying to catch fish.

"Why are we just standing like this?" Her voice cuts through the silence.

"Because this is how we catch fish."

"How do you figure?"

"You moved around too much before. You were basically dancing for the fish. They swam away because of it. They saw the threat and left."

"You're full of shit."

"Am I?" I step in even closer, and now my bare chest hits her back. She inhales, and I feel the vibration from where our bodies touch. "Then let's do an experiment."

Time passes slowly as she weighs my words with each pull of oxygen she takes, in each deep breath she expels at my proximity.

"How?" she finally croaks, probably because she thinks if she humors me in this, I'll let her go.

But I don't want to. Even if I wouldn't do this, I like how small she feels in my arms, and I'm not ready for her to leave yet. So instead of just teaching her, I will milk this for all it's worth.

I pull her close, leaning forward so that her head is in the crook of my neck. Her body trembles as my lips softly whisper in her ear to calm down.

"Inhale. Slowly and be still."

She does. Her shoulders rise and fall softly so as not to scare off the fish.

"How much longer?"

"I'll say this one time, dove. And I know you want to get angry with me, but trust me. Calm your heart. In life, this is an important message to learn. Every action has a consequence. If you are rash, it can have dire consequences."

The implication hangs in the air. I'm not talking about catching fish. No, rather, when she sneaked onto my boat. Now she is here on an island with me, stranded and having to fish for food.

She lets out a long, drawn-out exhale, finally accepting my advice.

We stand together for a long time with peace and tranquility all around us. It's odd what a difference a week can make.

Now, as I'm standing here, it brings me back to a time before, when I learned to fish this way. When I learned to survive by myself.

Now, I'll teach her everything I've learned. That way, if we do ever escape this, she can live through any challenge life throws at her.

# CHAPTER THIRTY-ONE

## Phoenix

**B**REATHING IS OVERRATED, RIGHT? BECAUSE I'M NOT.
It's a modern miracle I'm still standing upright. Well, I guess it's not a modern miracle, seeing as Alaric's holding most of my body weight.

His touch makes me dizzy. Light-headed. He holds me so close that his heat is all around me. I should insist he stop, but I can't. What I really need to do is turn over my shoulder and just kiss the man already. Put us both out of our misery.

I'm going to do it.

Right now.

The attraction is too strong not to. We are opposing pieces of a magnet, and the pull to each other is inevitable. This will happen, but if I kiss him now, it's on my terms.

Before I can second-guess myself, I move to turn my head over my shoulder. I'm in the crook of his neck, but he pulls back, our gazes locking.

I can see his desire.

His eyes read like an open book. They tell me of his wants and needs. We are so close now that his breath fans my lips. My eyes shutter closed, and I'm sure our lips will collide ... when suddenly, I feel a heavy weight in my arm, and then I'm tugged back. Or, well, at least my arms are.

My eyes jolt open, and Alaric is no longer staring at me. The moment is lost.

I turn my head back in the direction.

"There. We got one," Alaric says excitedly.

He helps me lift it up. The makeshift net is heavy as it comes out of the water. When it's high enough that I can see inside, an enormous fish is looking back at me, flopping.

A tinge of sadness enters my mind, but I push it away. I'm not a vegetarian or vegan by any means, but I have never hunted or fished before. But this is life and death for Alaric and me, so I continue to lift the net until it stops moving.

"You did it," Alaric says as he plants a kiss on the top of my head. I'm completely taken aback by the move. It's like how he kissed my head when I almost drowned. Caring. Proud.

It makes me feel warm inside.

"We did it," I say, looking back over it at him.

He smiles. No, more like beams. It's like a bright light in an unlit room. Blinding.

Alaric Prince is beautiful like this.

Like this, I can see an unfamiliar part, a part a woman could fall for.

I turn my attention back to the fish. I can't look at Alaric like that. I can't allow myself to believe any of that.

I'm not that girl for him. I can enjoy him, maybe even sleep with him, but I can't be getting crazy thoughts like that.

Nope.

That is one notion that will never be written in the stars.

---

After the first fish, Alaric went back to his rock, and I continued to fish alone. The one thing I have learned in the past few days is that time has no place on this island. There is only eating, hunting, and living.

We stay for a while until the bright blue sky morphs to a strange green color.

"We need to head back," he says, looking up at the forming clouds.

"Really, already?"

Alaric points to where he was staring. "See over there. That color?"

"Yeah," I answer, but I'm not sure why a green sky means we have to go.

"A storm is coming." He starts to walk.

"How do you know?"

"It looks like you will get survival class 2.0 now. When the sky turns green, a storm is brewing. But it's more than that. Look at the ocean. You see how it looks like squares are forming?"

"Yeah."

I have no idea what he's talking about, but I play along.

"Those squares show the riptide getting stronger. We need to get out of the ocean and back to camp. We need to pull the raft to a secure place, tether it, and then hope the storm doesn't cause it any damage."

"Shit."

"Yep."

Fear fills my stomach. If the storm is as bad as he's making it out to be, we could very well lose the only means to get off this island.

Without thinking twice, we are on the beach, grabbing our clothes, dressing, and then hurrying back to where the raft is.

"How long?"

"Could be anywhere from twenty minutes to an hour. Maybe longer. Look at the sky in the distance."

When I do, a strange foreboding feeling sweeps through me. A few miles out to sea, the sky is black. But worse than that is the funnel of clouds in the sky.

I must be lost in my head because I feel Alaric's hands cup my jaw and lift my face. Our eyes meet, and I see actual fear in his.

"I'm going to need you to listen to me. Can you do that?"

I nod, not being able to form words.

"Together, we are going to lift this raft. I will secure our stuff inside. It will be heavy. About sixty pounds of dead weight."

"Where are we going?"

"Toward the lake."

"Is that safe?"

"By the lake, no. But I thought I saw a cave the other day when I was in the water. By the waterfall."

"A cave?"

"If we can get there and if what I saw is correct, we can wait the storm out in there. I'm not going to lie. It will suck. It will be heavy, which is why I didn't attempt this before, but now we have no choice."

"Okay," I mutter.

When the time comes, and Alaric signals me to lift, I do.

Goddamn, that's heavy.

I grunt, my muscles flaring with the exertion.

It's way heavier than I thought, even with Alaric helping.

Alaric counts off, and we are walking. My feet keep slipping at this pace because my gait is much shorter than his.

I keep up even though the pain is immense. Even though my body screams to stop, I keep the pace.

Once we reach the clearing, Alaric stops.

"I'm going to put this down and run up ahead to make sure what I saw is accurate, and most importantly has room for the raft. If it doesn't, I'll have to tie it to a nearby tree."

"Be safe," I say, but he doesn't respond. Instead, his Adam's apple bobs, and then he's running toward where the waterfall is.

I expect him to run to the area where the water hits the lake, and I expect him to go underwater, but he's actually a few feet away by the rocks. From where I am standing, it looks like just black rocks and nothing else, but then I realize when he disappears, that's the cave.

A few minutes later, he comes out and jogs toward me. He's out of breath when he gets to me, and a thin layer of sweat drips down the side of his face.

"We are good to go. It's not very large. You might get your feet wet walking in, but once inside, it's dry."

"Okay."

"You ready?"

"Yes."

He reaches to lift the raft again, and this time, with an end in sight, it's less daunting. Until I hear the crack and the rumble of thunder. Large pellets of rain start to slap at our bodies. The sound of the water hitting the raft tells me the storm is coming fast. It's only a matter of minutes before it's a full monsoon.

"Faster!" Alaric shouts, and we set off into a run. I lose my footing often, but we keep going.

My lungs seize from the oxygen I expel.

Rain beats down on us. The sky is black, but I see the clearing.

Together, we push on, and now the water is higher at the mouth of the cave, but I don't care. My shoes will eventually dry, but who knows what the storm will bring. We are lucky to have a raft and shelter.

Once inside, I see what Alaric was talking about. In the first few feet of the cave, there is a small puddle of water, but then the rocks step up to dry land—well, stones but same difference.

We are safe.

"Help me flip it. Then we can unpack and start a fire."

"You want to start a fire in the cave?"

"It's the only way we will eat tonight. We just can't start it close to the mouth."

My mouth drops open. "And why is that?"

"Because if we do that, we risk the fire breaking apart the opening. At the opening of a cave, the rock is thinner."

Shock must register on my face because he reaches out and takes my hand, and a soft and reassuring squeeze comes next. "It will be fine. I'll start a small fire a few feet in where the ceiling is high enough that it won't be a problem. If the airflow is bad, we will know right away, and we will snuff it out if it gets too smoky."

"Good thing I got stranded on an island with you." My joke is lame, but he doesn't seem to mind.

"Yeah, anyone else, and you would be eating worms," he says, and I stick my tongue out at him and then turn away to assess the damage to my clothing. "You okay over there?"

I look down at the clothes that now cling to my body like a second skin. "Just cold. All my clothes are wet."

"I suggest you strip, and you can wrap yourself up with the blanket."

"It's a fantastic thing you have ... What did you call it? A ditch bag?"

"Yep, a ditch bag."

"Turn away," I order.

"Seriously, dove. We are stuck in a cave during a tsunami—"

I lift my hand and cut him off. "It's a tsunami?"

"No, it's not a tsunami. I'm just joking with you."

"Real funny, bro. I don't think I could handle that right now."

"Listen to me right now. We obviously didn't meet in the best of circumstances, but I can tell you without a measure of a doubt that you could survive. You are one of the strongest and most fearless women I have ever met."

His words stun me. They take me off guard so much that I have no answer for them at all. Instead, I remove my clothes until I'm left in my bra and panties, and then I reach for the blanket. Once I have it completely wrapped around me, I take them off too.

"At least I won't have to wash them. The rain did the job."

"See? Tough as nails and always seeing the bright side."

"Hardly, but what else can I do?"

"Not very much, considering the position we're in." He looks around the cave before pointing at a spot in the corner. "I'll set up the fire there."

"How are you going to start it? We are in a cave."

He smiles.

*He freaking smiles.*

Mister Nature has a plan.

"Okay, Mister I Know Everything About the Wilderness and Being Stranded on an Island, tell me oh, wise one, what's the plan?"

"I packed wood."

"Of course, you did." I roll my eyes. But with the sky so dark and the fire not started, he can't see.

"Dove, I know you are mocking me. I wouldn't do that if I were you."

"I did no such thing."

Before I know what's happening, he's shining the flashlight on my face.

"Damn ditch bag," I mutter.

"Damn ditch bag? That ditch bag saved your life. Apologize to it."

"The bag isn't Wilson. I'm not building a friendship with an inanimate object solely because I'm living the '*Castaway*' life."

"Don't insult Ditch." His voice is serious, and if I didn't know better, I would think he's serious. Seeing as Alaric Prince is sarcastic, I play along.

"Ditch? Seriously. You named the bag that?" Cue eye roll.

"Well, what else would you have me name her?"

This man is impossible yet entertaining.

"And now it's a her?" I mock.

Alaric's lips stretch wide across his face, his eyes gleaming with enjoyment. "She is."

"You are ridiculous."

"And she saved your life."

"Just light the damn fire already. Ditch would have been a better bag if she had a VHF radio. Who cares about a blanket or a flashlight? What we really need is a way to call for help." There, I said it.

"We were scared you would find it."

"See what a dumb move that was. The almighty Alaric Prince made a mistake."

With the flashlight now on the floor, illuminating the cave, I can see his face. His face is now serious and no longer playful.

"I did, Phoenix, and I'm sorry."

Phoenix. Not dove.

After that admission, I don't speak. I watch as he turns back to the wood and eventually makes a small but big enough fire. My own head tilts down, looking at the hard, dark earth beneath me. I feel bad for what I said. Alaric would have never done what he had if he knew what the future held. That's the thing I realize now. He's not the man I thought he was. Blinded by rage, he made bad decisions. But deep down, he's not that man. No. He's the man who saved me time and time again. There is no part of me that doesn't think he regrets his decision. It's still his fault we are trapped here, though, no matter how sorry he is.

"Are you hungry?" His voice pulls me from my inner thoughts.

My head lifts. "Not really."

"I'm not either, but we should eat to keep our strength up."

He's right. "As long as it's not the fish."

"Coconut?"

"Sounds amazing. What does your bag think of that?" I ask, trying to lighten the mood. With the future uncertain, there is no place for tension.

"She wants us to make the fish. I have vetoed her."

"Good call."

The fire is now up and running. The red embers drift around, warming the cave.

Alaric was right. It doesn't affect the air quality just like he thought.

We both settle around the heat, our clothes close enough to hopefully dry by the morning.

It's a good thing the cave is big and we could fit the raft inside the mouth. Just barely, though. It will be a bitch to get it out. Heck, it will be a bitch to carry back to the beach. But at least the boat won't tear, and we should be able to get it out to the ocean. Alaric had said it was meant to withstand the open sea. The only thing it can't withstand is thirst and hunger.

It really sucks that he didn't leave the radio in the raft, but I understand why he did it. He couldn't have expected ...

What am I doing? I keep going back and forth on how I feel about this. And now, I'm justifying what happened on his yacht.

The thing is, this all started because of me. Not true. The war started long before me. But this—being on his boat in the first place—all this started because of me.

Because I came up with a stupid and apparently transparent plan, and it backfired.

Royally.

From where I sit, I watch as he takes a knife to open the coconut. Then he collects the milk. I creep closer, not wanting him to spill any.

"Here," he says as he reaches over to me. The distance isn't far, and his hands touch mine. With the bottle in my hand, I sip—and I also freaking moan. It tastes so good. With all the adrenaline leaving my body, I realize how hungry I am. We hadn't eaten all day. Not since we left to fish.

We were so worried about getting to safety that I had forgotten or merely didn't realize.

"That tastes so good."

"I can tell." He chuckles.

"Don't make fun of me. Wait until you try it."

As if on cue, he lifts it to his mouth too and then swallows. "Fuck," he groans, and it's my turn to laugh. "You're right. That's fucking amazing right now."

"It really is."

When we are done drinking the milk, he cracks open the shell and takes the fatty meat out.

It tastes just as good as the milk. We sit in silence as we eat, other than letting out the occasional moan of pleasure.

"Wow, we are pigs," I say when there is nothing left.

"Are you still hungry? I know you don't want fish, but we have some other fruit in the raft."

"No. I'm good."

Again, silence falls on us. My gaze is on the fire, wondering what to talk about.

"Since we don't have stars tonight, there's no lesson," he says.

"That's a shame. Now what will we talk about?"

"We can talk about you."

"Or we can talk about you?" I counter.

"Didn't we already do that?"

He's right.

Maybe it's my time to open up.

# CHAPTER THIRTY-TWO

## Alaric

"The man you know as Michael is not my actual father," she says out of nowhere. "Hell, my name isn't really Phoenix. It's Sarah. We changed it when he adopted me."

I sit up from where I'm reclined on the raft near the fire.

Phoenix is still sitting across the raft from me, but I feel I need to be closer to her for what she is about to say.

I already knew he wasn't her biological dad, but I don't speak. This is her story, and I'm just here to listen.

She moves forward on the raft, closer to the warmth, as though talking about her past makes her cold. I can understand that. It's what I felt when I unburdened my childhood to her.

"When I was younger, I lived in New York with my family. We traveled a lot—more than most. Often, my father would take us to South America on his business trips. He was an international lawyer, and we went to Argentina during a time of civil unrest. War broke out. I don't remember much, but I remember that my family was caught in the crossfire. My parents both died. Michael was his client. He saved me that day and took me in when I had no one else. His life was too difficult, and he moved me around too much to keep me with him, so he sent me to boarding school, but he was always there for me."

I want to argue that doesn't stop him from being a

monster—that one good deed doesn't right his wrongs—but this isn't the time or the place for that.

That is a black cloud always hovering over us. If we let it in, it will destroy us.

Eventually, we will cross that bridge, but not now.

We both sit in silence after her story. There are no words to say that will help. We are both orphans who lost our family. We aren't that different.

"How long do you think the rain will last?" she asks, finally breaking the silence.

"A tropical storm like this? Probably a few days."

"This will set us back."

"It could," I admit, my voice dipping low.

It's worse than that. The waters will be unsteady, and although the raft can withstand open water, it can't withstand a storm like this one.

I don't say that.

The mood is already too somber to tell her any chance of us leaving in the next few days will have to be pushed back until we are sure another storm isn't brewing.

"Do you think we will die here?" she whispers.

It's dark in the cave, except from the fire dancing beside us, there's no other light, but I can see the way she trembles.

When I don't answer right away, she turns to look away from the flames and at me instead.

"You don't have to lie to me, Alaric."

"Probably," I admit.

"Because of this storm?"

I nod. "The chance that anyone will be looking for us or even know where to look was already slim. But if the weather keeps up like this, it could be days before we can do anything about it."

"If the storm lasts a few days, do we have enough food to last in here?"

Again, I go quiet. "Alaric."

"I'll give it to you straight. We don't have enough dry wood to last over two days. We have food, but if we eat it all, we'll basically have to start from scratch before we can leave."

"We are fucked."

"Not necessarily. It could end at any minute. It could be a fast, tropical storm."

She gives me a look that tells me she isn't buying what I'm selling. Good, because neither am I. By the look of the clouds …

"It's a hurricane, isn't it?" She cuts into my inner thoughts with exactly what I was thinking.

"The clouds looked that way."

"And how long do hurricanes last?" She levels me with a stare, a hard stare that demands me to be honest.

"If it's fast-moving, then a day or two, but typically, a week."

"And if it's terrible …?"

"Weeks." My words hang heavy in the gloomy cave. "I'm going to blow out the fire," I finally say.

"Why?" But she knows why. Tonight, even with the storm battering outside, it's not cold. We already used it to dry her clothes, the rest will have to naturally dry, but it's not worth the risk. Since it's almost time to sleep, we can't waste it.

"Okay," she whispers.

"Come here," I say, and her mouth forms an O.

"Without the fire, we will have to share the blanket."

If she wants to object, she doesn't. Instead, she scoots over to me.

This won't be the first time we have slept next to each other. Normally, we take separate sides of the raft and gravitate toward each other in the middle of the night.

When she's beside me, I move to remove my shirt.

"What are you doing?" she asks.

"You're naked under there. Let me give you my shirt at least."

She inclines her head and then nods. "That would be smart. Can't really share a blanket if I'm naked."

"I mean, you could ..."

She laughs and reaches for my shirt. When our hands touch, I let my fingers linger longer than I should. She doesn't pull away at first. Instead, she watches where we touch. Then she must snap out of the trance because she's moving away so she can put my shirt on. While she dresses, I put out the fire, and then I'm back in the raft with her.

"Thank you," she says as she lets it drop over the blanket. Once she's fully submerged in it, she lifts up, and the blanket drops away from her once naked body. "We should go to bed." I open the blanket, and she slips in. My arm is around her shoulder, and she is tucked into my chest.

"Sleep," I say as I kiss her hair.

She mumbles something, but I'm not sure what. It sounded like a thank you, but then I hear the soft inhale, and I know she's asleep.

Exhausted from the day.

I'm not faring much better because with Phoenix in my arms, protected, I feel at peace. I listen to her breathing, and before long, my own breaths match hers, and I too succumb.

# CHAPTER THIRTY-THREE

## Phoenix

*I*T'S DARK.

*There are so many people. My hand is in my mother's hand as she walks up to a familiar man. Uncle Michael. He's not my actual uncle, but he's Daddy's friend.*

*"Sarah." I hear my name, but I'm not sure where it's coming from. My hand drops from my mother's, and suddenly, I can't see anyone. Everyone is too tall. I move to find a higher ground to see.*

*Bang.*

*Bang.*

*Bang.*

*Rapid sounds over and over. Dust and smoke fill the air.*

*People scream.*

*Where's my mom? My dad.*

*Then I see him.*

*He's on the floor, gun lifted in the air. His finger keeps moving, but nothing happens. In front of me, on the ground, is my dad's other gun.*

*He's screaming for me to grab it. To fire. To save my mother. That's when I see her. She's lying on the floor, a man standing in front of her.*

*Before I know it, I'm grabbing the gun, my small hands wrapping around it. My mom looks at me, begging me, pleading with me.*

*I lift it, but I'm so scared.*

*I can't breathe. I can't move.*

*Frozen in place from fear.*

*The man shoots my mom, then my dad, and I do nothing.*
*Nothing but scream.*

My eyes open, but I can't see anything. Where am I?

"Shh," I hear from beside me, and that's when I notice the warm body holding me. The arms wrapped around me.

"Where ...?" I croak.

"We're still in the cave. Remember the storm?" he asks.

Suddenly, everything clears in my hazy mind.

The storm. Running for cover. Needing to put out the fire.

Alaric.

Holding me.

Keeping me safe.

Yet again.

He's mumbling something to me. Speaking into my hair as he gently strokes me, kisses me.

The gentleness he has shown me these past few days has my emotions amplifying.

Here I am, someone he thinks he should hate, and time and time again, he has put my needs first and taken care of me before everything else.

"You're okay," he says.

A sob breaks through my lips.

"Do you want to talk about it?" he asks before kissing my locks again.

"No."

I don't want to talk about it. I don't want to talk about the dream of the last time I saw my parents. The last time I held my mom's hand. That I could have saved them.

I want to pretend none of it happened and not think about how that one moment shaped the rest of my life.

I want to feel alive. I have been dead inside since they died, but now as I look my own mortality in the eyes, I can't let this be it.

Without allowing me to second-guess myself, I turn my head.

Still in his arms, I stare up at him. My eyes have adjusted to the darkness, and although I can't see him clearly, I can see his shadow.

Maybe this is for the best.

In the dark, I can be anyone I want to be.

Even the woman who finds comfort in Alaric's arms.

I move closer, securing my hands around his neck, and lean in until my lips fan his.

"What are you doing?" He breathes out, and the oxygen he expels tickles my lips.

"Forgetting," I say in truth, and he doesn't seem to object.

"You sure you want this?" His voice is deep and husky.

I lean in. "I do."

"Right answer, dove." Without a second thought, he crushes his lips to mine.

I open to him, allowing him to kiss me with a vigor I have never felt before. We are all teeth and tongue, moaning into each other's mouth. I have never kissed like this before.

It's not like the kiss on the boat. This one is primal.

He drags me on top of him until I'm straddling his lap. His hands run up my body, tugging at the bottom of his shirt. He pulls it up, never breaking from me, and exposes my breasts to him.

Time has no relevance when we kiss. I get lost in his mouth on mine. Seconds and then minutes pass, but we don't stop. We just get hungrier, more desperate. Until eventually, his hands move from where he's cupping my breast to lift the material.

Once the top is off, he pulls away. It's dark in the cave. I can't see much, but I can feel his desire and lust through each touch of his hands on me. Leaning forward, he presses his lips to the hollow of my neck and then works his way down.

He trails a line across my collarbone, grazing his teeth against my skin until he reaches my nipple.

With a swipe of the tongue, he makes me groan. He licks and tastes, and then a growl emanates from his mouth as he moves toward the other breast.

We continue this wicked dance until I'm grinding myself against him. He's hard and ready for me. The only thought now consuming my mind is what he will feel like.

He licks and sucks until my head falls back in ecstasy, and then I feel his arms bracketing around me, flipping me over until I'm on my back.

He hovers above me, his chest heaving.

"I need to be inside you." He groans, and I want nothing more.

With Alaric's shirt removed from my body, only his pants separate us.

In the dark, my hands search, and when I find the draw-string, I untie it.

It's not elegant as I try to maneuver.

It's hungry kisses. Desperate touches. Primal needs.

It's perfection.

When I feel him lift, I know he's rid himself of the pants.

I wait for him to crawl up my body. Instead, he fumbles more, and I'm not sure what he's doing.

But when the small flashlight illuminates the cave, I look at him.

What I see in his eyes takes my breath away.

"I wanted to see you." Then he's spreading my legs. Leaning up on my elbows, I watch as he crawls up my body but then stops.

His nose touches the inside of my thighs, and he looks up at me from where he's perched. "I wanted to see you when I did this." And then he looks up, a wicked gleam in his eye.

I moan my approval and lift my hips. He lifts my legs over his shoulders, and then he's going in, taking his tongue to my core in one long swipe. I gasp in pleasure.

"I…" I try to form words, but I can't. With me spread out before him like his own personal feast, it's difficult. My entire body quivers, courtesy of his tongue.

I press myself closer to his mouth, and the bastard laughs. His fingers part me, and he is pumping one and then two fingers in and out, causing my body to shake against him.

He mutters something, but I can't understand it. There's too much sensation as he continues to suck me into his mouth at the same time, building the pressure with each moment that passes.

My eyes flutter closed. Tingles run down my spine. Muscles tighten and tremble. My hands fist his hair, and my body starts to shake as I'm about to tip over the edge.

He stops.

"What are you doing?" I groan.

"I want to feel you come." He grows serious for a second, and I can see the giant elephant in the room.

"I'm clean. I don't sleep around," I practically beg.

"Me too."

It might seem reckless, but I'm desperate for the connection only he can give me right now.

"I'll pull out," he adds.

"You don't have to do that. I'm on the shot."

That must be enough for him because he grins at me like the Cheshire cat before starting to tease me where I need him most.

"You like this, dove?" he grits through clenched teeth. He's as desperate as I am.

"Yes," I answer, and then with a slow and steady thrust of his hips, he's inside me. It might be dark, and I might not be able to see anything, but I wish I could. I wish I could watch as he enters me then pulls back out.

He cups my backside and angles my body upward, slamming into me again and entering me fully, reaching deeper than I thought possible. He pulls back out before pounding back in. His strokes grow harder with each new thrust of his hips, and as I moan beneath him, his pace quickens.

I've never felt anything like this before. My nerve endings are on fire, igniting from within me. I feel myself being set ablaze, and then I'm falling over the edge. Alaric grits his teeth as he thrusts once, twice, and on the third pump, he pours himself into me.

Together, we both try to catch our breaths, and when we do, Alaric moves from on top of me. I miss his warmth instantly, but when he lies next to me and pulls me in his arms, my eyes grow heavy.

Once again, he kisses my head.

And once again, he says, "Sleep."

And like every time before, in the arms of my enemy, and the man who saved my life so many times—I do.

———————•———————

A warm heat causes my eyelids to flutter. I open my eyes to see that Alaric has started the fire.

I'm still in the raft, covered only by the small blanket.

Naked.

Last night plays in my mind on a loop, over and over again.

My cheeks warm and not from the fire now flaring next to me.

He hasn't noticed me yet, but I see him. He's going through the bag, pulling out a fish to cook.

Eating fish for breakfast might have at one point seemed gross, but now my stomach groans and my mouth waters to eat.

I watch as the muscles in his back flex.

I could watch him all day.

Probably will because there isn't anything else to do here.

Not that I'm complaining. He is rather gorgeous.

The memory of him being inside me has been branded into my brain. I can still feel him wrapped around me.

As if he can hear me thinking about him, he turns around. At first, his face is passive, but when he sees I'm awake, he smirks.

"Good morning," he draws out.

"Morning," I respond.

He puts down the fish and makes his way over to me. I'm shocked when he leans down to where I am and kisses me on the lips.

That wasn't something I expected. It's not that I thought he would go back to being a dick. He hasn't been a dick since we got to the island, but I also didn't think this would be a thing between us again.

I guess what I expected was for him to pretend nothing happened. It would have probably upset me, but I'd understand. Last night was different. I needed comfort, and he gave it to me, but today, in the light of a new day, I expected nothing.

He pulls back and smiles down at me. No one is more handsome than this man is when he smiles.

Sinful.

My heart beats like a drum, each beat reminding me how dangerous this man is to my health. I would have never thought that before, but now that I see the real him, I know that he's like the sun—beautiful, but if you get too close, deadly.

The problem is, no matter what I know, I still want to get burned.

"I'm going to make fish," he says, and it's just what I need to pull me out of my wicked thoughts.

"Sounds delicious." I laugh before looking toward the mouth of the cave. "Is it still raining?"

*Please say no. Please say no*, I chant over and over. Maybe that will make it come true.

"Unfortunately, I don't have good news."

I suck my lips into my mouth. That means we are stuck in here longer.

"I kind of need …"

"To go to the bathroom?"

"Yeah." I grimace.

"Right outside the cave, it leads to the lake. If you keep close to the rock, you can go in the lake or on the ground beside it. You won't get that wet because of the overhang of rocks. Plus, the trees give a big canopy."

"Is it safe?"

"For lengthy periods of time, no. But there isn't any lightning right now. It should be safe. The winds are powerful. Also, you can go farther in the cave if that makes you feel better. We have a little toilet paper left, and you can use some water we collected if you want to rinse."

"Can we risk the supplies?"

"We still have the lake. If worse comes to worst, I can collect more and purify it."

"I'll use the cave," I decide. No part of me has any desire to trudge through a storm right now. Maybe after, I'll wash off really quickly.

I grab the large jug of purified water and the flashlight and set off to walk deeper into the cave.

It feels kind of awkward, so I turn around and walk straight back to where he was.

"If this is our home for the next few days, I can't make it smell like pee," I admit. "That's gross."

"I feel that. Here, I'll walk you to the grass and then turn around. That way, you aren't by yourself."

"You'd do that … for me?"

Cue smile.

Cue butterflies.

This is not good.

The way he makes me feel can't possibly be good for my health.

It doesn't stop the enormous grin from spreading across my face or the way my insides warm as he takes my hand and leads me out of the cave.

It's still raining, but he's right. The rocks from the cave opening block most of the rain. Beside the opening to the left, there are rocks and grass. The lake is on the other side, a few feet away.

"You sure it won't get worse? No lightning?"

"I'm not sure of anything. But right now, the biggest issue is the wind. No lightning."

"Okay, ground it is. I'll be back."

Dropping his hand, I walk over to the grass. No longer under the rocks, the rain beats down on me. I had thrown on my tank and panties before walking out here, but that was stupid. Now, both are drenched, and I'll be spending the rest of the day naked again.

I guess I can think of worse things to do.

I take care of my business, and once I'm done, I head back to Alaric.

"If I have time, I want to jump in really quickly. Do I have time?"

Alaric looks up at the sky.

Dark gray storm clouds hover low in the sky, and the air smells sweet as remnants of the rain linger on the surface of the rocks.

My gaze skims over the distance. The rain seems to be slowing down, but the trees are still fiercely whipping around. But as long as I don't hear thunder, and I don't see lightning, it should be safe.

"You have a few. If we see anything suspicious, we'll get out. If the wind gets too strong ..."

"We'll get out."

"If we stay behind the waterfall, it will be okay. The rocks will cover most of everything."

"Sounds like a plan, but I would like to brush my teeth and get soap."

"Stay here." He walks away and comes back a minute later. "Hand."

I oblige.

He places a slight drop of toothpaste on my finger. Although it's not a lot, I'm happy for this luxury. I rub it on my tongue and teeth before spitting it out. After that, he throws the toothpaste back into the cave and then hands me the soap.

"Strip here. Soap up and then go into the waterfall."

"Here?" My eyes go wide. "You want me to get naked."

"Dove ... I have already seen you naked." He steps closer, his body touching mine. His hand reaches out and brackets around me, pulling me flush against him, and I feel the evidence of a now growing erection. "I have seen you, tasted you, and been inside you. I couldn't be more familiar with your body if I tried, and trust me—I intend to try many, many times. Bathing together hardly seems a problem."

He's right, and I'm acting like an idiot.

I lift the tank up and then pull my underwear off. Once I'm fully naked, I rub the soap all over my body before I go to hand it to Alaric, who is now also naked and sporting a very impressive length.

He rubs his body, and I swear it's the most erotic thing I have ever seen. Okay, that's not true, watching him wash and then touch himself might have been.

Once he also has soap on his body, he places the soap back and then takes my hand.

"You ready?"

"Yes."

Together, we walk closely against the stone until we are walking almost directly under the waterfall.

The water soaks us both, and then we are behind the falls in a pool of water. It's not as deep here, but just being underneath some water feels amazing right now.

I use the spraying water as a makeshift shower, and then I'm scrubbing my body.

It's only a few minutes later when I feel him. He's behind me with his hard body pressed against mine.

His lips are the first thing to touch me. They trail across my shoulders, placing small kisses on my skin. Next, his hands reach around me, pulling me flush against his body.

He's long and hard behind me, his erection resting on my back. He's leading me as he kisses me, leading me to the rocks that are no longer underwater.

"Brace yourself," he says. His hands are all over me now. Touching and teasing me everywhere.

A part of me wonders if this is safe with the storm outside, but where we are behind the waterfall, it's as if we are in our private grotto.

I lean forward and place my hands on a rock. It's slippery but no more slippery than if I was bracing myself in a shower.

His hands spread my legs, and then his fingers thrust inside me.

Preparing me to take him again.

He keeps up the pace before he pulls his fingers out, and then I feel him nudging at my entrance.

I'm about to tell him to hurry, that I can't hold myself like this forever, but then he thrusts inside me and takes all my words away.

I can't speak.

I can't think.

All I can do is feel.

He slams in and then pulls out.

The angle is so deep this way, I can feel every inch of him, and it's delicious.

With each thrust, I feel myself getting closer and closer.

This won't be long. This is a wicked frenzy. A need we both can't quench.

He fucks me hard, claiming ownership of my body, and I allow it. I welcome it. I give it to him freely.

I know he's close, which is good because I'm close too. I feel my legs tremble; I feel my body tightening, and then I'm flying off the side of the waterfall. I'm falling over my own cliff, and as Alaric bites down on my shoulder and tightens his hold, he falls over too.

He stays inside me as I catch my breath, and then he's slipping out and helping me stand.

I'm turned around before I know what's happening, and his mouth is on mine.

It's a tender kiss, soft and passionate, not hurried like before. Not claiming. No, this kiss is more than that. This is the type of kiss that holds promise. But I know deep down it can't. It's another lie we tell ourselves to survive on this island. But I shake those thoughts away. For now, I'll fade into the dream and pretend.

# CHAPTER THIRTY-FOUR

## Alaric

AFTER THE IMPROMPTU FUCK AT THE WATERFALL, I PULL her into my arms and lead her back to the cave.

Since we don't have towels, we sit naked by the fire to dry while we cook the fish.

With the storm still going strong outside, we don't have many options. As we wait for the wind and rain to pass, Phoenix regales me with stories of her life once Michael took her in.

The man she describes does not match the man I know.

But the man Phoenix has gotten to know on this island, the parts I have only shared with her don't match the man the world knows of me.

Here, I'm able to let down my guard. Here, my only responsibility is to keep us alive.

There is nothing else.

A part of me doesn't want to leave.

I'd never admit that, but things are simple here. Peaceful. There is no false pretense; all there is survival.

It's like all those years ago …

When my father dropped me on an island and told me he'd be back in a week.

There was no room to hate him, to hate anyone, when you just want to live.

It's refreshing.

Ever since my brother was murdered, ever since I got the call that my car was blown up parked outside the back of the building where my brother was, my life has never been simple.

"Am I boring you?" Phoenix asks. Her head is inclined, and her brows knit together.

How long was she talking?

And what the hell did she say?

"No," I respond.

Her lips tip up into a smirk. "Then what did I say, Alaric?" She winks.

Because she knows I wasn't listening.

"You said that I was devastatingly handsome, and that you wanted to f—"

"Now I know you weren't listening," she cuts me off.

"I was, but when you discussed your dorm room in boarding school, you lost me."

Phoenix gives me a timid smile. "Sorry about that."

"It's okay, I want to hear about it. We have nothing else to talk about it, so your dorm room isn't awful …"

"Why don't you tell me what you were thinking about?" she says, moving closer and taking my hand in hers.

"Because I can't," I admit.

"Why?"

I pull my hand away from hers and look at her—well, stare is more like it. Her eyes go wide with understanding.

"You were thinking about my father."

I nod.

"You were thinking about the war?"

I nod again.

"I know that this might sound strange, but do you want to talk about it?"

I cock my head this time and stare at her, really stare. "You want me to talk about why I want your father dead with you?"

She bites her lower lip. "I mean, if it's eating you up …"

"You would do that … for me?" I ask, not really understanding her at this moment. This is the man who saved her, and she wants me to discuss my feelings about him.

"Do I want you to hate him? No. Do I want to convince you that you shouldn't? Yes."

"That will not happen."

She lifts her hand. "I'm not saying it will. What I'm saying is, if I have my druthers, I would convince you otherwise, but since that's not going to happen, you can at least talk to me about it and explain."

"Explain what? That he killed my brother. There's really not much to explain."

Her mouth opens and shuts.

Instead of waiting for her to speak, I reach for her and pull her onto my lap.

"Dove, I don't want to bring that up here. I don't want to talk about real life here."

I look down at her. I know it hurts her for me to hate the man she loves so much, but it doesn't stop it from being true. It doesn't stop me from wanting revenge.

"But—"

"No buts. We are living in a different reality right now. Why bring the actual world into it? Why tarnish this? Can't we just live in the moment right now?"

At my words, her shoulders hunch forward, and she remains quiet. The silence stretches before she must mull over my words and decide I'm right because she looks back up at me. There's no mistaking my words hurt her, but neither of us can do anything on that front right now, so there's no point in talking about it.

"Agree not to mention it again," I say, placing a soft feathery kiss on her lips.

"Okay," she mumbles.

I sweep my tongue over the seam of her mouth.

"I can think of much better ways to spend our time."

"Is that so?" she purrs.

"Yes. If you're bored, I can entertain you …" My words hang in the air, dripping with innuendo.

"And what exactly can you do to entertain me?" Her hands reach around my body until she holds me closer.

"I can make you forget your name."

"But can you make me forget yours?"

"Never," I rasp, and then I force her mouth open with my tongue and plunge into its warmth.

She moans into the kiss, and I deepen it.

This is a much better use of our time together. There is no need to burden ourselves with the rest. There are too many things outside our control.

This is enough for now.

We kiss for a long time until we are both panting and needing more.

Still naked, I position her on top of me, straddling my lap, and then she slides down onto my cock.

The feeling of being wrapped up in her warmth is perfection.

It makes the world fade away.

She is more potent than any drug. I'm completely intoxicated by her.

With each rise and fall of her hips, I'm lost to her.

Completely and utterly lost.

# CHAPTER THIRTY-FIVE

## Phoenix

I STRETCH MY HANDS OVER MY HEAD AND LET OUT A LARGE and probably dramatic yawn.

It's been a few days since the storm hit, and it's still going strong. Whenever the winds die down, we quickly bathe ourselves in the lake. It's not ideal, but we make do.

Thankfully, we had a lot of fish, since we can't go looking for more food. But it also solidifies that once this storm is over, we will have to spend days recouping the food we ate before we can even consider escaping.

It's scary.

A part of me thinks we should stay here.

But this island isn't ideal.

Although the cave is helpful, we can't stay here indefinitely.

Alaric seems confident we'll find another island, as long as we have enough food and water to last ten days. According to him and the map he showed me on the boat, there are plenty of islands near where we are.

He says that even if no one finds us, we should be able to find shelter on another island regardless, and maybe that one will have a better food supply.

Fish and coconuts and the occasional starfruit aren't enough for us to live here long term.

Eventually, we will get sick.

The only option is to try.

There is an actual possibility we will die, but we both agree we would rather die fighting.

Which brings me back to the here and now.

We have spent days wrapped in each other arms, losing ourselves repeatedly in each other's bodies.

I have never felt pleasure like what he has given me.

Since my life is hanging in the balance, I don't think of what any of this means, so I just enjoy him.

Enjoy the comfort I can get from him, even if that means pretending.

It's not really a lie.

I'm just ignoring the truth.

Looking to my side, I see that he's still asleep. After our last romp, we both passed out.

The man certainly has stamina. I don't think I have ever had this much sex in my life.

But when he's inside me, I feel like anything is possible.

I feel like surviving is possible.

Again, with that lie.

Now the only question is, what will happen if we do?

What will it mean for us?

Nothing.

It will mean nothing.

It will just be two people who needed to find peace in Hell.

As if he knows my gaze is on him, he stirs.

A yawn leaves his body, and his arms reach over his head.

He opens his eyes to catch me staring at him.

"You're up?" he asks as he rubs the sleep from his eyes.

"I am."

His face grows serious as he watches me where I am. "It's rare someone gets the drop on me."

"You've taught me well."

"Yes, your survival skills are really coming along. The fire you started today was good," he says.

"It was on point," I fire back before smiling.

"If you say so."

"I do." Reaching for my tank top, I move to put it on, but he shoos my hand away. "Don't you think we need a break?"

His hand reaches out, and his fingers form a circle around my nipple.

"Speak for yourself. I never need a break." He leans into me until his tongue is tracing the column of my neck.

"Be serious, Alaric." I push him off and move to an upright position.

"I'm always serious about sex."

"Sex … is that all that matters?" I huff as I reach for my tank top again, finally managing to put it on.

"Don't start that right now."

"Start what? Having feelings. Not wanting to be used."

"Cut the shit, dove."

"Dove. Dove. Dove!" I shout, acting like a petulant child, and I'm not even sure why. I knew that this wasn't serious, so why am I acting like this? But as much as I tell myself to calm down, I find my emotions are over the place as I say, "Fuck that shit." I move to a standing position and look down at him and snarl. "I'm not some little dove. I'm a goddamn Phoenix, no matter what happens. No matter who burns me, I'll rise."

I pace the little cave, and I'm not sure where my anger is coming from or when Alaric wraps his arms around me. But he does.

"You're right."

I stop moving.

This seems to be Alaric's favorite way to hold me, my back to his front. He's always holding me like this. Like I am a dove that's trying to fly away.

"You're not a dove. You are a Phoenix. I just like the way it sounds now. Habit."

"As long as you know what I am."

He spins me around, his hand reaching beneath my jaw and tilting it up.

"I know exactly who you are, Phoenix, no matter what nickname I call you. This isn't just sex, but I don't know what you want me to say."

"We talk about everything but the truth."

"Is it wrong that I don't want to rock the boat?" I glare at him for his comment, and he smirks. "Terrible choice of words."

"You think?"

"We're taking pleasure in each other, not just physical but also emotional, and to go there would ruin this little ecosystem. Neither of us knows what the future will bring."

"I know. I know you're right ... But—" I take a deep breath, trying to find the right words to convey why I am upset and what I want. "I can't help but want to talk about it anyway."

"Fine. But not now."

"Why not ...?"

"Because we just got into a fight. Our first fight and I want to make up."

I level him with my stare.

"What?"

Placing my hand on my hip, I shoot him daggers with my eyes. "You know what."

"Fine." He leans down and kisses my mouth. It's a chaste kiss, and it lightens the mood. "Let's eat something and then venture outside to see about the storm."

"Do you think it's safe?"

He walks over to the area where his clothes are, and I watch his ass as he walks.

I shouldn't judge him for always wanting to have sex. The

man is a modern sexual miracle and his ass a work of perfection. Cut from marble. The truth is, I want nothing more than to touch him, but I don't say that. Instead, I just ogle him longer before turning away.

"It might not be perfectly safe, but the last time we were outside, the winds were much weaker. It's still raining, but the storm might be passing. If that's the case, we can safely fish again and replenish everything we've eaten."

"You would feel comfortable leaving this shortly after the storm?"

I turn back to look at him. His face is serious. "No. But I don't think we have a choice."

Even though my head nods, I'm not sure how I feel. He's right. Long term, this island isn't the right move, but I'm still not sure when to leave.

"Let's not think about this now. We can decide in a few days."

"Yeah, probably a smart idea."

It is. But a part of me still wants to know more about what he thinks my father did. I understand he thinks he killed his brother. My father said as much, but I can't help but need to know more of that story.

But right now isn't the time. There might never be a moment that will make sense.

That will just be something I have to deal with.

# CHAPTER THIRTY-SIX

## Alaric

THINGS HAVE BEEN TENSE EVER SINCE THE SHOWDOWN with Phoenix yesterday. We went outside. The storm is definitely passing.

I estimate it will be gone by tomorrow, which means today is my last full day with her in this cave before we start to prepare.

Tonight, I'll leave the fire going all night. There's no reason to snuff it when we can gather more wood tomorrow.

I sit down on the floor and get the twigs to ignite. Phoenix sits in front of me.

"Do you ever wish we had marshmallows?" she asks as she takes a seat next to me.

"I never pictured you as a roasting marshmallow type of girl."

"What kind of girl did you picture me as?"

It's a hard question, and now that I know she was raised alone in a boarding school, it's even harder.

"Honestly."

"Of course. At this point, after everything we have been through together, how can you even ask."

"I picture you as a loner. Not much different from me. But while I was not by myself by choice, you were. In the end, we ended up being similar. You choose to be alone because, in your mind, everyone who you cared about left you. Including Michael." I say his name even though it's bitter on my tongue. "Even if he saved you, he left you. So you never tried."

Her eyes are wide and glassy.

"I-I ..." She seems flustered by my words. "I never thought of it like that. But I guess you're right."

"Trust me, I understand. I've never really had anyone. I was also left by choice. I trusted no one. My brother, a bit, but not for a long time."

"Why? What happened there? You seem to really have loved your brother."

"It's a long, complicated story."

"I have time." She gives me a warm smile. "A lot of time."

A part of me wants to tell her. Another part wants to push it down and pretend that part of my life never happened.

The thing is, as I look at her large blue eyes, the ones that say I can talk to her, that I can unburden myself to her, I really want to.

"Damian hated me when he died." Saying the words out loud feels like a giant weight has been lifted from my shoulders. I've never admitted that to anyone. Never admitted I knew, or that I cared.

The truth is, I had no one to tell. Besides my brother, I had no one. Ever.

The pain of his death feels like a sucker punch to my heart. It feels like the walls of the cave are closing in.

"Why did he hate you?" she asks, her voice low and unsteady.

"There was this girl."

"Isn't there always?" she mumbles.

"We all grew up together. My brother was only one year older, but as I said before, he was the one who was supposed to take over. My father was grooming him. This girl was the daughter of my father's closet business partner. They had this dream to combine businesses. An agreement was set. The families would join."

"An arranged marriage."

"I know it must sound crazy, but that's the way most families in this line of work handle things. They need to know they can trust the person they bring into the mix. It was understood that Grace would marry my brother, Damian. It was fine when we were children, and the older we got, it was all my brother ever wanted. But for Grace, it wasn't. She wanted to marry into my family, but—" I stop and take a deep breath. "Just not to him."

"She loved you."

"She did. She was relentless. Anytime I was home, she would come find me. She wanted to be with me, but my brother was so in love with her."

"She only had eyes for you." I nod at her statement.

"The thing is …" I swallow through the lump in my throat. "When we were young, after one of the many times I was forced to survive in the wilderness alone, Damian was sent to retrieve me. I was hungry, delusional. I was feral."

"What happened?"

"I sliced his face with a knife." Lifting my hands, I cover my face—another thing to feel guilt over. The guilt I have inside me is suffocating.

"You were a kid. That wasn't your fault."

"Damian never saw it that way, and after that moment, neither did Grace. She couldn't look at him. It got worse as we got older. She hated to look at him and wasn't attracted to him. She only wanted me. I tried my best to let her down easy, but one day it all came to a head. She tried to kiss me, and I pushed her off. I told her she was to marry my brother. She said she would never marry him."

"I was a dick. I laughed in her face. I didn't know," my voice cracks.

"What didn't you know?"

"She didn't want him and claimed she only loved me. She didn't want to live a life married to a man she didn't love. She didn't want to marry a monster."

"That's what she said?"

"Yeah."

"What did she do?"

I stand from where I'm sitting and start to pace. I'm surprised when Phoenix rises too, and this time, it's her hands that wrap around my middle from behind.

"What did she do?" she presses, not letting go. Stubborn, stubborn dove.

"She committed suicide."

Phoenix inhales sharply. "I'm so sorry," she whispers.

"No one knows of my rejection. No one knows what happened."

"But I don't understand …"

"She blamed me in her letter. Like an ultimate fuck you for rejecting her. But the problem was, she made it seem like I hurt her, that she couldn't live with what I did …"

"And he blamed you."

"He blamed me for hurting who he saw as his fiancée. For making her take her own life from grief. Damian used to have this quote he would say. '*Only the dead have seen the end of war.*' He was right. Grace was the only one who knew what her death would bring."

"Why didn't you explain?"

"At first, I tried, but he wouldn't hear me, so lost in his grief, and then he hated me, so there was no point. It was my word against his dead love. Nothing I could say would bring her back. I didn't want to tell him she chose death rather than be with him."

"You played the villain to keep him from getting hurt."

We both fall silent, her arms still wrapped around me. I can feel her heart beating against my back.

"You were right," I whisper after a minute.

"Right about what?"

"When you called it my tarnished empire. It always has been, long before I even made the decision that would ultimately lead to my brother's death, it was broken."

"It wasn't your fault."

"It feels like it."

"You were being a good brother. Through all of this until the end … you were being a good brother."

When I don't answer, she turns me around.

She places her hands on my shoulders, and I look down at her.

"You are a good man."

"I'm not."

"I beg to differ. Trust me on that, I would love to be in the Hate Alaric camp."

"How can you say that? Look at where we are. You're here because of me."

"I'm here because I got this crazy idea to snoop, and you decided to be a dick and not let me get away with it."

"I'm a dick."

"Yeah, you are. But every now and then, you do something that redeems you …" She pinches her fingers. "Just a little."

"That's good to know. And here I thought I was a full dick." She lets out a laugh and continues to hold me to her.

I take a deep breath. "He went crazy after that. Drinking. Drugs. He fell off the radar and abandoned us. He went so off the rails that my father changed his will. When my dad died, he left me everything …"

Anger rises in my lungs as I think about the next part. I shouldn't tell her the rest and just leave it at that, but I don't.

"He came back. He forgave me … He wanted to be a part of the business. He wanted to be my brother. He wanted me to give him a chance, to trust him and I did. *I* sent him in my place."

I turn and look at Phoenix. Her face looks pale, and she's nibbling her lip.

"He went in my place to a meeting with my competitor."

"My dad—"

"Yes, your dad. Damian went to the meeting in my place, and he never came back. There was a bomb." My voice cracks and I can't go on. I can't talk about that day anymore.

"I-I …"

"Don't." I lift my hand to stop. "There is nothing you can say, so please don't. Not now."

She surprises me when she finally speaks. "I'm sorry."

No words leave my mouth.

"I'm so sorry," she says again, and this time, she raises on her tiptoes and places a kiss on my back. "It might not be the same, but I know what it is to lose your only family. To not have anyone in the world who belongs to you."

Her words have me turning. When I'm standing in front of her, I look into her large blue eyes. Like the endless ocean, I could get lost in those eyes if I let myself, and right now, that's exactly what I want to do. Get lost in her.

I lean down.

Our mouths meet, but unlike every time before, this isn't rushed. This isn't a frenzy of kisses. No, this is soft. This is me bleeding in front of her. Me finally letting go of the guilt and hurt I have felt over the years, and this is her showing me the light.

She wraps her arms around me and gently pulls me to the ground. Neither one of us even attempts to rid ourselves of our clothes. We just kiss, and somehow, it's exactly what I need.

When I wake up the next day, we are both dressed and still lying entangled with each other.

She moves in my arms and then lifts up to see me. She looks like a goddess looking down from Heaven, and after last night, I'm not sure she isn't. "Hi," she whispers.

I rise and place my lips on hers.

"Morning," I groan against her mouth. "Are you hungry?"

"Has it stopped raining?"

"I'm not sure."

"Should we find out?"

"We should, but first, I want to do what I didn't do last night."

"And what pray tell is that?" she jokes.

"I want to ravish you one more time before we get to work."

She removes her clothes and looks up with sultry eyes, spreading her legs to give me a perfect view.

She's breathtaking, captivating, ethereal.

The need to consume courses through my veins.

A sweet elixir tempting me.

One taste will never be enough.

I don't know how long I devour her, or how long I find peace in her body, but by the time we are both spent, I know it's time for us to both eat food and get dressed.

We don't talk while we nibble on fish, or when we walk out of the cave. Nor do we speak as we head back to the beach.

The landscape around us has changed since the storm. Tipped over trees. Scattered branches. The ground is soft with mud. We would never have survived this without the cave's protection. We keep walking while I cut through the debris with my knife.

It takes longer than usual to make our way back to the lagoon where I taught her how to fish.

The weather isn't great, and the water is choppy, but we are running out of food, so we have no choice.

Phoenix stays to the shallow parts, and I go deeper.

The sun still isn't out. The sky is still darker than what I would like, but we should be able to leave in the next day or two.

A part of me wants to stay after last night and live in this bubble a little while longer. But it's time to go home.

Across the water, there is a small pile of fish forming near where Phoenix stands. It's a bigger pile than one would imagine for a newer fisherman. Impressive actually. She's right.

She is a phoenix. It doesn't matter what happens to her or what challenges life throws at her, she rises.

The pile of fish is a testament to that.

"You ready?" I shout from my position.

My pile isn't large, but my catch is bigger.

"Yep!" she hollers back.

The fish are still on my stick as I walk over to her.

"Are you done for the day, or do you want to look for fruit?"

"Since we are out, we might as well. Who knows what tomorrow will bring?"

Again, she's right.

The future isn't certain.

We could face a war on the ocean. And as Damien used to always say, "Only the dead have seen the end of war."

I hope that's not the case.

# CHAPTER THIRTY-SEVEN

## Phoenix

Six days have gone by since that night with Alaric. The night he told me everything. The night he purged his guilt.

It wasn't his fault that his brother died, but I'll never be able to tell him that.

He would never let me say that.

A part of me doesn't understand the story. My father might be a lot of things, but if he called for a meeting, he is not the type of man to double-cross you.

He reminds me of Alaric in that sense.

Alaric was honest about my part in this from the beginning. He was even honest with my father when he brokered what should have been the trade of my life for his. My father is the same way.

He wouldn't set up a meeting under false pretenses.

There's no way.

I know I can't bring it up, though. With today being the day we leave, I can't risk Alaric's mental state.

We both need to be on our A game.

It's risky. But I trust him. If he believes there is a shot, I know there is.

As much as I have grown to enjoy the moments I've spent in his arms, I know we can't stay here.

These past weeks have been the best in my life. To some, that might sound strange, but that doesn't stop it from being true. It's not just the sex, either. Yes, we've had more sex than I can even count, but it's more than that. We talk. I've opened up to him about myself, and more importantly, he's opened up to me.

Alaric and I aren't much different in the end. We are kindred spirits, each living through a profound loss and growing into the people we are today.

It hurts my heart to leave this place after all we have been through together.

I think it's been at least two weeks since we arrived, but the days have blended, so I'm not sure if it's closer to three. Despite not wanting to go home, I know it's time. No one is looking for us now, so this will be our only shot.

A part of me wants to tell him I've changed my mind, and we should stay. That's not in the cards for us, though.

We wouldn't make it more than a few months. And what if something went wrong? What if one of us got hurt?

Yes, there is a good chance we will die, but at least we are making one last stand.

If we die, we die on our terms.

Or at least that's what I tell myself as I watch Alaric load the raft.

He's arranging the supplies and pulling out the red canopy that comes with it, just in case we head into rain. Better to set it up now than in the middle of a storm.

The paddles that Alaric whittled are in the raft.

I didn't even know what whittling was until I met Alaric. I didn't know how to pick fruit and not die, or how to fish, or even how to start a fire.

In the few short weeks we have been here and the month I have known him, Alaric Prince has changed my life.

And I would like to think he's changed me for the better.

A lot can still happen, but if I die today, I know my life is better because of him.

Some might say I'm crazy.

That he kidnapped me.

He never kidnapped me, though, because I stowed away on his boat. Maybe my brain is messed up, or maybe I'm confusing things, but I don't hate him, and I don't blame him.

He saved my life, and I will forever be in his debt for that.

What will happen to my dad?

I'm not sure. We might not even live long enough to find out.

Our only worry needs to be living.

We will face the rest when we need to.

"You ready?" His deep voice cuts through my thoughts, and I turn to look at him.

"Not yet." His brow lifts in confusion. I take a step up to him, and when I'm close enough to touch him, I reach out. He gives me his hands, and I take a deep breath. This is harder than I thought it would be to say, but I need to do this. "There is one more thing I want, no need, to do before we go."

Now, he looks even more perplexed by my weird rambling. I'm not sure how to explain this to him, but since honesty is our policy, I blurt it out.

"Teach me how to fire a gun."

Alaric's head cocks to the side as he studies me. He's never asked about my previous aversion to learning, and he doesn't ask now. That's the thing about him, he understands what I need, and he gives it to me. No questions asked.

"Come stand here." With my hand still in his, he leads me away from the raft and toward the open sand in the opposite direction. He's probably worried that I'll accidentally shoot a hole in it. I don't put that past me. Alaric and I haven't had the best of luck.

Once I'm at the correct location, Alaric steps behind my body, and his hand reaches out to guide me.

The air is heavy around us, my untold story lingering between us.

And I decide right then and there that I want to tell him everything, purge my soul, show him my truth.

"Thank you for not asking before." My heart starts to beat at a faster clip as Alaric places the gun in my hand. The cold metal sends a chill up my spine despite the heat.

"You can do this," Alaric says from behind me. His words tickle my ear right before he kisses the nape of my neck.

I'm not sure if he's talking about shooting or finally voicing what happened that day so many years ago.

I choose the latter.

"The day my parents died …" I pause, trying to find my words.

"You don't have to tell me more."

"That's the thing, I don't have to, but I want to. I want you to know all of me."

His lips place another kiss on my bare skin. "Then I'm listening."

"I could have stopped it. They were being shot at, but I could have stopped it. There was a gun. I-I …" A sob breaks through me. A cry I have been holding onto since I was a little girl. "I had the gun, and my parents, they begged me to shoot."

"It's not your fault. You were a child."

"I froze. Don't you understand? I froze. I had the gun in my hand, and instead, I watched them die."

His hand lifts and turns my jaw to face him.

"It's not your fault. You need to forgive yourself."

Looking into his eyes, I see his own feeling mirrored in him. He's struggling with the same guilt as me. A deep-seated guilt that leaves a stain on your soul.

A stain that will only go away with forgiveness.

Inhaling deeply, I pull in the oxygen around me. I breathe in the warm salty beach air. Then I exhale. "I'm ready."

"Me too," he whispers, his eyes darker than normal, filled with years of pain begging to be released as well.

With his help, I aim the gun, wrapping my fingers around the trigger.

"Strength is struggling but refusing to surrender. You got this, Phoenix. You are the strongest woman I know."

I allow my eyes to close for a beat, and when they open, I gather all the strength inside me to push past all the resistance.

I shoot.

The moment goes slow. Like a movie scene where the camera fades out and time stops for a beat.

"You're incredible," I hear Alaric say, and as my heart beats frantically against my breastbone, I feel at peace.

Neither of us speaks for the next few minutes as both of us bask in the weight of the moment. Eventually, I step away from where his arms are wrapped around me and turn to face him.

"Now?" he asks.

My eyes linger on him, soaking in every last inch as we prepare for this journey. After I nod, my gaze moves back to the island.

This small but beautiful island.

It's the type of private paradise that if I could, I would buy it and build a house. Plant my own garden and live in peace. And a working boat, of course.

With a soft tug at my heart, I turn away from it and step into the raft and sit.

"We are going to have to paddle to get away from the land." He hands me the paddles. "I probably won't need your help. But here, just in case."

"If you are the one doing the work, do you want the good ones?"

"I'll be fine. Remember, I can build a coconut radio." He smirks.

"Wait, a minute … I thought you couldn't." I laugh.

"I only said that to make sure you were stuck with me."

"And why would you go through all that trouble for little old me?"

"Because you are worth it," he says, and there is no humor in his voice.

For a second, I'm wondering if I'm imagining his comment, but his face is soft and thoughtful.

Then he turns back toward the island, one more look.

One more glance.

Before we put it all in the past.

"I'm going to miss it," I admit. "Is that weird?"

"No. Me too." His voice is so low I think I imagined his comment.

After that, we don't speak. Alaric is deep in concentration, paddling us out to sea, and I stare into the horizon, a lonely tear dripping down my cheek.

I'm not sure why I'm crying, but I am.

One tear leads to two and three, and then they pour out of my soul.

When we are finally far enough out, he places the paddle down and then pulls me into his arms. He holds me tight as if it might be the last time. It might be.

Together, we hold each other, and with each second that passes, the island becomes one with the sky, lost in the deep blue ocean. A mirage.

If my heart wasn't breaking, I would almost think this was all a dream.

# CHAPTER THIRTY-EIGHT

Alaric

IT'S BEEN HOURS SINCE WE LEFT. I HAVE THE CANOPY HALF down to steer, not that I know where I'm going.

If only I knew where I started.

The last time I looked at the map, there were too many tiny islands that I couldn't pinpoint where we ended up.

On the ocean, we are a small speck, like a tiny grain of sand in a never-ending beach.

I'm not sure which way to go.

Even when the sky goes dark with the stars above us to guide, I'm not sure what direction home is in.

It makes me feel useless.

Something I hate.

It's not that I'm a control freak. Okay, I am, which makes being lost in the ocean my biggest nightmare.

At least if I had something to go by … I'm resourceful, but this is a whole different level of fucked.

Phoenix has been quiet.

Eerily so.

This isn't easy for either of us, but for me, I'm used to having to survive. I spend every day of my life doing so.

She, on the other hand, doesn't.

"Are you hungry?" I ask.

There is no way to cook out here, but we cooked all the fish we caught before we left. It will most likely taste like shit, but hopefully, it will be enough to give us a chance to live.

"No, not really."

"You have to eat eventually."

"I know."

There isn't much room in here, but since it's a six-person raft, there's enough that she's on the other side.

"You don't have to sit so far away."

"I'm afraid."

Her words make me tilt my head. "Afraid of what?"

"That the raft will capsize. What if the—"

I shake my hand at her, cutting off her words. "That won't happen. They built this to last. It has weight stabilizers; it won't flip."

"Not even in a storm?"

"Not even in a storm," I say.

The truth is, that's how it was sold to me, that it won't flip in the ocean, but under the right circumstances, it might. I won't tell her as much. I already know how scared she is.

She weighs my words in her head, and then she moves closer.

Not too close, but close enough that she can rest her head on my shoulder.

From the angle, we both have an unobstructed view of the sky.

The stars above twinkle down on us like tiny tea lights.

I point out into the distance.

"You can't see it now, but did you know there is a constellation called Phoenix?"

"Really?"

"Yeah, it's a minor constellation in the southern sky." I pull back and look at her. "It was obviously named after you."

She laughs, and the sound lightens the thick air. "Or it's named after a mythical bird."

"I like the idea that it's named after you. A mythical creature who brought down the beast."

"And what beast are you referring to?"

"Me."

My hand reaches out and lifts her chin. Our eyes meet. There is little light, but enough that we can see into each other eyes.

"You did, you know."

"Did what?" she asks, her expression confused.

"You brought down the beast. Made me care."

"About?" she whispers, her voice low and unsure.

"You."

In the darkness of the night, the words I have held inside me slip out. Normally, I would hold back, but with the future unsure, I don't have that luxury. If we are to die here, I want her to know that she changed me, so I tell her just that. "You changed me."

"No, I didn't."

"You did. Knowing you. Spending time with you. Surviving with you … it changed me."

"You act like we're going to die out here and these are your last rites …" She narrows her eyes at me, her jaw tight. She doesn't want to ask what hangs in the air, but she does. "Are we going to die?"

I answer the best I can. "Not if I have anything to say about it."

Together, we stare at the stars, and we both stay silent, the weight of all that's happened sitting heavy on top of us. Through the endless darkness of the night, stars twinkle from above, the vastness humbling. A reminder of how small we are and how fleeting life is. I pull her tighter to me, encasing her in my warmth.

A part of me wishes this moment could last forever, that it could be endless like the glittering sky above us.

I count seconds that pass by the breath she takes, and finally, when her inhales soften, I know she's fallen asleep.

My mind won't shut up, though.

Endless possibilities of where I will steer us tomorrow play on a loop.

If we go north, will we find someone?

South?

Not knowing drives me mad. A part of me just wants to leave it to fate. Don't steer and just hope.

That part of me is foreign. I've left nothing to chance. My upbringing fights with my subconscious over what to do.

In the end, I decide I will try to move us northeast. When the sun peeks out against the horizon, I will use it as my guide.

I remember the islands from the map and better than that, civilization.

It might take a few days, but if we are lucky, we might stumble upon about another boat on the way.

There's no way we won't.

Or at least that's what I tell myself as I close my eyes. I won't sleep long. Just enough to be ready for tomorrow and whatever it will bring.

# CHAPTER THIRTY-NINE

Phoenix

T HE SOFT ROCKING OF MY BODY STIRS ME AWAKE. AS MY
eyes open slowly, I don't remember where I am at first. But
now that I can see, and all I see are dark skies, I remember.

I'm on the raft.

Adrift at sea. With Alaric.

I turn to find him. He's looking out into the ocean from the
opening of the canopy. What he's looking for, I'm not sure, but
he seems tense.

His shoulders are tight, and his jaw even tighter.

"What's wrong?" I ask, and that's when he turns around and
looks at me.

His face has been on edge.

It's pale. His eyes are large, and they seem hollow.

"What's wrong?" I ask again.

Something isn't right, but then something dawns on me.
"What time is it?"

The sky is black, but there are no stars. There's no sun either,
just endless black clouds above us.

A storm.

"How long until it hits?"

As if Mother Nature answers us, a bolt of lightning cuts
through the sky in the distance.

"Sooner than I had hoped."

"This is bad, right?"

"This raft can withstand it," he answers, but the monotone way he says it gives him away. Maybe when I first stowed away on his boat, I wouldn't have heard it, but after endless hours of getting to know him, I hear in his voice everything he doesn't say.

This is a very big deal.

"With our track record, it's going to sink," I deadpan.

"It won't sink." He is tight-lipped again.

"And you know this how?"

"Because I did my research before purchasing it. Just in case something like this happened."

"And what did you find out?"

"The raft can survive the open sea."

"Good to know. But for how long?"

"I'm not sure. The longest anyone has been on a raft like this at sea and lived to tell is seventy-five days … I imagine the rest died."

"Well, that's reassuring." I shudder at the thought. "So … what you are saying is we should be fine."

"Hypothetically speaking."

I groan. "Oh lord, Alaric, just lie to me."

"Do you really want me to?"

"No."

We stare at each other, neither of us knowing exactly what to say. This storm changes everything. Although there was a good chance this plan wouldn't work, the storm makes those chances even higher.

"I'm going to seal this up." He points to the canopy on top of us, to the hole he unzipped for us to look out of. "It will protect us from the rain that will come."

He moves to his knees and closes it. Soon, we are bathed in darkness, none of the gray skies showing anymore.

"Now what?" I ask.

"Now we wait. It could be hours, or it could be minutes. The water will get rougher."

"Great."

We both sit on opposite sides of the raft as we wait, each needing our own space to come to terms with what is about to happen. As time passes, I can feel the swells of the ocean getting larger.

The sound of raindrops hitting the covering echoes around me.

With each second, the sounds intensify, as does the beating of my heart.

The air in my lungs tightens until it seems it's becoming nearly impossible to breathe.

Alaric must sense my distress because he's up and next to me before I can even open my mouth.

"Breathe," he orders. "Inhale deeply and then exhale. You are having a panic attack."

I want to scream, *No shit, Sherlock*, but I can't find it in me to voice those words, let alone find my voice.

"I have you. Breathe."

He does, I know he does, but it still feels like a weight is sitting on my chest.

"Everything will be okay."

*But how?* I want to shout.

How will it be okay?

As if the universe is playing a wicked trick on me, the raft thrashes around, each wave making us sway back and forth. When a big one hits, I find my voice in the form of a gasp or maybe a scream. I'm not sure what leaves my mouth.

Tears roll down my cheeks, and his fingers wipe them away.

"This isn't just a storm, is it?"

I look up at him, and when he doesn't answer right away, I know what he's not saying. It's not. It's much worse.

"We're going to die." My limbs shake, and he holds me.

He holds me as I cry, as I tremble in his arms, and he tells me repeatedly that he has me.

All the things I've never done, all the missed opportunities, all the things I will never do play out in my brain.

And then, as my tears dry up because I have nothing left inside me to shed, I look at him.

I look at this beautiful, broken man. This man who has shown me more comfort and compassion in the past couple of weeks than anyone else ever has.

I never questioned my father's love, but even when he took me in, he never took care of me like this.

I'm not ready to say goodbye to Alaric.

At that moment, as the raft hits wave after wave and the sounds of thunder and rain beat around me, I look at him and see a future I'll never have with him.

At that moment, I realize I want that future.

That I want to go back to the island and just be with him.

That I want to love him.

My tearstained eyes look up at him with unshed tears threatening to fall when we lock gazes.

"Alaric ..."

He must see it because he shakes his head. "Not like this."

"Then when?"

"Dove ..."

I lean forward and place my lips on his. "We *will* die," I say against his lips.

"We might."

"I don't regret it." His brow pinches at my confession. "I don't regret any of it. Not one minute of the time I have spent with you."

"Phoenix," he says my name like it's a benediction. Then he takes his hands and pulls me closer, his mouth sealing over mine.

He tells me without words that he feels the same way.

No matter what the outcome, we wouldn't change it. No matter the pain, hurt, lies, and death … whatever brought us here, we welcome.

He kisses me as if I'm his oxygen. And as if he needs me to survive, I kiss him back. The raft tips to the left then back to the right. It moves like a ball in a pinball machine, bouncing around the ocean with nothing left to hold it steady.

Our outcome is unknown, but if I die in his arms, I'll be okay.

Neither one of us profess our love, but we don't need to. It's written in every touch.

Maybe because saying it would be too final.

Maybe admitting you have fallen in love with your enemy is too much right now.

"Phoenix Michaels, no matter what happens, I will never regret you," he whispers against my lips.

And then we hold each other.

Silently waiting for the end to come.

Knowing if it does, we will have forever been changed by each other, and that is enough.

# CHAPTER FORTY

Alaric

A SOUND PULLS ME FROM THE DEEP BLACK ABYSS OF MY MIND. It sounds like a motor.

I jolt up, my eyes still hazy from sleep.

"Phoenix …" I shake her, and her eyes flutter open. "Do you hear that?"

She wipes the sleep from her eyes. "What's going on?" she asks, and I place my finger to my mouth.

"Listen. Do you hear that?"

We both go quiet, and then I hear the sound of the engine or motor or whatever it is again.

Lifting my body up, I move to open the top.

Rain pours in. The storm still rages, but we didn't die last night. The ocean is rough, the raft still bouncing around under dark gray clouds, but in the distance, I swear I hear something.

I don't see anything because the hazy sky is too dark, but I can't mistake the sound.

Water continues to pour down on us, and I know I need to act fast. If there is anyone out there, we can't risk losing them, but at the same time, I can't risk taking on too much water.

"Flare gun," I shout, and Phoenix grabs it and hands it to me. "Cover your ears," I say, and then I fire into the distance. As soon as the gun fires, I move to close the top.

"What are you doing?" Phoenix asks as I close it completely.

"I can't risk too much water coming in."

"But what about the sound?"

"We have to hope they see the flare. I can't see where the sound is coming from, so I won't be able to steer there, regardless."

"We just wait and see?"

"Yeah."

The look in her eyes tells me she is thinking what I'm thinking. To have come this far only to be teased with rescue would be a cruel joke.

I don't want to think about it now. There is no part of me that is ready to let her go, but I have to if they come back for us, which I know they will.

When we are rescued, that's exactly what I will have to do. I'll also have to put this all behind me.

No matter what Michael did, my feelings for Phoenix are too intense to act on them.

I'll need to call off the hit.

When Phoenix slipped into my life, I meant to do it because him dying by another man's hands didn't seem right.

When everything first happened all those years ago, I just wanted revenge. I placed a hit on him. In turn, Michael went into hiding.

Now …

I shake off the thoughts in my head. If this is my last moment with Phoenix, I'm not going to spend it thinking of her father.

My feelings are a storm inside me. It's as if the ocean water is rising, and there is nowhere to escape. It pounds against me, but when she takes my hand, she's the calm. She makes the tide recede.

With our fingers entwined, I grab her and pull her toward me. Her pupils grow large as my hand cups her jaw, and I bring her mouth to mine.

There are so many words I want to say, but I can't. It wouldn't be fair. Instead, I kiss her, telling her with no words what I feel.

Phoenix opens to me. Her small hand unclasping and wrapping around my neck. She kisses me with the same desperation I feel, pouring all her emotions into me.

Time stands still as we kiss, and then it's only when she's panting against my mouth, and her heart is beating against mine, that we pull apart.

"Do you think they will find us?"

"Yes."

"And if they do …?" Her voice dips to an inaudible octave. Rescue. Making it out of this. That was never something either of us thought would happen. What does that mean if we do? For us.

# CHAPTER FORTY-ONE

## Phoenix

I WANT TO ASK HIM.

But then I remember he made no promises for the future.

"Alaric …"

"Yeah?"

"I know you don't want to talk about it, but with the chance of—"

"Don't."

"For what it's worth, I don't think it was my father who betrayed you," I say before I can regret it. "And I know that nothing I say will convince you, but the man I know, the man I have come to care for, the man I-I …" The words I have never said before sit heavy in my chest. I weigh out what to do, what to say, but in the end, I don't know what will happen. We might have heard a boat, or maybe we were hallucinating; this could be my last chance, so I do it. I cut into my chest and give him my heart. "The man I'm falling in love with would find out the truth." His eyes are wide. I don't expect him to say anything back, but it's as if he can't speak at all. Then he blinks and swallows.

"And if it was him?" he says through a clenched jaw, words tight … and a part of me dies. I know he made no promises, but a part of me breaks anyway.

"Then I will understand," I say, my voice low and sad.

He looks down at his hands, clenching them into fists. He opens and shuts them, and then relaxes, his gaze finding mine. "Dove …" he says, but then a loud sound has us both jerking upright.

It's getting closer. The sound is getting closer.

Whatever Alaric would have said is forgotten as he springs into action and pulls down the top. It's a risk to let this much water in, but it's a risk worth taking.

As soon as it's mostly down, and the rains pounds against us again, the sound is clear as day.

In the distance, gaining speed, is a small motorboat.

They found us.

We're saved.

I fall into Alaric's arms, fresh tears finding their way out.

We are saved.

---

They bundle Alaric and me up in towels on a fishing boat. We both shiver as we try to dry off.

It was a whirlwind of activity as we were rescued.

But now, as the boat heads toward land, I can't help but shake.

I'm not even sure why I'm shaking.

Cold? Nerves? Both.

We don't speak as we get closer and closer to the land in the distance. I'm not sure how long it's been since we got on the boat, but Alaric was right. Eventually, we would have found land, but whether we would have lived through the storm had the fishing boat not seen us is a different question.

A question we thankfully will never have to answer.

Other questions linger on my tongue, but I don't have the energy to ask them.

I know that when we were first rescued, they took Alaric to the captain where, I have to assume, he tried to reach his men.

He doesn't tell me what they said.

I don't ask either.

I don't know what will happen when we hit land, but I'm too afraid to find out.

Things happen fast from that moment on. One minute, we are on the boat, and the next we are docking.

Where Alaric's men await.

I'm shocked to see Cristian is one of those men, but I'm not shocked to see he's the only one from the yacht crew.

The rest must all be dead.

If Alaric knew this already, he didn't tell me. Actually, he hasn't said anything at all to me since we got on the boat.

I feel like my tongue is heavy with questions, but none will leave my mouth.

Did he know most of his men died?

Was his yacht ruined? Not that a material item would matter compared to the lives lost, but I still want to know.

Maybe that's why he hasn't spoken to me.

Maybe he still thinks this is my father's fault. Maybe he's blaming this all on me. That his men are dead because I stowed away on his boat.

I still believe my father is innocent in all this, but Alaric doesn't.

It feels like a weight is crushing me. I watch him when he sees his men; it doesn't look like a surprise. He knew who would be here.

The boat edges closer, and then one of the crew members from the fishing boat jumps off to help tie the rope onto the dock.

I wait for Alaric to say something to me, but he continues to pace the deck, waiting. His shoulders are tense, and for a minute when the boat docks, I think he will get off the boat without saying a word to me.

Him leaving without saying goodbye has my heart thumping rapidly in my chest.

He wouldn't do that. Would he?

Then I get my answer as he walks. I sit in silence as he's off the boat and hugging Cristian.

He … he left me.

It will be okay.

When I'm off the ship, I'll call my father. I'll figure something out.

I don't even know where I am.

Again, I'm shaking. Again, I feel the tears forming behind my eyelids. But I hold them back. I won't let him see me cry.

I'm about to get up and move to leave when he turns and looks at me. Our eyes lock. Then he's storming back to me.

I'm startled by the ferocity of his movements.

He grabs me forcefully, and his mouth is on mine.

He kisses me with a desperate passion, and I know this is it. This is his way of saying goodbye. The tears I've been holding back pour out of my eyes, and he pulls back. His gaze trails down my face, watching me cry.

He lifts his hand up and wipes one away.

"Your father is on his way," he says

"You called my dad."

"I did." My back goes ramrod straight, and he slides his finger along my jaw. "Don't worry. This isn't a trap. I won't hurt him."

"Why?" I whisper, still against his lips.

"Because of you. Because of what he means to you. I could never hurt you like that, dove." His breath tickles my mouth, but his words make me go warm.

"I thought you were going to call me Phoenix," I whisper.

"I lied." He laughs. "You will always be my dove." And with that, he pulls away. I want to hold him to me. Beg him not to leave and tell him we can make it work regardless. But as I see a car approaching in the distance, I know who it is, and I know why he's leaving. My legs grow weak, and as I watch him walk off into the distance without a goodbye, I feel like I might fall.

Nothing about me will ever be the same after my time with Alaric.

That much I'm sure of.

And I'll be better for it.

When he's gone, the car stops right in front of where the boat is. It is barely set into park before the door is flying open.

My father comes running out of the car. I have known Michael since I was a little girl. Longer than I can ever imagine. My earliest memories are of him, but never have I seen him like this before.

He grabs me in his arms, emotions playing on his feature. I stay in his arms, hugging him for a few minutes, before he pulls back and looks me up and down, trying to make sure I'm okay. I'm sure I look like a mess. I haven't bathed since the island days ago. Yes, Alaric and I still brushed our teeth on the raft, but that was the end of personal hygiene because of the storm.

"Are you okay?" he asks, scowling. "What did that bastard do to you?"

"He did nothing."

"Like hell, he didn't."

"Dad …" I take his hands in mine. "He never hurt me. He saved me, actually."

"You wouldn't have had to be saved if it wasn't for him."

"Now that's not true." My father looks at me like I'm crazy. "I snuck onto his boat, remember? I came with a plan. A malicious one."

"And he kept you. He could have let you go."

He's right there, but I've moved past that fact a long time ago. I have made my peace with both Alaric's and my involvement in what happened to us. Neither one of us were innocent, and there is no point dwelling on the past.

Together, we walk to the car. I'm not sure where we are, what island, but I don't bother asking anything. I don't want to know. I just want to go home.

I'm exhausted. I can barely breathe, and the truth is, I'm on the verge of falling apart.

It doesn't matter because thankfully, I don't need to do anything or say anything. The car is silent as we drive to wherever we are going, and then we are pulling up to a Gulfstream jet.

I'm in a daze, and maybe he is too, or he understands I've been through enough today.

Before I know it, we are on the plane, and then we are landing. I must have fallen asleep because the next thing I know, my eyes are opening, and the plane is no longer moving.

"Where are we?" I ask.

"New York," he answers. His answer takes me off guard. Normally, because of business, my father keeps a residence in Miami, so why are we in New York?

He must read my question because the moment we are alone in the back seat of his car, he leans forward, his arms resting on his knees.

"When you disappeared, so did the deal with Alaric."

The deal that paid off his debt.

"You've been hiding in New York this whole time. Did you even try to find me?" My voice cracks.

"Of course. I did, but after a week …"

"You thought I was dead." He looks down at my words, distraught. I reach my hand across the car and take his hand in mine. "You couldn't have known, and you wouldn't have found us."

"How?" He shakes his head, and I know he wants to ask how I am alive, but he's too emotional to do so.

"Alaric. If it wasn't for Alaric, I would be dead."

He grits his teeth at my admission. It's obvious there is still bad blood between them.

Not wanting another confirmation, I turn to look out the window. For the first time since I have been rescued, I let my mind wander, and my thoughts go straight to him.

In my mind, he's beside me, and it makes the pain spreading through my body more powerful.

Everything hurts.

My father must notice because he turns and says, "The doctor will be waiting at the apartment ... at the hotel."

"You've been staying at a hotel?"

"No, I was somewhere else. Where no one could find me."

"And now?"

"When you were rescued, one of the men who worked for Alaric told me where you would be and that my problem was taken care of. He would honor the original deal and that what he did to you was enough."

My father's fists are clenched, and I can only imagine what he must think. What he must think Alaric did to me.

"Dad—"

"No, I don't want to know. I don't think I can live with myself if I knew."

My teeth bite down into my cheek. I don't say anything, though. The truth is, that's a conversation for a different day. I don't have the energy to go there anyway.

Soon, we are pulling up to the hotel, and I'm being whisked away.

My brain is going a mile a minute, and I can't even take in all that's happening. My father doesn't just have one room for us; he has rented the whole floor. A hotel security guard waits for us as we exit the elevator.

"Is this really necessary?" I ask, but he doesn't respond.

When I'm finally alone in the suite that I'll be staying in, the first thing I do is strip naked and stare at myself in the mirror.

I knew I lost weight, but now looking at myself, I can't believe how much.

I look skeletal. My skin, although sun-kissed from the days fishing in the sun, still looks pale. Like my body was starved of nutrients, which it was. My hair is brittle and no longer shiny, but as I stare at my hip bones, I don't think about anything other than the fact that I lived. Looking at myself, I now see how close I was to dying.

Turning on the shower water, I step in once it's hot. A moan escapes my mouth. After weeks of bathing in a lake, a warm shower feels like heaven.

I let the hot scalding water wash away the past few weeks, and by the time I step out, I feel a little more like myself.

Like a Phoenix.

Reborn after death.

# CHAPTER FORTY-TWO

## Alaric

IT'S BEEN THIRTEEN DAYS SINCE I'VE SEEN HER, AND I STILL look around as if she is just up the beach from me.

Leaving her was much harder than I thought it would be. But it was also the most necessary thing I have ever done.

Despite what she says, her father killed my brother.

I can't be with her.

Despite what I needed for myself, I put her first and let her father live. Then like the fucking lovestruck pussy that I am, I paid off his debt and let him go free of any consequences.

The only one being that his life was in my hands, and I gave it back to him.

For a man with as much pride as Michael Lawrence, it's almost enough.

But for me, it's not, so I have to stay away.

I'm sitting on my newly refurbished yacht in the port of Miami when Cristian approaches.

"How is she?" I ask because no matter what I say, I have my men checking in on her.

"No one has seen her."

That makes me lift my brow. "What do you mean?"

"She refuses to leave the hotel. Apparently, she stays in her room, and if my contacts are correct ..."

"Yes?"

"She's been sick."

My brain thinks of everything she ate while we were on the island when we were together. Could something—or *some-one*—have hurt her?

Did she get sick? An infection? She got hurt … was that what happened? Did I not see it? Is she okay? Maybe it was the starfruit? It can be deadly for people suffering from kidney problems.

*Shit.* That could be it.

As much as I know I shouldn't see her, I need to know if she's okay. I have to see what's wrong with her.

"Did you call Matteo and tell him to remove the hit on Michael?" I ask, settling back into my chair.

"I wasn't able to get a hold of him, but I told Lorenzo. I'm sure it will be taken care of."

Looking away from him, I stare off into the distance. This is where I caught her. I wonder if I'll ever be able to look at this boat—hell, even the ocean—and not think of her now.

Turning back, I see Cristian staring at me. "Tell the captain we're sailing to New York," I say to him.

"I already did," he says, and I level him with my stare.

"That was a little presumptuous, don't you think?"

"Yes, but I have been with you for years. I see how you have been since you've been back. I knew you would want to see her."

"You were right. But, Cristian …"

"I know. I know."

He walks out of my office, and I look around. This room isn't any different. Of all the damage that was done to my yacht, it wasn't completely ruined.

The lives that were lost, though, those lives will haunt me for the rest of my life.

It's become very obvious that someone else was trying to kill me that day.

They weren't after Phoenix, after all. That doesn't mean Michael didn't kill my brother, but it leads me to some questions.

A part of me wonders if there is more to this puzzle I'm not seeing. Like a colossal piece is missing, and I'm just not finding it.

It takes us ten days to sail from Miami to New York, but instead of staying there, we make the trip a little further, ending up at Cyrus Reed's instead.

On the way to New York, I tried to call Phoenix every day. Every time I did, I was met with a dead end.

Michael has her locked away on the top floor of a posh hotel in the city. Despite my best efforts, my attempts to get in contact with her have been futile. This is why I find myself on a detour. If anyone can help me, it's Cyrus.

When we are docked, I find my host standing on the edge of his property, waiting with his arms crossed.

He really is a prick when he wants to be, but I can trust him, and trust is hard to come by in my business.

"Alaric Prince, to what do I owe this honor? The last time you just stopped by, you unloaded a shit ton of guns and then never picked them up."

"Hello to you too, man. Aren't you glad I'm alive?"

"As if getting lost at sea could stop you? Now, cut the shit. As much as I like you, and I do, you are kind of interrupting."

"Trouble in paradise?"

"Fuck no, but now that I have Ivy, I don't really like to be bothered with anyone else."

"Duly noted, but for the amount of money I pay ..." I raise an eyebrow.

"And this is why I haven't pulled one of your guns from my basement and killed you."

"And to think we are friends. How do you treat your enemies?"

His lips tip up. "Bullet in the brain."

"I do remember that." I chuckle, and then Cyrus does something I don't expect. He chuckles too.

Sick bastards, the both of us.

We both start to walk toward the house, toward my ... scratch that Michael's guns.

"So now that you're here, tell me what exactly I can help you with?"

"The guns."

He stops walking and turns to face me. "Are you finally taking them?"

"Not exactly." When I don't elaborate, he starts to walk again, and so do I.

He leads me toward his office, and once inside, he gestures for me to take a seat. He pours himself a cognac and me a glass of scotch, and then after we both drink, he levels me with his stare, telling me with no words to proceed.

"I need you to give them to Michael Lawrence."

That makes him put the glass down, the liquid spilling over the rim and onto his desk from the force.

"The fuck? You mean the bastard who killed your brother?" Cyrus asks, his brow furrowed and his jaw tight.

"That's another thing," I interrupt. "I need to look into that and into the attack on my yacht."

"Okay, but I'm confused."

Leaning back in my seat, I focus my gaze out the window. Although you can't see it clearly, that's where his island is. Where Ivy is. For all intents and purposes, they shouldn't be together, yet they are. Maybe, if what Phoenix says is true, maybe there is a chance. But first, I need to know. I put my cards on the table for Cyrus. "Maybe I was looking at this all wrong. Michael has always claimed his innocence."

"This is about the girl?"

"I don't know what you are talking about." I'm so used to denying it, so it slips out of my mouth, but it sounds like a lie. I can hear it, and by the way Cyrus looks at me, he can hear it too.

"Cut the shit, Prince. You were stranded on an island with his daughter, and then you come back with this bullshit. No way is that a coincidence."

"Shut the fuck up." I grunt.

"That's not a no." He grins, and I'm not sure what Ivy has done to this man, but now he's grinning too. I guess anyone can change. Can I? *I already have.* The fact that Michael isn't dead yet speaks of that, and now I'm here bartering a deal to give the man, who has been my enemy for as long as I can remember, his guns for a girl. Yep. I've changed. It's pretty obvious I also handed in my man card somewhere on that island.

"Can you do that for me?" I ask, needing to get out of my own inner rambling.

"I can. Anything else you need?"

He probably will hate himself for asking that question in five, four, three, two, one.

"Can you throw a masquerade party and invite him and his daughter?" Now that the hit has been called off, Michael will not have to stay in hiding. It's the perfect plan to lure her to me.

The look on his face is worth a thousand words. "What the fuck, Alaric? You know I hate people."

"This is true, but in my plan, this is necessary. He won't let me anywhere near her. I wouldn't put it past him to shoot me on the spot if he saw me. This is the only plan I can come up with that allows me to speak to her and not get killed. Trust me, if this wasn't my last option, I would never ask." His hand runs through his hair as he thinks about what I'm asking. "Plus, who are you kidding, Reed? As much as you hate everyone, you always have them here, so this time, you just have to make it a little bigger."

"You'll owe me."

"The fuck I will. I helped save your girl's life."

"Touché." He lifts his glass and takes another swig. "Tell me the plan."

# CHAPTER FORTY-THREE

## Phoenix

THE DOOR TO MY ROOM FLINGS OPEN, AND MY FATHER STEPS into my room.

"How are you feeling today?" he asks as he crosses the space to get a better look at me.

"Like shit still," I mumble.

"The doctor said that after what you've been through, that would happen. You just need to give it time."

"It's been four weeks." I groan.

Four miserable weeks. Four weeks of a broken heart, and apparently, a parasite I had picked up on the island.

Only me.

When I returned, I was severely malnourished, and my body has been paying the price for it ever since.

I now know without a shadow of a doubt, that if it wasn't for Alaric, I would have died.

He saved me.

I owe him my life, and I will never see him again to tell him that.

For the first few weeks, I expected Alaric to come for me. Or at the very least call. But after a month, I now know I never meant as much to him as he did to me.

He never did tell me he loved me.

Here I was, crazy and stupid in love with him, and I was just a way to pass the time.

My heart still hurts when I think of him.

No matter how much time passes and how much I beg my brain and my heart to move on, I can't.

I'm now resigned to the fact that it will never happen, and I'll just die from the apparent parasite I got from my ill-fated trip.

"When do you go back to the doctor?"

"Not for another few weeks. He thought it would pass naturally, but I feel weak."

Luckily, the vomiting stopped, but now I'm tired all the time.

Since I haven't left the hotel, my tan from the island has faded, and now I just look pale and sickly.

A part of me wonders if it's just my broken heart that has made me feel like this.

"I'm happy you are feeling better. That's actually why I came to talk to you—"

I sit up in my bed and raise my brow. "What's going on?"

"I need you to come with me to a fundraiser."

"I thought … I thought you didn't want to be seen in public with me. That you were afraid of one of your enemies hurting me?"

"The only enemy I had was Alaric Prince, and he's been off the radar."

A sharp pain resonates through my leg as I realize my fingernails are biting into the skin of my thigh under the blanket.

"Off the radar? What do you mean?" I can't help the way my voice rises, and my father doesn't miss it. His eyes narrow into thin slits.

"No one has seen him. And without him breathing down my neck and ruining my business, my life is better. Both our lives are better without him in it."

It's a pointed comment. He has asked me about my time with him and if he hurt me. My answer was never to tell him.

At first, it was to protect and hold dear our time together. Now, I'm embarrassed I meant so little to him.

"What did you want to talk about?" I say, changing the topic, annoyed that I have to think about Alaric at all—and that hearing his name made my heart flutter a little faster.

Damn treacherous heart.

Falling in love is for idiots.

Or, at the very least, masochists.

"A masquerade party. They are raising money for an adoption agency. I thought it would be a good idea for you to come."

"A political idea."

He stands quietly, and I wonder what he is thinking. My comment is uncalled for because my adoptive father has never in my life used me for his own gain. He has always protected me, but my wounds over Alaric are still deep.

"You have never been that to me. This is important. Not just because of the topic, but also because of business. I know it might seem like it's political, but seeing as this is near and dear to our hearts, the host invited you. The money being raised is for children like you. Children whose parents have died. The difference is, they don't have anyone to take them in. I thought you could use this because you haven't left this room. I thought that maybe"—he swallows—"that after what you have just been through, you might be feeling alone and miss your parents. I thought this could help, that helping others like you could help, and I thought we could do this together."

Tears well in my eyes at his words. I feel like a complete ass for attacking him. I was lucky to have Michael, but so many children aren't.

"Okay," I whisper, but then another thought pops into my head. "I have nothing to wear."

"Don't worry, I'll make sure that everything is taken care of. I'll hire a stylist and hair and makeup to come to the hotel. You won't have to worry about anything."

Maybe I need this.

It can give me a purpose.

Which is something I need right now.

# CHAPTER FORTY-FOUR

Alaric

EVERYTHING IS IN PLACE, INCLUDING THIS GOD-AWFUL mask.

However, I can't complain because it was the only way this plan would work.

Michael Lawrence has been keeping his daughter on a short leash. She still hasn't left to go anywhere.

Not even to get ready for tonight. Her father hired a team to go to the hotel and get her ready.

Yes, I am keeping tabs.

Phoenix would probably accuse me of being a stalker, which I am.

I don't care what anyone thinks. I need to make sure she's okay. My men give me updates, and I know they want to ask more, but they know better.

Instead, they play their part in this ruse. The ruse that I don't care about her.

It's all a lie, though.

I can finally admit it.

I love that fucking girl.

Now what to do with this information is a completely different matter.

Which brings us to the here and now.

A party to lure a man and his daughter into my world when they are both known to be notorious recluses.

In typical Cyrus fashion, the party in his grand mansion in Connecticut is over the top.

This place is ridiculous, but then again, I have no use for a house, mansion, or even an apartment. I'm happy living on my yacht and moving from port to port. There's only one place that I was ever happier than when on the sea …

With her.

In the cave.

But this place, Cyrus's place, isn't even where he lives now.

Now, he is only with her.

A spark of jealousy fills my veins. That's what I want.

It's not going to happen, though, not after everything.

Then why the ruse? Why make all this happen if I'm not going to cage the dove?

Because I just need to see her again.

Then I'll let her fly away.

I move around the room, scotch in hand. Even with the masks on, I see familiar faces, and I head over.

"Tobias, James, Matteo, good to see you."

They must not have recognized me at first. My mask covers more than theirs, but for my plan to work, Phoenix can't know it's me right away.

"Likewise, we all thought you were dead?" Matteo says, reaching his hand out, which I shake.

"Did you cry?" I mock.

"Yes. I thought I would have to find someone else to supply me. You know how much I hate negotiating."

"Asshole."

"Good to have you back, mate," James says, next shaking my hand, followed by Tobias.

I spend the next few minutes talking shop with them before I pull Matteo aside.

"Thank you for taking care of that thing for me." I'm referring to the hit. Matteo cocks his head in confusion, so I lean closer, so only he will hear me. "The hit on Michael Lawrence. Lorenzo said he'd take care of it."

"Then it must have been."

I nod and step away. It's only a moment longer before I am excusing myself to find Phoenix.

The room is filled with people milling around with drinks, appetizers, and masks covering their faces.

It should be impossible to find her in this mess, but it's not.

I see her right away.

Like the Red Sea parting, there she is, across the room, standing by herself.

She looks gorgeous. Her long gown is the same color as her eyes and also the same color of the lagoon where we fished.

A part of me wants to believe that's why she chose it.

It dips low in the front, showcasing her small but pert breasts, the material clinging to her tiny frame.

She looks smaller than when she was on my yacht. It appears she hasn't gained back any of the weight she lost on the island.

Anger flows through me. She's still unwell, even after all this time.

I should have been there. I should've made sure she was okay.

Guilt spreads through my veins, and before I know what I'm doing, I'm striding toward her.

I'm halfway there before I slow my pace.

She hasn't seen me yet, and here I am, moving like a caveman—no pun intended—toward her. If I go in guns blazing, I'll ruin everything. She will alert her father, and I will never get to speak to her.

As it turns out, even though I know where she is currently, I don't put it past Michael to see me as a threat and hide her away. He did manage to hide her from me for years.

Now walking at a normal clip, I make it appear that I'm looking elsewhere when I make my approach.

I'm not sure if she sees me, but when I finally stand in front of her, she gives no indication that she knows it's me.

Reaching out my hand, I offer it to her.

A silent invitation to dance.

Her large blue eyes find me, and she squints, and I think this is when she figures it out, but with my whole face covered, even most of my eyes, it would be nearly impossible.

She looks around the room, maybe looking for her father to help her.

My game will be over before it starts, but then she inhales deeply and offers me her hand.

Once encased in my own, I walk us toward the dance floor.

I had forgotten how small she was in my arms, and now that I have her in them, I'm not sure I will ever be able to let her go again.

The music changes, and I pull her close.

My hand rests on the small of her back as I lead her around the room.

With the orchestra playing the melody, I move us to the beat, slowly shuffling us closer to the door, to our destination.

Her eyes are closed as she sways.

Probably lost in her own mind, like I am so often.

She doesn't notice when I lead us to the outskirts of the room—or when I step through the open door, still dancing.

She doesn't notice when the door starts to shut because the music continues to play in this room. It isn't until we stop moving, and I place my lips by her ear that she does.

"Did you miss me, little dove?"

# CHAPTER FORTY-FIVE

## Alaric

W HEN SHE DOESN'T ANSWER, I PRESS HER FARTHER INTO the room.

"How?" she finally asks, her breath coming out in ragged bursts.

"I would know you anywhere, little dove," I respond.

She steps back.

I step forward.

Trapping her against the dining room table, I continue my advance until my legs press against hers.

"I missed you." I look down at her, watching as she inhales deeply at my words. "Did you miss me?"

"No. Not one bit," she hisses.

My hand reaches forward and cups her jaw, my fingers trailing her exposed red lips. "And that's what I missed the most. Your fiery little mouth."

"Stop touching me."

I trace her skin, remembering every delectable thing about her. I'm not supposed to be doing this. I'm supposed to be saying my piece and then walking away, but now that she's in my grasp, I can't.

"You can't do this to me."

"Do what?"

"Touch me. Pretend you care."

"But that's where you're wrong. I do." My hands start to lower, trailing down her neck to the hollow of her chest. I follow the line of her dress, dipping low between her breasts. She shivers at the touch.

"You didn't try to see me."

"I did."

She shakes her head in confusion, but she doesn't say anything as my fingers press against her heart.

"This right here is mine. It beats for me. Only for me."

Her breath catches at my words. She shakes her head and rights herself. "I'm not yours. You made that clear."

"I tried to see you, dove."

Her eyes are darker than normal, hollow, lacking the usual spark. "Then why didn't you?"

I lean forward and swipe my tongue against the shell of her ear. "Ask your father."

"I don't think so, Prince." Her hand lifts to push me away, but I grab her wrist, encasing her delicate skin in my fingers. "He wouldn't lie to me."

"And now I'm Prince?" I ask, her chest heaving angrily at my words.

"Well, you're certainly not a king …"

"Oh, so we are back to that again? Do you need me to remind you who you belong to?"

"Funny, and here I thought I belonged to no one."

"That's where you were wrong, dove." I step back, and then with no warning, lift her under her arms and place her on the table, her dress bunching at her hips.

Once she's where I want her, I rest my hands on her thighs.

I move in, sealing my mouth to hers. I wait for her to push me—and she does put her hands to my chest, but when I sweep my tongue against the seam of her lips, she doesn't. Instead, she opens on a sigh, and being the asshole that I am, I kiss her deeper. Taking full advantage of her, needy and pliant, I let my hands explore her, lifting her dress, touching the scrap of underwear covering her.

My finger strokes the fabric. "I've missed this." With more pressure, I keep up my ministrations until she starts to writhe beneath my touch.

"I want to be inside you." I groan against her lips. "Do you want me? Do you miss this?"

"Yes," she pants as I rip her thong off her body.

"Tell me I can fuck you."

"You can fuck me." She starts to shake, and I know she's close. With my free hand, I move to unzip my pants, and then once I'm free, I place myself at her entrance.

I give her one more second to object, but when she wiggles her ass on the table and pushes herself forward, I'm lost. With one quick thrust, I'm inside.

*Being inside Phoenix is like coming home.*

At first, my movements are slow and leisurely. We haven't been together for a month.

I allow her to adjust to me, but once I feel her relax around me, I start to move, pulling out and then thrusting back in.

My movements are still slow. A torture we both need after our separation. Slowly, I drag my cock out and then let it hover at her entrance before sliding back in.

I pull out again and then push back in.

My hips circle and thrust as my hand reaches between us.

In. Out. In. Out.

The slower I go, the more she moves her hips, begging me without words to pick up the pace and give her what she needs.

But I can't.

I can't take her fast. I need to savor every minute with her.

As if she knows I'm teasing her, she tilts her hips up and pushes me in deeper.

"Faster," she begs.

I swivel my hips again but don't pick up the pace. Instead, I look down to where our bodies are connected, and now I watch us.

There is nothing better than watching me fuck her, watching her small body take me, watching as she lets me own her. Mind, body, and soul.

I pick up my pace, needing more, needing to see more. My thrusts become harder and deeper. As she begins to tighten around me, her breath coming in short bursts, I know I won't be able to hold on much longer. Brutally intensifying my pace, I fuck her hard enough to imprint me in her soul.

I hope it does.

But as we both come down from our highs, and her blue eyes look up at me—first with lust, then with confusion, and then with anger—I know she's the one letting me go.

I thought I'd be okay, seeing her and saying goodbye, but the longer I stare, the more I know I'll never be done with her.

She seems frazzled as she starts to rearrange her dress.

"Get off me," she says, and her hands reach for my shirt to push me off her.

"Stop." I level her with my stare. "We need to talk. Are you sick?"

Phoenix pushes again, and I step away even though separating our bodies is not something I want to do yet. I'm not ready for her to walk away.

"Wow. Thanks, do I look that bad?" she hisses.

"No. You look beautiful. But we still need to talk," I say again, this time more forcefully.

"There is nothing to talk about."

I look between us. The evidence of our tryst is still front and center. "I beg to differ. I tried to call you. I tried to see you. Why do you think I put on this whole ruse? I knew your father wouldn't let me near you, so I had Cyrus Reed throw a masquerade ball. That way, Michael wouldn't know I was here. I did all of this"—I gesture my hands around the room—"just to see you."

"See me? Don't you mean have sex with me? Seems like a lot of work to get laid ..." she snaps "... in a ... what is this? A dining room?"

"Yes."

She's quiet for a moment, her eyes narrowing. "When did you try to contact me?"

"Since we left Miami to head to New York." My vague answer isn't lost on her as her jaw tightens.

"And before that?"

"Phoenix, it was wrong of me to disappear when we first got off the island." She lifts a brow at my words. "I wanted to give you space to think, to heal, but now I want to talk."

"And you thought this was the place. Spoiler alert, it's not." She stands, fixes her dress, and starts to walk away. My hand reaches out to stop her, but I think better of it. You don't try to cage a frightened bird. Her flight-or-fight has kicked in, so I need to give her time.

"You can run away all you want, but you can't hide from me, little dove. I'll always be there to catch you."

# CHAPTER FORTY-SIX

## Phoenix

"THIS IS ENOUGH ALREADY. I DON'T KNOW WHAT HE DID TO you, but you need to talk to me. If he hurt you ..." my father says, stepping farther into my suite on the top floor of the hotel that he's rented.

"He didn't hurt me." Not a lie, technically. He never hurt me physically. Not emotionally either, if I'm being honest with myself.

"He did something. You have been hiding in your room for a month."

"Since when is that a problem? Before this, you hid me in a boarding school and then Switzerland."

His mouth opens and shuts, and I realize I may have gone too far. "I didn't mean it like that."

He shakes his head and looks down before lifting his gaze to reach mine. What I see reflected on his face makes me stumble. "I'm sorry. I was wrong to say that. It was never because of you. It was because of that man. Everything that has gone wrong is because of that man."

"Dad—"

"No. Don't Dad me. It's true. You would never have gotten on that boat if it weren't for what he did to me. And for what? His hatred for what? An unwarranted vendetta. The man is garbage, plain and simple."

If I ever had any bit of doubt about my father's part in Alaric's brother's death, I don't now. My father is a proud man, an angry man when need be, but never a liar. If he were involved, he would understand Alaric's need for vengeance.

"If I could, I would have him killed. The world would be a better place without him in it."

I'm about to object and defend the man who only a few minutes ago, I was hating, but a wave of nausea hits me hard, and I feel my lunch rising up my throat. Without another word, I bolt from the door and into my bathroom. Everything I ate today comes right back up.

I hear his footsteps from behind me.

He hands me a towel, but I'm too weak to say anything.

"Enough of this. I know you didn't want to go to the doctor, but you are. Now."

I wipe my mouth before standing up and walking over to the sink. I fill a glass and then spit.

"I'm not going now. I'm going to bed."

"Like hell, you are, Nix. We are going to the hospital. This parasite or bug or whatever you caught on that island has been going on too long. It's obvious you need medical attention."

He doesn't let me say no. Instead, he's ushering me to the door.

All I want to do is crawl back into my bed and hide, but apparently, that is not in the cards right now. Because the next thing I know, I'm in the car, and I'm on my way to the hospital.

From that point on, I'm in a daze.

I'm taken to a private room.

I guess money and connections can get anything done. Next, I'm poked and prodded.

It's awful. Not only do I just want to sleep, but they've taken so much blood I'm sure I will pass out.

Now, I'm lying on a gurney with a flimsy gown on, waiting

for someone to come in and tell me what the heck is going on. Some doctor I don't know is the one to finally walk into my room.

He's holding a clipboard, and right behind him, a nurse is wheeling in a machine.

What the fuck is going on?

My heart starts to race frantically in my chest.

"Hello, Phoenix. I'm Dr. Reynolds."

"What did you find?" I blurt out, my heart and brain not able to take the wait any longer. "You found something, right?"

"Well, that's what I wanted to talk to you about. We did."

"Just tell me. I can handle it."

"I wanted to ask you, when was your last period?"

My eyes grow wide. Why would that matter? All of a sudden, my limbs feel weak, and I'm sure I will pass out. "I-I ..." The blood in my veins throbs as I try to think back. My periods are less frequent since getting the shot. "I'm on the shot," I say forcefully as if that should make a difference.

"I see that in your records. Were you up to date on your shot?"

It feels like my stomach is hollow as I realize I'm not. I was supposed to get another shot ... but when I got back, I was sick and forgot.

"I know this might come as a shock, but both the urine test as well as your blood sample reveal ... you are pregnant, Phoenix."

He speaks, but I can't hear a word he says because it sounds like I'm in a wind tunnel. My heart hammers in my chest, and the sound is so loud that I can barely make out what he's saying.

"What?" I whisper, shaking my head.

"I'm going to give you an ultrasound. I'm not sure how far along you are, so to make sure I'm thorough, I'll be doing a transvaginal one. We will measure the baby and see how far along you are. How does that sound?"

I don't know if I even answer, but then the ultrasound technician walks closer to me, wheeling the machine next to my bed. The sound of the tires is loud against the quiet of the room. Next, she pulls out a wand and places something over it.

"Now just lie back. This might feel a little weird." With my legs spread open, she places that thing inside me. Tears well in my eyes. I can't believe this is happening. I can't believe I'm pregnant with Alaric's baby. This has to be a mistake. But as the doctor points at the screen, I know without a measure of a doubt that there is no mistake.

There amongst the dark screen is a little something flickering.

"That's your baby."

All the tears I was holding at bay start to fall.

*That's my baby.*

———— • ————

Sitting in my suite, I feel so alone. I have no one to talk to about what is going on. I know I need to tell Alaric, but can I? He's the father of the baby, but he's in a war with my father. Another person I can't talk to. He would never understand.

Standing, I start to pace the large living room with my phone clutched in my hand. I don't even have a way to reach him.

Even after the party, I never got his number.

What do I do?

Looking down at my phone, I open it and scroll through my contacts.

That's when I realize how selfish I've been. Hannah. My one friend. My best friend. I still haven't called her.

She probably doesn't even know I went missing. I just left when my father called and never looked back.

She probably hates me.

Before I can second-guess myself, I'm dialing her number.

"Where have you been?" she answers, and hearing her voice feels like a warm blanket being draped over me when I'm cold.

"I'm so sorry," I blurt out. I can already feel moisture gathering in my eyes.

"Are you crying?"

A sob breaks through my mouth, confirming that yes, I am, in fact, crying—more like having a nervous breakdown.

"I am," I hiccup.

"Talk to me. Nix, what's going on?"

My hand reaches up and wipes the tears from below my eyes. "My dad needed me."

"And you couldn't call to check in?" There is no mistaking the doubt in her voice.

How do you tell someone that everything they thought they knew about you is a lie? Do you just blurt out, *My father's an arms dealer, just as we always suspected.* I guess that's what you do. "Everything we thought about my dad was true."

The line goes quiet.

"Hannah?"

"Everything?" she whispers into the line as if someone's listening.

"Everything. I left to help him …"

"What does that mean?"

Taking a deep breath, I sit down on the couch because this might take a while. Over the next thirty minutes, I tell her everything. I tell her about the plan to seduce Alaric to find the guns. I tell her about the island, and then I tell her the last part. The most important part.

"I'm pregnant."

Once again, she's silent. I know she's still on the line because I can hear her breathing.

"Is it his?"

"Yes." My voice is low, low enough I'm not even sure she hears me, but then she speaks.

"Fuck."

Her words are exactly how I feel. I hug my knees to my chest, and my body starts to shake. "I know. What do I do?"

"Do you love him?"

"I think I do. Before all this, before we were rescued …" I swallow hard. "I was falling in love with him."

"I can't believe this." She speaks in a broken whisper, mirroring the emotions inside me.

"You and I both." My gaze lowers to my belly, to the flat skin. On instinct, my hand reaches down and touches it. Touches the life Alaric and I made. "I have to tell him."

She inhales deeply before exhaling. "You do."

"What if he's not happy? What if this thing between us doesn't work? He's the villain in this story, after all. Can you survive loving the villain?"

"We make our own stories. We write our own endings. Only you can decide."

Her words echo through me. She's right. I'm not sure how this will turn out, but only we can decide.

"Thank you."

"For what?"

"For always being there for me. Even when I was a crappy friend."

She laughs at that. "I love you, Nix. Now go rest. It sounds like you need it."

"Gee, thanks."

"Just speaking the truth."

"Love you."

I hang up the phone a moment later.

I have a lot to think about.

# CHAPTER FORTY-SEVEN

## Alaric

I T'S BEEN ONE WEEK SINCE THE PARTY. ONE WEEK SINCE I HAD Phoenix in my arms. I'm driving myself crazy. I sound like a pussy, but I can't get her out of my mind. It's obvious my pacing back and forth is driving my men nuts as well. To make matters worse, Matteo called me the other day. Apparently, he can't get in touch with his man hired to pull off the hit.

Now I'm desperate to make sure she's safe.

Cristian keeps shaking his head.

The thing is, despite my attempts to see her again, she hasn't left the goddamn hotel. That was until today.

Yes, I'm stalking her.

No, I don't give a fuck.

It might make me crazy, but here I am, pacing a room in the hotel where she's staying.

From what my man staking out the front desk has said, she left, went to the hospital, and isn't back yet.

I'm ready to fucking kill someone.

Someone needs to tell me what the fuck is going on.

Cristian, however, is laughing at me. He said it's probably a routine checkup, and I can't just storm her car when she arrives.

Not that Michael is a threat any longer, but I'll never get Phoenix to talk to me if he's around.

The problem is, who knows how much longer she will be?

"You will wear a hole in the carpet," Cristian says, holding back his chuckle.

My hand forms a fist as I turn to face him. "Fuck off, Cristian. If you know what's good for you."

I turn and go back about my business of walking back and forth in the suite I'm staying at.

In the background, I can hear my men talking, but I pay them no mind.

Why is she at a hospital?

I've never felt this helpless in my entire life.

No, that's not true. I felt this helpless when Phoenix and I were on the raft, and the storm hit.

I thought we were going to die. Back then, I was an idiot. Deep down, I knew how I felt about her but didn't say it.

It took me a long time to admit that I can't live without her. Way too long. The truth is, she deserves better.

Another truth: I don't give a fuck.

She's mine.

It takes four hours for my phone to ring, and once I know she's back, I wait until her father is gone.

In my possession is a key to her room, and I plan to make her see me, regardless of what she wants.

It's midnight when I first make my approach. I've paid off the security guard to tell me when Michael has turned in for the night and to let me pass.

The walk from my room to hers isn't far—just one floor up.

Yes, I'm insane enough that I booked the whole floor beneath theirs.

When I'm standing in front of her door, I knock once. If she doesn't answer, I'm still going in.

I can hear the sound of feet walking and then a soft voice. "Yes?" She sounds confused but not asleep.

"Dove."

That's all I say for an announcement.

"Go away, Alaric. I'm not ready to speak to you yet. I need to think."

"I didn't want to have to do this," I warn as I place the key to the pad and then let myself in.

"You're nuts," she says, mouth open and hands on her hips.

"Yes."

"You can't just—"

"Can't just come in? Sure, I can." Standing a few feet away from her in the foyer, I smile. "See?"

"You're such an ass."

She looks beautiful when she's angry, her blue eyes more vibrant. They are the exact color of the lagoon on a clear, sunny day.

Being this close to her brings me back to that time. "I didn't realize how much I would miss it."

Her brow furrows. "Miss what?"

"The island. Being with you on the island. Life was simpler then."

"Yeah, there were no guns to sell."

I move closer to her. "I was happy."

"And now?"

"I'm not."

"That's not my problem. You left. I know at the party I gave you mixed signals, but I'm not in this for a quick screw on a dining table, island, or whatever you think you're doing in my hotel room at midnight."

"I'm not here for that."

She lets out a deep breath before stepping aside and letting me pass.

Once I'm in the living room area of her suite, I look toward the couch, and she nods.

Taking a seat on the couch, she takes the one farther from me as if it will protect her from me. She crosses her arms across her abdomen and sits down. She still looks pale, beautiful but pale.

"Are you okay?" I ask, and she nods, but she no longer looks at me.

She looks tired and scared, and I know I'm supposed to sit my ass on the couch, but instead, I find myself crossing the distance and squatting in front of her.

"What is going on?"

She has tears in her eyes, the water shimmering in her irises, making them look iridescent.

"Talk to me."

"I can't." The look reflected back at me is unlike anything I have ever seen. She looks downright petrified, more so than when we were on the raft during the storm.

I remove her hands from where they sit on her belly and start kissing her fingers.

"I didn't tell you before, and I realize now that makes me a coward. But somewhere on that island, I fell in love with you. Not just any love. A heart-stopping love. A devastating love. One that has consumed every fiber of my being. I thought if I left you, you were better off. The war with your father ... My need for revenge. I thought I was being selfless by letting you go."

"And now?" she whispers, tears still heavy behind her lids.

"You are my peace. Even after the island, I would wake up expecting you beside me, hoping that this was all a nightmare and I was still on the island with you. Because that's my dream. To be back there, with you. But I walked away, and it might have been for what I thought was the right reason, but I was wrong."

"You left."

"I know. I'm selfish. I can't let you go. I might not have been there then, but I am now. I might be too late, but I couldn't go without telling you, without demanding you listen."

"Then say it," she says.

"I love you. I loved you then, and I love you now. Looking back, I knew on the raft. I knew if I was going to die, if you were in my arms, I would die in peace."

I lift to place a kiss on her lips, and she doesn't fight, but she doesn't kiss me back either.

A sinking feeling settles in my gut. Am I too late?

She won't look at me. No, instead, she keeps glancing at a table. To her phone, maybe? Without asking, I stand, and she reaches her arm out. "No."

Anger courses through me. What is she hiding? Without waiting for her to say more, I storm toward the table, where a piece of paper rests, and then I see it.

Everything I think I know comes to a halt. Everything I ever thought was important smashes to the ground because nothing else matters but this.

I don't hear her as I stare at the paper.

I barely feel her as she places her hand on my shoulder.

But when a tear drops from my eye, I blink. I turn to see her, her own tears now spilling down her beautiful face.

Her lip trembles, and I hold up the paper.

"A baby?"

She nods.

"My baby."

"Yes."

"You're having my baby?"

More tears slip down her cheek as she nods.

And then I'm dropping to the floor. My mouth to her stomach. I lift the hem of her shirt and kiss her flesh. I kiss my baby.

I'm not sure how long I kneel in front of her, but eventually, I stand and walk her to the couch. Once she's sitting, I don't sit. I don't presume to stay either because we still have too much to do before I can.

"I won't lose you," I tell her. "I'll talk to your father."

"He hates you."

"You're mine. That baby in your belly? Mine. Your thoughts and dreams are mine. I will make your father understand, or I will take you from him. Even if I have to tie you up in my boat."

"You already tried that." She inclines her head. "How did that work out for you?"

"Pretty well, seeing as you're having my baby." I grin back.

"Shh." She laughs.

I bend down and place a soft kiss on her lips. "This is not where our story ends, little dove. I will fight for you."

# CHAPTER FORTY-EIGHT

## Phoenix

Last night, Alaric told me he loved me. Words are just words without action.

Today, I have to speak to my father. Alaric might be calling him to form a truce, but I need to speak with him first.

We've never spoken about the island, and it's time.

It's time for me to tell him everything, including that I'm pregnant.

When I'm standing in front of the room my dad stays in, I knock once before he answers.

He's dressed and ready for the day. Me, on the other hand … I'm still in my pjs. I didn't want to risk missing him.

"Phoenix, are you okay?"

"I lied to you yesterday."

He moves aside and lets me in. I walk past him and sit down at the table.

"About the hospital?" he asks as he stands behind a chair across from me. His fingers wrap around the top, and I can see his knuckles are white. "What did you lie about?"

"The doctor did tell me what was wrong, or rather—" I stop and take a breath. "I'm pregnant."

As soon as I utter the words, I hear the crash, and the chair is on the floor now.

"The bastard." He starts to curse and pace. Then he's reaching into his pocket. The next thing I know, he's pulling out a gun.

"What are you doing?"

"I'm going to kill him. I might not have protected you then, but I'm—"

"Stop!" I scream, and he looks up at me in shock. "You will do no such thing. I love him, and he loves me, and it's about time you listen and hear me. If you touch Alaric, I will no longer be in your life."

"But—"

"No buts. We haven't talked about the island, but it's time. It's time you know he saved me. Not once, not twice, but three times. I fell in love with him. He's not the man you know, and for me, you will form a truce. He is the father of my baby. I love him, and you will talk to him. And if you think this is one-sided, it's not. For four years, he thought you killed his brother—"

"I didn't."

I hold my hand up. "I know that, but he doesn't. I told him, but whether he believes it or not is irrelevant because he still is willing to sit down with you. To talk and to move forward because he loves me that much. Now the question is, do you love me enough to do the same?"

"Of course."

"Then call him and set it up."

"I will do this for you because I love you, and you're my daughter. But that doesn't mean I will ever trust him. If he so much as lifts a finger wrong where you are involved, I will kill him. Do not ask me not to."

"Understood."

---

My father does as I ask. Today, we are all going to meet. Where, though? Not on Alaric's boat and not here in the hotel. Someplace public, maybe? In the end, we decide against all of that. We are all only as good as our word. If Alaric hurts my father, he won't be in our baby's life and vice versa.

The dock by the yacht is the destination. Alaric has parked his boat at a private one close to the city, so we will meet there.

It's a beautiful day without a cloud in the sky. As soon as we pull the car down toward the boat, I see him.

His hair looks lighter in the sun. I had forgotten that when the sun hits it, he has blond highlights scattered through the brown.

"Are you ready?" my dad says to me, and I nod. Together we walk down to where Alaric has set up a table. There are three chairs. I sit between the two men as a buffer.

It's tense at first.

"I love her," Alaric says, and I'm shocked he starts there. "I'm here for her. For my baby."

"I'm here as well."

"Then I'm going to ask you this, and I need you to be honest—man to man. I will not seek vengeance no matter your answer, but I need to know. Did you order the hit on me four years ago? Did you kill my brother in my place?"

"No," my father says without hesitation.

"Okay."

I look at the two men I love most in the world, and then I focus on Alaric. He has spent years trying to seek justice for a death that should have been his, and he is willing to take my dad at his word.

"Now what?" I ask.

"If your father says he didn't do it, then I trust you, dove, to know that he wouldn't lie to me. He wouldn't risk you. But the question still stands … who tried to kill me? There have been two attempts on my life, both involving you," he says to my father.

"I had nothing to do with either attack. But certainly not the one that almost took Nix from me."

"I'm inclined to believe you there." He looks off into the distance at the water. His tense shoulders seem to ease. "Someone is trying very hard to make it look like it was you, and I want to know why."

"Competition," I blurt out.

Alaric raises a brow. "Your father is my only competition, so how does that make sense?"

"There has to be a third party," I state. "Someone who must have been just starting out back then. It would make sense. He tried to kill you, his plan failed, but in turn, it still worked."

"How do you figure? I was alive. My brother was dead. How did that work?"

"Because you were focused on my father. You spent all these years focusing on the wrong person."

"If what you're saying is true, I was focusing all my resources in the wrong place, then what was the objective with your father?"

"They probably thought your men would retaliate, which you tried to for years. My father has been in hiding ever since. I was in hiding. But then I stepped out … Perfect bait." I use his own words.

"For more than just you …" my father says, his hand lifting to rub his temples.

"What?"

"This war flushed me out too."

Everything goes slow from that moment on. I hear Alaric scream. I watch horrified as he jolts from his chair, jumping in front of my father, pushing him out of the way … and only then do I register the red light that was shining on my father's chest.

# CHAPTER FORTY-NINE

## Alaric

THE FIRST THING I DO IS MAKE SURE PHOENIX IS OKAY. THEN I scream for Cristian.

The rest of my men are running toward the table.

"You hit?" I ask Michael. His face is pale, clearly in shock.

"No … you saved me."

"I did." My voice is monotone.

This is my fault. Phoenix is here, and there's been an attempt on Michael's life because of me.

My stomach turns violent as I realize I might have put my baby and the woman I love in danger.

"You're bleeding?" Phoenix shouts, and I look at my shoulder, and sure enough, there is blood.

"It's just a graze." I look at Cristian. "Get the shooter. He couldn't have gotten that far."

I need to find him and make sure there will never be another attempt on Michael's life.

"Where do you want me to bring him?"

I look around, noting the buildings around me. Although this is private, I can't run the risk. "The boat." He nods, knowing exactly where I want him.

Once Cristian runs off, Michael turns to me. "I want in."

"That can be arranged. He did try to kill you, after all." I don't say it was on my authority, but I'll cross that bridge when I need to.

Phoenix goes to speak, and I lift my hand. "Nope, you will be sitting this one out."

"But—"

"You need to rest."

"I'm not helpless." She groans.

"I know you're not. Fuck, you are one of the strongest people I know. But you are pregnant with my baby, and even if this is the only time you listen to me, you will listen. You will go to my stateroom and wait for me there."

She pouts, but she doesn't object.

After I wash off the blood, I head down to the lower level of the boat. To the room I built especially for this.

For anyone asking, it's a storage room.

Storage for what … now, that depends.

Sometimes, I store equipment. Sometimes, it's guns. Today, it's a man tied to a chair.

As I'm about to enter, my phone rings … A text.

Matteo: It was called off.

My movements halt as I stare at the phone.

Me: Are you sure? Because there was just an attempt made on his life.

Matteo: 100% sure.

Fuck. Then who do we have in my storage room? More confused than before, I place the phone back in my pocket and swing the door open and stride inside.

"Do you know this man?" I say to Michael as he follows behind me and then walks to where I am.

"Do you?" he asks.

"Never seen him before." Moving to where he is, I'm not standing directly in front of him. "Who do you work for?" He smiles but doesn't answer.

"You think this is funny? You won't find it funny after I torture you."

"Do your worst." He snickers.

I step forward, my fist flying and hitting his face. When I pull back, he spits blood, and this time, when he smirks, his mouth is full of blood.

Stepping back, I signal for Michael. "He tried to kill you. It's only fitting that you torture him."

Gun in his hand, Michael steps in and fires a bullet into his shoulder. The man lurches forward, but with his limbs tied, there isn't anywhere for him to go.

"I have seven more bullets. Something tells me you'll eventually talk," Michael says, but by the crazed look in this man's eyes, I'm starting to think we should just throw him overboard.

Six more bullets. Blood drips from everywhere as I stand beside Michael.

"What's it going to be …?" I ask, and Michael lifts the gun. The final bullet. The kill shot.

This man will die if Michael fires again.

"Who do you work for?"

Silence. Just that damn smirk. Like he knows the outcome regardless of the games we play.

"Are you ready to die for this? Is that how this will end?"

"Enough of this shit!" Michaels says, finger on the trigger.

"I am okay with death." A sick twisted smile spreads across his face as Michael pulls the trigger. "Only the dead have seen the end of war."

The words he utters are cold needles stinging my body. "No!" I shout, rushing over to the man, but as I do, his eyes flutter closed, and then his head hangs limply. I lift it, his eyes are open, but there is nothing behind them. "No … Wake up." I turn to Cristian. "Get the doctor. We need him to live."

"It's too late for that."

My knees give out.

"What the fuck just happened?" I hear from behind me, and I turn to see Michael looking down at me.

"I don't know," I mutter because I don't.

I have no fucking clue what is happening.

Like a zombie, I find my way out of the room and back up to the main deck.

Phoenix is there waiting for me, her eyes wide with fear, and it is only then I realize I am bathed in blood.

"It's not mine," I grit out.

"What happened?"

But I have no words to explain it. Nothing makes sense. Nothing at all.

It takes me a while, three glasses of scotch and a few long breaths, to calm the hell down.

After every last drop is gone from my drink, I slam the glass down.

"Can someone tell me what the hell just happened?" Phoenix asks.

Cristian and Michael both look at me, but neither speaks. This is my story. My freak-out. This is on me.

"Did the man tell you who he works for?" she asks.

"No." The tone of my voice is brash, and Phoenix shivers.

"Did he say anything?"

"Yes."

"What did he say?" Her question is simple, but my answer isn't.

"'Only the dead have seen the end of war.'"

Her eyes go wide, and I know she remembers. I know she knows that only one man has said that to me. Only one man used that sentence, over and over again. It was only one man's motto …

"Your brother."

"My brother," I confirm.

"What does this mean?"

"Beats the fuck out of me, but I have every intention of finding out."

Standing from where I'm sitting, I look over at Cristian.

"Get Cyrus on the phone," I say.

He nods and sets about doing that. Michael and Phoenix look as confused as I feel.

"Alaric," Michaels says. "Thank you. I owe you my life."

"You mean something to Phoenix, and she loves you. That's enough for me." As I'm about to say more, as I'm about to apologize for everything I did to him for those four years, Cristian comes back and hands me the phone.

"What's going on? I didn't think I would hear from you so soon."

"That incident with Ivy ..." Out of respect for him, I won't talk about that in front of my men or Michael.

"What about that?" he fires back, angry over it still and rightfully so.

"The guy who helped you ... Jason. Jack—"

"Jaxson?"

"Yeah. I'm going to need you to get me in touch with him."

"What's this about?" he asks.

"Better you didn't know."

"Duly noted. I'll get you his contact info."

I hang up and sit back down. I'm going to need another drink before I make this call.

Two minutes later, I'm on the phone with Jaxson Price and I'm telling him what just went down.

"Can you explain that one more time?" he asks over the line.

"Four years ago, my brother died ... and I have reason to believe ... Fuck. I don't know what I believe."

304

"A man hired to kill the one man who can confirm he didn't kill your brother is dead. Am I getting this straight?"

"Yes."

"And the one man, he quoted your dead brother?"

"Right again. I'm thinking that when my brother was estranged, he might have worked with whoever is doing this. Maybe for revenge?"

"That sounds plausible. Crazy but plausible."

"Maybe this person wanted our businesses and killed my brother to start the war." That's the explanation that Phoenix came up with, and it seems more plausible now.

"It definitely appears that way. So, you need me to track all your brother's acquaintances before he died, and see if there are any hits?"

"Yeah. I'm going to be sending you a care package. Let me know what you find." I probably should warn him it's a finger. "You're going to want to open it by yourself. That's your warning."

He lets out a chuckle. "Easy enough and duly noted. I'll make sure no one can see whatever you placed in the box. I'll have the information back to you within a few days."

Now to see if the real bastard who killed my brother covered his tracks.

Once I hang the phone up, I walk into my room. Now that I'm alone, it hits me.

It's the same feeling I have felt for years, but different.

Guilt.

An uncontrollable guilt.

For years I have harbored guilt in my soul over my brother's death, a death that should have been mine. The only thing that kept me going was revenge.

Today changed that.

Today changed everything.

In my life, I have done many wrong things. I have done horrible things, but never have I become my father.

Never have I been that cruel, that sick and depraved.

My hands are stained with death, but until today, they were never tainted with a death that did not belong to me.

George.

I killed an innocent man.

He was never meant to die.

I reach for the decanter in the corner of my room, pulling the crystal stopper out and downing the contents.

His life was not mine to take.

# CHAPTER FIFTY

## Phoenix

IT FEELS LIKE AN ETERNITY AGO THAT I WAS LAST ON THIS yacht. Things have changed epically in only a matter of months, but here I am, back here, and I'm okay with that. The truth is, I'm more than okay. I'm finally happy again.

Today was a hard day for everyone on this boat, but in truth, for Alaric, it is so much more than that—the past four years of his life were a lie. Now, I can't find him on this giant boat. I need to make sure he's okay.

I start to wander through the decks, and then it dawns on me the one place I haven't checked—his stateroom.

It's funny. I was on this boat for two weeks before, and I still can't find my way around it.

As I'm walking, I see Cristian. He must note my confusion because he points behind him.

"He's that way. The door all the way at the end." As I begin to walk, I feel the boat move.

The last time the boat left port, I was desperate to get off, but this time, I'm not worried about how I'm going to get off. It would be fine with me if I never had to again.

I just need Alaric.

As soon as I open the door to his stateroom, I see him. "Are you okay?" I ask as I approach. Alaric is sitting on the bed with his back toward me.

But it doesn't take a rocket scientist to know he's stressed out. I can't even imagine what he must be thinking.

"No. Not really," he admits as he turns to face me.

My tongue feels dry in my mouth as I take in the expression on his face. There are not enough words in the dictionary for me to help him. The only words I can conjure are, "I'm sorry."

He gives me a tight smile, silently thanking me for trying, but knowing it's not enough. Nothing will be. Not until he finds out what happened all those years ago. That day still haunts him, and now, his wounds are open and gaping again. They are old scabs that are bleeding again.

"It's not your fault," he says, and although it's true, it's not my fault, I just want to help him.

"Talk to me."

"I'm a monster. You were right. I don't know how to do this." He buries his head in his hands.

"Do what?"

"Forgive myself. I don't know how you can even look at me."

I stare at him and shake my head. "I don't understand—"

"George," he whispers, and it feels like someone punched me in the chest. I step closer, my legs touching his. "I thought"—he takes a deep inhale—"I thought it was justified." He looks up at me, his blue eyes dull and hollow. "My father, he killed for sport. I vowed to never be like him." His head drops down toward the ground, breaking our stare.

"You're not."

"Aren't I?"

"Listen to me, Alaric." I place my hand under his jaw and make him look up at me. "You are nothing like your father."

"How do you know?"

"Because you feel guilt. Because you feel remorse. Because of this." I place my hand on his heart. "What can I do to help?"

His hands wrap around my thigh. "Love me."

I lean down and kiss the top of his head. "I already do. I didn't tell you because I needed to know you would fight for us ... I should never have doubted you, and for that, I'm sorry. I loved you then. I love you now, and I'll love you forever." I place his hand on my belly. "We both will.

"Let me love you, then," he says, and I look down at him to meet his gaze.

The color of his eyes reminds me of the ocean on a stormy day, dark and endless. "Okay ..." I take a step back, his hands dropping to his sides, and he watches as I remove my shirt and then my pants. He stares at me without blinking, until I'm naked and then walking to the bed.

Then I'm on it, but he still hasn't moved. He doesn't undress, and I wonder if I read this wrong, but when I move to cover myself, he shakes his head.

"Just because I'm still dressed doesn't mean I don't want you, but right now, I just want something different," he says, and I level him with my best fake glare.

"And what would that be? Because I'm not doing anal."

Alaric breaks out into a boisterous laugh, and the sound warms my heart. Even though my joke is stupid, it's exactly what Alaric needs to pull him out of the daze he's in.

"Good to know, but no, that's not what I meant," he clarifies.

"What did you mean, then?"

"Here, let me show you." He crawls onto the bed and lies down beside me, resting his hand on my belly. I'm not showing yet, but it doesn't matter to him.

"Thank you," he says.

"For what?"

"For giving me something to look forward to, something to want to live for. I have spent the past few years never caring if I lived or died, but now, because of you, because of the baby ..." He lowers his body and places his lips on my stomach.

My eyes fill with tears.

"I already love you," he says to my invisible bump. "I will always protect you. I will do everything in my power to keep you safe." He looks up at me, his eyes glassy and full of emotion, and then crawls back up until he's face-to-face with me. He leans over and kisses me. "After this, I'm done."

When he pulls back, I look at him. "What do you mean?"

"I'm out. I'll tell your father. Either he can buy me out or I'll offer it to Cristian."

I shake my head in confusion. "Why?"

"There has been too much death. I don't want you or the baby in the crossfire anymore."

"What will you do?"

His lip tips up into a smirk. "Maybe Cyrus is hiring?"

"Isn't his job just as bad?"

"Hardly. Ever since he settled down, he really only focuses on the money aspect. He's given all the rough shit to Matteo to handle, and the investments now go through Ivy's brother Trent. Cyrus is just a stern face to keep the assholes in line."

"Holding the mob's money still seems pretty rough."

"True. Fine, I'll just retire."

His words take me off guard, and I think I stare at him for five minutes before I blink. "Can you do that—"

His hand reaches up and touches my face. "After this, yes." Then the movements stop, and his jaw is tight. "Before I figure out who really killed my brother, no."

"What do you think happened?"

"To be honest, I think after Grace died, Damian was in a bad place. I wouldn't put past him to have gotten into bed with some bad people over grief."

"Maybe someone from her family," I mutter to myself, but his eyes go wide at my suggestion.

"Maybe that's it. Maybe that's the piece of the puzzle I'm

missing. Maybe he got into bed with her family and convinced them it was my fault. Fuck!" He grunts, his fist hitting the bed beside us. "Why hadn't I seen it before?" He reaches across the bed and grabs his phone.

"What are you doing?" I ask, lifting my back and resting my weight on my elbows to stare at him.

"I'm telling Jax this new information. It makes the most sense. Her father lost his in when his daughter died. Maybe this was his second shot to get into the family business."

He leans down and kisses my lips.

"What was that for?" I ask.

"That was for always listening and loving me regardless of what I say."

I wrap my arms around him and bring him closer.

"Always," I say against his mouth as I continue to kiss him. Then I tell him with my body just how much I love him.

# CHAPTER FIFTY-ONE

## Alaric

AFTER KILLING THE MAN ON MY YACHT, WE DRIVE OUT TO sea. Then we weigh the body down and dump it.

When this is all over, Phoenix and I will need to go somewhere no one can find us and just be together. Maybe we can dock by our island.

I'm lost in my own head when Cristian walks into my office.

"We are going to be docking soon."

"Any word from Jaxson?"

"Nothing yet, but it's only been two days. I'm sure as soon as he has anything, he will let us know."

"Phoenix wants to see her dad," I say as I stand from my desk and move past him.

"You sure that's wise? The last time you were all together, there was a near attempt on Michael's life."

"True. No, it's not wise. But at the same time, what will you have me do? Keep her locked up like a prisoner on this boat. I already tried that, and we all know how that ended."

Cristian smiles. "Congratulations, by the way."

I laugh. "Thanks. I'm going to walk away after this," I say.

He nods. "I figured."

"I'm going to talk to Michael about it today, but if he's not interested, would you want it?"

"You would trust your business to me?" Shock registers on Cristian's face.

"I would."

He nods. "Then yes."

"I'm going to see if Phoenix is ready. Find a place for us to meet. Someplace safe. If she's going to be with me—"

He understands.

---

It's a few hours later, and Phoenix and I are driving toward the spot where we are going to meet Michael.

My phone rings in my pocket on the way. I look down to see a name.

"Jaxson. What do you have for me?"

"First off"—he pauses—"thanks for the package." There is no confusing the sarcastic bite to his voice. "However, it was very useful, no matter how unpleasant it was."

"Go on …"

"It didn't take me long to figure out who the finger belonged to. His name was Vincent Keller. And it appears you were right."

My hands tighten into fists. "How so?" I grit out.

"Before his death, he was employed by Leonard Moreno. Father of Grace Moreno. Business associate of your father and before his death your brother was associated with him as well."

*I was right.* I knew that this was a possibility, but it doesn't lessen the sting. My enemy is someone I once considered family. How the fuck did everything go so wrong.

"I need to catch this bastard. What else do you got?"

"A few addresses."

I lean forward in my seat, shocked that I might actually be able to find him today.

"You have addresses, plural?"

"I do. In Jersey. A few different buildings. Most look

abandoned, but they were all purchased under a shell company. I was able to trace them all back to Moreno."

"Fuck." From beside me, Phoenix takes my hand in hers and gives me a reassuring squeeze. It's exactly what I need right now. It reminds me to calm down.

"Yeah, I thought you might say that."

"Text me the addresses." I hang up the phone and take a deep breath.

"What's going on?" Phoenix asks.

"We were right. It is Grace's father." I turn to face her and find her pupils are wide and her mouth is hanging open. "Jaxson has a list of addresses. He's sending them to me now."

The phone chimes again, and there it is, the addresses that can potentially lead me to a man I've known all my life. I stare at it for a few minutes.

"Are we going?" Phoenix asks.

"You aren't—"

"Stop right there. I'm not some weak girl you need to hide away in a tower."

"That's where you're wrong."

She rolls her eyes. "Be that as it may, we are going to check it out." Then Phoenix does something I don't expect. She grabs my phone from my hand, looks at the address, and calls her dad.

"Change of plans. We have a few leads," she says to him, and after she gives him the list of addresses, she hangs up.

"You will not enter any of the buildings."

"Fine, but I'm coming. I'll wait in the car. We can't risk him finding out if Jaxson ran checks. The longer we wait, the better chance he finds out we are looking for him."

She's right. I just hate the fact that she is here with me. Maybe Cristian was right. Maybe I should have kept her locked up.

We sit silently as we pull up to the first building. Michael isn't here yet, but I don't wait. Time is of the essence. I leave

Cristian in the car with Phoenix, despite his objections. The first building looks vacant. There are no cars in the parking garage, and when I peek in through the window, there is no movement at all. Walking up to the door, I jimmy the lock and then kick it open, gun in hand, ready to fire.

The place is completely empty.

There's not one piece of furniture, no trash, no sign of life.

It's a small office space with faded white walls that are now cream, and dark, dingy carpet. This place looks as though it's been abandoned for years.

The next address is even worse.

At least the first building we went to had carpet. This one looks like it's been condemned for even longer.

Where the other building was vacant, this one has trash everywhere. The smell is foul. I don't even bother to look around—as soon as I open the door, I'm closing it.

I probably should suck it up, but if I go in there, no way can I get back in the car with Phoenix. She's finally not feeling sick; the stench from this place would set her off.

When I step back in the car, Phoenix sniffs me. "What is that smell?"

Her pregnancy nose is on point. She's like one of those bomb-sniffing dogs.

"Nothing compared to what the inside of that place smelled like," I say as I gesture to the building. "Cristian, head over to the address on Washington." I turn to Phoenix. "Tell your father to meet us there. These have all been dead ends. I'm sure this one will be too."

When we pull the car up to the next location, something is not right about it.

This whole thing feels wrong. Like we are walking into a trap.

But what other choice do I have?

Go back.

Take her someplace far away from all this.

No. I need to know. I need to look the bastard who killed my brother in the eye and understand why. Was it for a part I never played in his daughter's death? Was it just greed?

We park the car, and it's only a few minutes later when Michael's car pulls up.

I take out my phone and call Jaxson back.

"Is there anyone in the building?" I ask.

"From the heat signature … no. It's empty. But that could be wrong. The building next door has movement."

I look at the building in front of me.

"As long as it's not coming from the building we're searching, we should be okay."

"Be careful, man. This feels almost too easy."

"Like a trap?" I ask.

"Yes."

"I agree, but I have no other choice. This is the only lead we have."

"Understand. Good luck."

I hang up the phone and turn to Phoenix. "No matter what happens, you don't leave this car." Her lips form a thin line. "Dove … say you understand me."

"I understand you."

"But you didn't agree?"

"No. I didn't. If you are in trouble—" She's about to go on, probably to lecture me, when Michael knocks on the window.

"Stay here," I say again before swinging the door open.

As soon as I leave the car, I turn to him. "This could be a trap."

"It's most definitely a trap. Sure you want to do this?"

"I don't really have a choice. I need to know who set us up. Phoenix and my baby will never be safe until I do."

"On that, I agree." After he speaks, he starts to walk, and I follow. Like the last few, this one is also empty. We search each floor, yet again we find nothing.

"This whole day is a waste."

"No, not necessarily," Michael responds. "Now where to?"

"I have to head over to a new property I bought. It's not too far from here. Got to make sure the construction is coming along. Come with us, and we can talk there. I have some things I need to discuss with you." He nods and we both head out of the building. "I'll text you the address."

"That was fast." Phoenix smiles when I step into the car a minute later. "Find anything?"

"No. But I felt my phone vibrate, so maybe Jaxson has more intel."

Pulling out my phone, I find a few more addresses to look at, but those will have to wait until tomorrow. I'm done with this day and still need to talk to Michael about my plans to retire. Closing out Jaxson's message, I send a text to Phoenix's dad with where to meet.

It doesn't take us long to get there, and when we arrive, I turn to face Phoenix.

"I'm not waiting in the car." She narrows her eyes at me like she means business.

"You are. No objections. It's a shithole in there. Half the floors are missing. The top floor doesn't even have walls. You're staying, and that's final."

"Were you always this bossy?"

"Yes," I deadpan.

"And I still fell in love with you."

Leaning across the back seat, I seal my lips over hers. "Damn straight, you did. Now be a good little dove and stay put." With one final kiss, I fling the door open and step out of the car.

Michael is already standing there, waiting for me. We both

start to walk, and when we are almost by the door to the building, he stops, turning around to look at me.

"Before I go in there with you, what did you want to talk to me about, Alaric?"

"I'm out," I say, and his head shakes in confusion. "I'm done. After this, I'm retiring ..."

A myriad of emotions plays across his face, and it almost appears as though he might cry. "After Nix's parents died—" He stops talking and takes a breath. "Her father was my best friend and business partner. It cost him their lives. I should have put her first." He nods again. "I-I wish I could have seen that then. Thank you for putting—" His words are cut off by a deafening sound, a gunshot. Someone is firing at us. I turn to look at where the shots are coming from. A building next to mine. "What the fuck?"

Michael is quick to move too, taking out his gun and aiming high. "This is crazy."

"Get to the car," I shout. Cristian is running in the direction of where the gunshot rang out, and I'm about to follow when I hear Michael shout something back. I don't register what's happening until Michael is pushing me out of the way.

Another series of gunfire.

I turn back to where the car is parked on the side of the building to make sure it's not under fire too. It's bulletproof, but still. Luckily, it's hidden from the war that's currently happening. My ears are ringing, and I try to make out where it was, and then I see him.

Michael.

On the floor, not moving.

I move toward him.

In the distance, I can hear Phoenix yelling. The door is open, and she's running toward us.

"No!"

Even though I know it's not good to move Michael, I pull his body behind the cover of the building away from the gunfire.

When I'm sure that we are safe here, I move to look at Michael's wound.

His shirt is stained red, the spot growing with every second that passes.

"Why?" I ask as I place my hand over the wound.

"Be-because now it is my turn to save you," Michael gurgles.

That bullet was for me. Michael saved me.

# CHAPTER FIFTY-TWO

## Phoenix

EVERYTHING HAPPENS IN SLOW MOTION. FIRST, I SEE ALARIC and my father talking, and then …

My heart beats heavily in my chest, the blood in my veins running cold.

There's gunfire. Someone is shooting, and then I see my father push Alaric out of the way.

Everything stops.

My world stops as my father, the man who raised and loved me with all his heart, falls to the ground.

I don't think twice before I'm throwing open the car door and running toward them.

The car is parked on the side of the building, so it should be out of range of a gun, but I don't even care. I need to get to my father now.

As I start to run in the direction, I see Alaric is pulling his body toward me, out of the range of the gunfire.

I'm in front of my dad now, and his eyes are barely open, glassy with unshed tears.

"No," I whisper as I take in the large wound on his chest. The wound gapes with blood. "No, you ca-can't—"

He reaches his hand out, smiling a tight and sad smile at me. "It's my time." Blood leaks from his lips, and a sob erupts from my mouth.

"You-You can't leave me." Tears start to pour down my face like a dam burst.

"It's my time. I needed to save him. It's his time to take care of you. To take care of your baby. You allowed me to be your father. You honored me with your love. You taught me how to be selfless. This is my gift to you. For everything. I die happy, knowing you and the baby will live."

I want to cling to him. Beg him not to leave me. Beg him to stay.

But I can see the light fading from his eyes.

He turns to Alaric and raises his hand. "Teach your child better. Do better."

"I will. All of my remaining breaths will be for your daughter, for your unborn grandchild."

"Thank you." His voice has faded to nothing more than a whisper. He lifts my hand that holds his, and I look into his eyes. A tear slips out, his face paler than a moment ago. "You are going to be the best mother," he says. "I love you."

Tears pour from my eyes as he closes his eyes. His chest rises and falls, and then there is nothing.

Falling forward, I clutch him to me. Blood soaks my skin, but I don't care. I just want him back. "I love you, Dad. I love you so much more."

Sobs rack my body, and then I feel Alaric's hand on my back.

"I know you want to stay here, but I need you safe in the car."

"Where are you going?" I hiccup through my sobs.

"I need to end this, dove. I need to know you will be safe."

There is no strength left in me to object. I allow Alaric to lift me, but I look back down to my father. "We have to move him."

"When this is over," he answers as he continues to lead me to the car.

Alaric leans over and places a kiss on my lips.

"Be safe," I say, and then he's running into the building and into the unknown.

# CHAPTER FIFTY-THREE

## Alaric

S PRINTING TOWARD THE BUILDING WHERE THE SHOTS WERE fired from, I see Cristian when I enter. He lifts his hand up to his mouth, then motions up.

This building is abandoned too. The stairs are concrete, and they look like a war zone, like it's falling apart.

How the hell did Grace's father know to come here? He must have been following us all day. Waiting for the moment our guard was down. If he wanted to get to me, why shoot from here, why not ambush me inside my own property?

The more I look around, the answer is clear. Now I know more than ever that this was a well-thought-out plan. You can die just stepping foot in here. The floors are broken, and not one part of the stairs is up to code. One last trap and I walked us right into it.

I've been so blinded by my need for revenge that I didn't realize I was walking myself into what will probably be my own death.

No.

I shake my head. There will be no dying today. Not when I have so much to live for. Nothing will take me away from her.

I take the stairs two at a time, doing quick work to see where he might be hiding.

Each floor is worse than the next. Open floor plans of mass chaos are what greet me. Something tells me this fucker is all the way on the top. I motion to Cristian to check the other direction while I continue up to the top floor.

There is nowhere else he can be.

When I make it up to the last floor, I see the shadow of a man in the distance. I don't have a clear shot, so I step closer, getting the angle I need to take him out.

"It's over, old man," I say. I lift my gun and am about to fire when the man speaks.

"It's just like I've always said, Alaric ... Only the dead have seen the end of war." He turns to face me, the scar I gave him so many years ago marring his face. A face I thought I would never see again.

I stumble forward. "Damian."

"Very good, dear brother. Did you miss me?"

"I don't—"

"Understand?" he asks before I can finish speaking, and then I realize my mistake. In my shock, I never notice the gun now trained on me. He has the advantage. "Yes, I figured it would raise some questions."

"You're alive."

"Look at you. So smart. Maybe Dad was right to leave everything to you." He snickers.

"Is that what this is about? The business?"

"It was never about the business." His voice cuts through the air like a dull knife cutting through meat.

My brother is alive ...

"It was you?"

"Ding. Ding. Ding. You are finally getting it." A sardonic smile on his face. "*How did I escape? With difficulty. How did I plan this moment? With pleasure,*" he says, quoting *The Count Of Monte Cristo*.

"You are no Edmond," I fire back, but in his sick, twisted mind, he thinks he is. He thinks this is his revenge. For what? And then it hits me. For her.

This is all for Grace.

I lift my hand to him. "It's not what you think. You never had the full story."

"I don't want to hear your lies. I have plotted this moment for years, since her father showed me the note. He helped me, you know. Helped me orchestrate all this."

"Ask him. He knows the truth."

"It's too late for that."

"What do you mean?" I ask, knowing the best way to disarm someone is to keep them distracted.

*Keep him talking.*

"I had no use for Moreno anymore. It wasn't supposed to take so long, and he was growing on my nerves, so I killed him. But he was the perfect scapegoat, the old fool. This should have been over years ago, maybe he would have lived if the original plan had worked."

"And what plan was that?"

"I was going to start a war between you and Lawrence, and then while you fought, I would take everything. I wanted you to see what it was like to lose everything you cared about, and since I was all you had, I started with my death. Then I would take my business back. The only snag was Michael went into hiding …" He looks downright insane now. His smile makes the scar across his face look mangled. "But now I have a better plan. I'm going to take Michael's daughter. I'm going to take the woman you love."

Without even thinking, I start to run toward him. I catch him unaware because his eyes go wide as I attack. His gun drops to the floor. I go to raise my own, but he's too fast, and mine falls as well.

Each of us struggles to get control.

Fists fly.

Blood sprays.

I don't want to kill him. I just want him to understand.

"It's not what you think." He punches me again. "Just listen to me, Damian. Grace committed suicide."

"Yes, because you hurt her," he spits.

"But not the way you think."

"You broke her."

"No!" I shout. "I never touched her. Her father broke her. My father broke her. You broke her."

He shakes his head at my words, and I use the opportunity to tighten my grip and fling him down.

"She didn't want to marry you. She killed herself because—"

"The letter," he fires back, rabid. Out of control. "You're lying."

"I'm not. The marriage was a noose around her neck. She came to me. She didn't love you. She knew she would be forced to marry someone in our family, so she proposed that she marry me instead. She thought she lov—"

"Enough!" he screams, scrambling around to get to me. "You'll say anything."

We circle each other. No weapons, just our hands.

"Think about it. Why would I lie now?"

"Because of your precious little dove. Don't worry, Alaric, I won't leave her in a cage for long, just long enough to clip her wings."

That's all it takes. I'm throwing my body onto his. We twist and turn, the edge of the construction site getting closer and closer.

"Stop!" I shout through our punches, but Damian is a man possessed, and then he's flying through the air, trying to hit me. I'm quick to step out of the way, but then I hear him scream. He can't stop, and he's going to fall.

I run to grab him, my body sliding across the concrete. Skin rips as I move, but my fingers catch onto his.

"I have you," I say, my torso now hanging over the edge of the building, the only thing keeping my brother from falling is my hand. "Give me your other hand." I'll need both to save him.

Damian looks at me with clear eyes for the first time.

"Why are you trying to save me?" he asks.

"Because I love you," I answer truthfully, and his brows knit together. "Give me your hand." He doesn't, and it gets harder and harder to hold on as my fingers lose their purchase.

"Is it true? Is what you said true?" he asks.

"It is. I'm sorry. Now give me your hand so we can move past this."

He starts to lift his hand up but then stops.

"Goddammit, Damian, give me your hand."

I see the moment it happens … when his eyes grow wet with unshed tears.

I shake my head. "No, Damian. Please—"

"Too much has happened."

"That's not true. Please give me your hand. Regardless of the past, I love you …"

"How can you love a monster like me?" he says, and then he lets go.

"No!" I try to grab him, but it's too late. My torso starts to slip, but then someone is tugging my leg.

"I got you," I hear Cristian say as he continues to pull me back until my body is secure on the concrete.

My brother is dead.

This time, for good.

# CHAPTER FIFTY-FOUR

## Alaric

After what we have both have been through, I decide there is still one more thing we have to do before we can move forward with our lives. Now that I have given the business to Cristian, time is a luxury I have, and I plan to spend every moment with Phoenix and my baby when he or she comes.

Since Phoenix is still fairly early in her pregnancy, this is the safest time for me to take her this far from shore.

We are both still grieving even though it's been a month.

The first few weeks on the yacht were hard. But eventually, we both found a way for our hearts to heal.

I never did tell her where we were going, and when the island comes into focus, I wonder how she will react.

There is a very important question I need to ask her, and I can't imagine another place to ask.

The boat stops, and we drop anchor. Since the island isn't developed yet, we will need a tender to get back there.

"Where are we?" she says from behind me, and I turn to face her.

"You know where we are," I say, moving closer and taking her hand in mine. I lift it up and place a kiss on each knuckle.

"What are we doing here?"

"I thought you might like to see it. With eyes no longer clouded by fear."

She inclines her head and thinks about it for a minute. At first, I think she might say no. That it's still too soon or she needs more time, but then she nods.

It doesn't take us long before the Zodiac pulls up to the beach. I get out first, and then I lift my hand out to grab her.

The island is exactly how we left it. Still uninhabitable and it never will be. That's the beauty of the island. It's not meant to sustain life, just give it. And that's what it did. It gave me life. It gave me Phoenix, and most importantly, it gave me the baby we will have soon. The island will never be a place that we can call home, but it can be a place that we hold in our memories forever.

A place where all my dreams were born.

Together we walk the grounds, remembering every moment we were together, and then we get to the cave.

So right there, in the cave where I first made love to her, I get down on one knee.

Her mouth trembles as she realizes what I'm doing. Then I take her hand and place an oval diamond on her finger.

Tears stream down her face. "I love you. I want to spend the rest of my life with you. Will you marry me?" I ask, and then stand.

"Yes," she says through tears and then lifts up on her tiptoes to kiss me. "Where and when?"

"I was thinking back on the yacht?"

"Like now?" she asks.

"Well, we would have to leave. Are you ready to leave?"

She looks around the cave and then nods. "I'm ready to put this part of our lives behind us and move forward with you, wherever that may be."

"Good. Let's start now."

We don't stay on the island much longer, and before we know it, we are on the deck of the boat.

"Are we really doing this here?" I smile at her question, and she furrows her brow. "What?"

"I actually had another plan." The look of confusion has my lips splitting wider, and she rolls her eyes.

"You're enjoying this way too much." She has a scowl on her face, but I know Phoenix secretly loves this. After everything we've been through, she trusts me completely. I would never give her reason not to. She's the most important person in my life. Her and my baby in her stomach.

I'm still not sure how I got so lucky. Sometimes, I'm afraid this is all a dream because no way after all the shit I've done do I deserve her love.

The guilt sometimes creeps in, but Phoenix reminds me that I need to forgive myself. Sometimes I do, other times it's harder, but she's always there to help me when the shadows of my past creep in and threaten to ruin everything.

I owe her my life.

From our island, we take the Panama Canal then head down the coast until we reach Peru. Phoenix doesn't ask any questions, I'm sure she's dying too, but she knows better.

When we're finally off the boat and heading to our secret location, on a private plane and then by jeep, she's done with my game.

"Tell me where we are." Her hand reaches out and swats me playfully. I catch her by her wrist and turn her palm up, then place a kiss on her pulse.

"What fun would that be?"

Phoenix stares out the window as we drive. The closer we get, the darker it becomes outside. My hope is that by the time we get there, the night sky will be pitch-black except for the stars.

Finally, we reach our destination. I step out of the car first then help Phoenix down. It might be dark, but I can see her eyes go wide.

"What is this?" she whispers in awe, and I know without turning around what she sees. The stars above reflect off the watery mirror of the land below, creating the illusion that we are walking on stars. There is no telling where the night sky meets the earth.

I wrap my arms around her until my hands rest on her belly. Her back to my front, I lean down and whisper in her ear.

"We are at the El Salar de Uyuni."

"I don't—how is it—" I can hear the confusion in her voice. I place a kiss on her hair and explain.

"This was formed by a prehistoric lake that went dry. It's considered one of the most remarkable places on earth. A thin layer of water is beneath us." Her head drops down, and she takes it all in. Stars are above us and beneath our feet. "Right there"—I point up to the stars twinkling from above—"That's the constellation Phoenix. I wanted to bring you here, under the stars you were named after, to marry you." I turn her around and place my hand under her chin until she's looking up into my eyes. "I didn't just want to marry you under the stars, but I wanted you to stand on them too."

Her eyes glisten with tears, but not tears of sadness. Tears of joy. They are full of love, an unconditional love that I have been searching for all my life. I never expected to find it—her, but life has a funny way of playing out. Phoenix has taught me that. You can find love and happiness anywhere, as long as you're willing to let it in. That and to forgive yourself. I owe my life to this remarkable woman. I will spend the rest of my days proving that, by loving and breathing for her.

"I feel like I'm flying." Her voice is filled with awe, and it makes me smile.

"You are, my little dove. And from this moment forward, I want to fly with you." Even in the darkness, I can see her eyes fill with tears, the soft sound of her silent sobs the only noise in the still of the night. "From the ashes, you rose, Phoenix. Rekindled from a spark. You are fire. You are hope. You are everything I need and everything I love. I'm irrevocably in love with you. Will you marry me here? Now. Be mine forever."

Her arms wrap around me, and she places her lips on mine. "Yes."

And there underneath the stars, with just the driver officiating the wedding, we say our vows. Sealing our lives to eternity.

# EPILOGUE

## Phoenix
*One year later*

I<small>T'S BEEN ONE YEAR SINCE MY FATHER LEFT US. ONE YEAR OF</small> having to figure out a way to live without him in my life.

Alaric has been my rock. He has loved me unconditionally and given me exactly what I've needed.

Even today, as I hold our daughter in my arms, I still need Alaric's strength holding me up.

Together, we walk up the hill to the stone that says his name.

Michael Lawrence.

Beloved Father.

He might not have been my biological father, but he loved me with all his heart, and that's all that matters.

"Hi, Dad," I say. "I'm sorry I've haven't been here in a while. I was having a baby, so I think you'll forgive me."

Alaric places the flowers that I had him pick up on the way to the grave.

"I'm here right now because I want you to meet your granddaughter." I step closer. "Dad, this is Michaela. She is everything that is perfect in this world. She has shown me what true love is. You would have loved her."

Michaela makes a cooing sound, and I know it in my heart that she is saying hello to her grandfather.

We stay at the graveyard for some time. Eventually, Alaric takes Michaela in his arms when she gets fussy and walks back to the car with her. When I'm alone with my dad, I begin to tell him about everything.

I tell him about Damian. I tell him once Damian was dead, I had to bring Alaric back to life. But every day, he got better. We sailed for some time during my pregnancy, and then when I was about to be in my third trimester, we came back to New York so we could be around the best doctors in the world. Alaric was insistent about that.

Life has been calm since Alaric left the business. At first, I thought he would resent me for making him stop, but he never did say anything. In fact, since he's given it up, he seems at peace.

When I'm done talking to my father, I head back to the car. I find Alaric in the back seat, whispering sweet nothings to our baby.

"What are you doing in here? What are you telling her?" I laugh.

Alaric places a kiss on his daughter's head and looks up at me with a large grin on his face. "I'm telling her all about the time her momma stowed away on my yacht."

*This man.* "You would, wouldn't you?" My eyes roll as I shake my head in mock disgust.

"What?" He shrugs. "It's a great story."

As much as I want to tease him some more about what he tells our daughter, I can't because he's right. "It is, isn't it?"

"The best."

Alaric places Michaela in her car seat, and then we both get into the front seat of the car.

"Where to now?" I ask.

"Home," he responds.

"And then ...?"

"Wherever the tide will take us. As long as we are together, I'm home," he says.

And it's true. In Alaric's arms, I've found a home.

We give each other a place we both belong—filled with hope, love, peace—and most of all, a family.

And when you have those things, time holds no meaning, and the possibilities are infinite.

*Like the sea.*

# ACKNOWLEDGMENTS

I want to thank my entire family. I love you all so much.

Thank you to my husband and my kids for always loving me. You guys are my heart!

Thank you to my Mom, Dad, Liz and Ralph for always believing in me, encouraging me and loving me!

Thank you to my in-laws for everything they do for me!

Thank you to all of my brothers and sisters!

Thank you to everyone that helped with Tarnished Empire.

Jenny Sims

Angela Smith

Amy Halter

Marla Esposito

Champagne Formats

Hang Le

Viviana Izzo

Thank you to Philippe Leblond for being the perfect Alaric.

Thank you to Sebastian York, Ava Erickson, Kim Gilmour and Lyric for bringing Tarnished Empire to life on audio.

Special thank you to Nina Grinstead and everyone at Valentine PR.

Thank you to my AMAZING ARC TEAM! You guys rock!

Thank you to my beta/test team.

Parker: Thank you for everything you do for me.

Leigh: Thank you for always being there.

Livia: Thank you for everything!

Sarah: Your input and feedback is always amazing! Thank you!

Kelly: Thank you for all your input and proofing my audio.

Lulu, Christine and Suzi: Thank you for your wonderful and extremely helpful feedback.

Jill: Thank you for all your help.

Melissa: Thank you for everything.

Harloe: Thanks for always being there.

Mia: Thanks for always plotting.

I want to thank ALL my friends for putting up with me while I wrote this book. Thank you!

To all of my author friends who listen to me complain and let me ask for advice, thank you!

To the ladies in the Ava Harrison Support Group, I couldn't have done this without your support!

Please consider joining my Facebook reader group Ava Harrison Support Group

Thanks to all the bloggers! Thanks for your excitement and love of books!

Last but certainly not least…

Thank you to the readers!

Thank you so much for taking this journey with me.

Made in the USA
Las Vegas, NV
18 May 2023

72239244R00199